KILL ME
IF YOU CAN

JAMES PATTERSON is one of the best-known and biggest-selling writers of all time. He is the author of some of the most popular series of the past decade – the Alex Cross, Women's Murder Club and Detective Michael Bennett novels – and he has written many other number one bestsellers including romance novels and stand-alone thrillers. He lives in Florida with his wife and son.

James is passionate about encouraging children to read. Inspired by his own son who was a reluctant reader, he also writes a range of books specifically for young readers. James has formed a partnership with the National Literacy Trust, an independent, UK-based charity that changes lives through li_____ ____ ____ __ ___ voted Author of the Ye_____ook Awards in New

Also by James Patterson

STAND-ALONE THRILLERS

A list of more titles by James Patterson is printed at the back of this book

JAMES PATTERSON
& MARSHALL KARP

KILL ME
IF YOU CAN

arrow books

Published by Arrow Books in 2012

3 5 7 9 10 8 6 4

First published in Great Britain in 2011 by Century

Arrow Books
Random House, 20 Vauxhall Bridge Road,
London SW1V 2SA

www.randomhouse.co.uk

Addresses for companies within The Random House Group Limited can be found at:
www.randomhouse.co.uk/offices.htm

The Random House Group Limited Reg. No. 954009

A CIP catalogue record for this book
is available from the British Library

Typeset in Berkeley (12/16 pt) by SX Composing DTP, Rayleigh, Essex, SS6 7XF

Penguin Random House is committed to a sustainable future for
our business, our readers and our planet. This book is made from
Forest Stewardship Council® certified paper.

Printed and bound in Great Britain by Clays Ltd, St Ives plc

In memory of my good friend and partner in crime, Joe Drabyak—M.K.

Prologue

THE GHOST

One

SOME PEOPLE ARE harder to kill than others. The Ghost was thinking about this as he huddled in the deep, dark shadows of Grand Central Terminal. A man named Walter Zelvas would have to die tonight. But it wouldn't be easy. Nobody hired the Ghost for the easy jobs.

It was almost 11 p.m, and even though the evening rush was long over, there was still a steady stream of weary travelers.

The Ghost was wearing an efficient killing disguise. His face was lost under a tangle of matted silver-and-white hair and shaggy beard, and his arsenal was hidden under a wine-stained gray poncho. To anyone who even bothered to take notice, he was just another heap of homeless humanity seeking refuge on a quiet bench near Track 109.

He eyed his target. Walter Zelvas. A great hulk of a man with the nerves and reflexes of a snake and a soul to match. Zelvas was a contract killer himself, but unlike the Ghost, Zelvas took pleasure in watching his victims suffer before they died. For years, the ruthless Russian had been an enforcer for the Diamond Syndicate, but apparently he had outlived his usefulness to his employer, and the Ghost had been hired to terminate him.

If he doesn't kill me first, the Ghost thought. With Zelvas it was definitely a matter of kill or be killed. And this would surely be a duel to the death between them.

So the Ghost watched his opponent closely. The screen on the departures monitor refreshed and Zelvas cursed under his breath. His train was delayed another thirty minutes.

He drained his second cup of Starbucks cappuccino, stood up, and crumpling his empty cup, deposited it in the trash.

No littering, the Ghost thought. That might

attract attention, and the last thing Zelvas wanted was attention.

That's why he was leaving town by train. Train stations aren't like airports. There's no baggage check, no metal detector, no security.

Zelvas looked toward the men's room.

All that coffee will be the death of you, the Ghost thought as Zelvas walked across the marble floor to the bathroom.

A half-comatose porter, mop in hand, was sloshing water on the terminal floor like a zombie tarring a roof. He didn't see Zelvas coming.

A puddle of brown water came within inches of the big man's right foot. Zelvas stopped. "You slop any of that scum on my shoes and you'll be shitting teeth," he said.

The porter froze. "Sorry. Sorry, sir. Sorry."

The Ghost watched it all. Another time, another place, and Zelvas might have drowned the man in his own mop water. But tonight he was on his best behavior.

Zelvas continued toward the bathroom.

The Ghost had watched the traffic in and out of the men's room for the past half hour. It was currently empty. *Moment of truth,* the Ghost told himself.

Zelvas got to the doorway, stopped, and turned around sharply.

He made me, the Ghost thought at first.

Zelvas looked straight at him. Then left, then right.

He's a pro. He's just watching his back.

Satisfied he wasn't being followed, Zelvas entered the men's room.

The Ghost stood up and surveyed the terminal. The only uniformed cop in the area was busy giving directions to a young couple fifty feet away.

The men's room had no door—just an L-shaped opening that allowed the Ghost to enter and still remain out of sight.

From his vantage point he could see the mirrored wall over the sinks. And there was Zelvas, standing in front of a urinal, his back to the mirror.

The Ghost silently reached under his poncho and removed his equally silent Glock from its holster.

The Ghost had a mantra. Three words he

said to himself just before every kill. He waited until he heard Zelvas breathe that first sigh of relief as he began to empty his bladder.

I am invincible, the Ghost said in silence.

Then, in a single fluid motion, he entered the bathroom, silently slid up behind Zelvas, aimed the Glock at the base of his skull, and squeezed the trigger.

And missed.

Some people are harder to kill than others.

Two

WALTER ZELVAS NEVER stepped up to a urinal unless the top flush pipe was made of polished chrome.

It's not a perfect mirror, but it's enough. Even distorted, everything he needed to see was visible.

Man. Hand. Gun.

Zelvas whirled on the ball of his right foot and dealt a swift knife-hand strike to the Ghost's wrist just as he pulled the trigger.

The bullet went wide, shattering the mirror behind him.

Zelvas followed up by driving a cinder-block fist into the Ghost's midsection, sending him crashing through a stall door.

The Glock went skittering across the tile floor.

The Ghost looked up at the enraged colossus who was now reaching for his own gun.

Damn, the Ghost thought. *The bastard is still pissing. Glad I wore the poncho.*

He rolled under the next stall as Zelvas's first bullet drilled a hole through the stained tile where his head had just been.

Zelvas darted to the second stall to get off another shot. Still on his back, the Ghost kicked the stall door with both feet.

It flew off its hinges and hit Zelvas square on, sending him crashing into the sinks.

But he held on to his gun.

The Ghost lunged and slammed Zelvas's gun hand down onto the hard porcelain sink. He was hoping to hear the sound of bone snapping, but all he heard was glass breaking as the mirror behind Zelvas fell to the floor in huge fractured pieces.

Instinctively, the Ghost snatched an eight-inch shard of broken mirror as it fell. Zelvas head-butted him full force, and as their skulls collided, the Ghost jammed the razor-sharp glass into Zelvas's bovine neck.

Zelvas let out a violent scream, pushed the Ghost off him, and then made one fatal mistake. He yanked the jagged mirror from his neck.

Blood sprayed like a renegade fire hose. *Now I'm really glad I wore the poncho,* the Ghost thought.

Zelvas ran screaming from the bloody bathroom, one hand pressed to his spurting neck and the other firing wildly behind him. The Ghost dived to the floor under a hail of ricocheting bullets and raining plaster dust. A few deft rolls and he managed to retrieve his Glock.

Jumping to his feet, the Ghost sprinted to the doorway and saw Zelvas running across the terminal, a steady stream of arterial blood pumping out of him. He would bleed out in a minute, but the Ghost didn't have time to stick around and confirm the kill. He raised the Glock, aimed, and then . . .

"Police. Drop it."

The Ghost turned. A uniformed cop, overweight, out of shape, and fumbling to get his own gun, was running toward him. One squeeze of the trigger and the cop would be dead.

There's a cleaner way to handle this, the Ghost

thought. The guy with the mop and every passenger within hearing distance of the gun-shots had taken off. The bucket of soapy mop water was still there.

The Ghost put his foot on the bucket and, pushing it, sent it rolling across the terminal floor right at the oncoming cop.

Direct hit.

The fat cop went flying ass over tin badge and slid across the slimy wet marble floor.

But this is New York—one cop meant dozens, and by now a platoon of cops was heading his way.

I don't kill cops, the Ghost thought, *and I'm out of buckets.* He reached under his poncho and pulled out two smoke grenades. He yanked the pins and screamed, *"Bomb!"*

The grenade fuses burst with a terrifying bang, and the sound waves bounced off the terminal's marble surfaces like so many acoustic billiard balls. Within seconds, the entire area for a hundred feet was covered with a thick red cloud that had billowed up from the grenade casings.

The chaos that had erupted with the first

gunshot kicked into high gear as people who had dived for cover from the bullets now lurched blindly through the bloodred smoke in search of a way out.

Half a dozen cops stumbled through the haze to where they had last seen the bomb thrower.

But the Ghost was gone.

Disappeared into thin air.

Book One

THE ART STUDENT

Chapter 1

I SWEAR THIS is true. My name is Matthew Bannon, and I'm a Fine Arts major at Parsons in New York City.

The first thing you resign yourself to when you decide you want to dedicate your life to being a painter is that you're never going to get rich.

It goes with the territory. Vincent van Gogh died without a nickel, and that guy could paint rings around me. So I figured I'd spend the rest of my life as a starving artist in a paint-spattered loft in SoHo—poor but happy.

But that fantasy took a total nosedive when I found millions of dollars' worth of diamonds inside a locker in Grand Central Terminal one night.

That's right. *Found.*

I know, I know. It's hard to believe. I didn't believe it, either. I felt like a guy must feel when he wins the Mega Millions lottery. Only I didn't buy a lottery ticket.

I just reached inside locker #925, and there it was.

A leather bag filled with millions and millions of dollars' worth of diamonds.

One minute I was planning a life of poverty; the next minute I was holding a small fortune in my hand.

Growing up in Hotchkiss, Colorado, I saw my share of rich people. None of them lived there. They would just be driving the scenic route on their way to Vail or Telluride and they'd stop for gas or something to eat at the North Fork Valley Restaurant.

Hotchkiss is about half the size of Central Park, with fewer people than you'd find in some New York City apartment buildings. But it's in the middle of God's country. It's everything John Denver sings about in "Rocky Mountain High."

It's where I learned to hunt, fish, ski, fly a plane, and do a whole lot of other macho stuff that my father taught me. He was a Marine. So were his father and his father before him.

My artistic side comes from my mom. She taught me to paint.

My father wanted me to carry on the family's military tradition. My mother said one uncultured jarhead in the family was enough.

So we compromised. I spent four years in the corps, with three active deployments to Iraq and Afghanistan. Then I saved up enough money to move to New York. Now at the age of thirty, I was in one of the best art programs in the country.

And suddenly my days of worrying about money were over.

I was rich. Or at least I could be rich if I decided to keep the diamonds. And why not? The guy who owned them wouldn't come looking for them.

As far as I figured, that guy was dead.

Chapter 2

YOU MIGHT THINK that finding a bag full of diamonds would be the best thing that happened in my life.

But you'd be wrong.

The best thing was finding Katherine Sanborne.

We met at the Whitney Museum.

The Whitney is one of my favorite places in New York, and I was staring at one of my favorite paintings, *Armistice Night,* by George Luks.

And then I saw her. Midtwenties, a heart-stoppingly beautiful face framed with auburn hair that fell to her shoulders in soft curls. She was escorting a group of high-school kids. As they came up beside me, she said, "George Luks was an American Realist."

"And I'm a Puerto Rican romantic," one kid said.

Big laugh from his teen cohorts.

Another kid jumped right in. "And I'm a Jewish pessimist," he said.

Within seconds, half a dozen kids were vying to see who could get the biggest laugh. Katherine just grinned and didn't try to stop them.

But I did. "None of you is as funny as George Luks," I said, pointing at the painting on the wall.

"You think this picture is funny?" the Puerto Rican romantic said.

"No," I said. "But the guy who painted it, George Luks, was a stand-up comedian and a comic strip illustrator. Then he teamed up with seven other artists and they became known as the Ashcan School."

"Cool," the kid said.

"He *was* pretty cool," I said. "Until one night he got the crap kicked out of him in a barroom brawl and was found dead a few hours later. Now, if you paid attention to your teacher, you could learn a lot of cool stuff like that."

I walked away.

A half hour later Katherine found me gawking at Edward Hopper's *Early Sunday Morning*.

"Where's your class?" I said.

"I'm not their teacher," she said. "I just do volunteer work at the museum every Wednesday. The kids liked you. They were sorry you left."

"I'm sure you handled them just fine," I said.

"I did. But I was sorry you left, too. How do you know so much about art?"

I shrugged. "I just do. It's not a very exciting story."

"I love to hear what other people think about art," she said. "If I bought you a cup of tea and a pumpkin muffin at Sarabeth's Kitchen, would you tell me some of the least boring parts?" She smiled and her soft gray eyes were full of mischief and joy and promise.

"I couldn't do that," I said.

Her smile faded and her eyes looked at me, more than a little surprised.

"But I could buy *you* a cup of tea and a pumpkin muffin at Sarabeth's Kitchen," I said. "Would that work?"

The smile flashed back on. "Deal," she said, extending her hand. "I'm Katherine Sanborne."

"Matthew Bannon," I said. Her hand was warm and soft and about half the size of mine. I held it for only a second, but it was long enough for me to get that jolt that goes through your body when you touch someone who has touched your heart.

We had tea.

I told her about my dream to be a painter.

"Maybe I can help," she said. "I teach art. I'd love to see your work. Maybe you can bring some samples to my office tomorrow after my class."

"I thought you said those kids in the museum weren't your class."

"They're not. I don't teach high school."

"Oh, okay. That makes sense," I said. "You're pretty young. You probably wouldn't want to put up with a bunch of hormonal teenage boys all day. What grade do you teach?"

She smiled. "It's not a grade," she said. "It's a master's program. I'm a professor of Fine Arts at Parsons."

It was now official: Katherine Sanborne was beautiful and brilliant.

I was totally out of my league.

Chapter 3

I SPENT HALF that night trying to figure out which of my paintings I should show her. Was this one too predictable? Was that one too boring? Or worse, completely pedestrian? I was seeing my work in a whole new light. Not just was it any good, but was it good enough for Katherine?

The next day I was in Professor Sanborne's office with fourteen photos of what I hoped was the best work I had done thus far. I doubt I'd ever felt more vulnerable and exposed in my life.

"No wonder you knew so much about the Realists," she said after she looked at them. "Your work reminds me of Edward Hopper. In his early days."

"I suppose you mean back when he was finger-painting in kindergarten?"

She laughed, and I decided it was gentle humor, kind humor, rather than the savage variety some professors strive to perfect.

"Not that early," she said. "As you know, I'm sure, Hopper is legendary for his ability to capture reality. But his early works are so impersonal. That's where you are now. In my opinion, anyway. Over time, Hopper's paintings began to take on emotions—loneliness, despair, gloom. *Nighthawks* is probably his best work—my favorite—and he didn't paint that till he was sixty."

"I hope it doesn't take me that long," I said, "to do something half as good."

"It won't," she said. "Not if you study at the right school."

"Like where?" I asked. "Any suggestion you have would be so helpful. Honest."

"Like *here*," she said.

I shook my head a couple of times. "I don't think I have the talent to be accepted at Parsons."

"I'll bet you do," she said. "Loser buys the winner . . . I don't know—dinner at Peter Luger. I love Luger's."

Six months later, Professor Katherine Sanborne and I were having the porterhouse medium rare at Peter Luger in Brooklyn.

I paid for dinner.

We started seeing each other regularly after our celebratory dinner, and six months after that, I was in her Group Critique class at Parsons. We did a pretty good job of keeping our relationship a secret from the other students, I thought.

The best part of Group Critique was being able to be near her three times a week. The worst part was enduring the critiques by my so-called peers.

The morning before I found the diamonds, my latest painting was being thoroughly trashed by Leonard Karns. Karns was short, round, pretentious, and bitterly, unnecessarily nasty. He waddled over to my canvas and explained to the rest of the group why it sucked and, by proxy, why I sucked.

"So it's a bunch of nobodies in line at an unemployment office," he said. "But do we really care about any of them? I could take the same picture with my cell phone camera. It's like the German playwright Bertolt Brecht said, 'Art is not a mirror held up to reality, but a hammer with which to shape it.'"

"And you don't think Mr. Bannon has shaped this piece?" Katherine said.

"No," Karns said. "But I think he should take a hammer to it."

If he was hoping for a laugh from the rest of the class, he didn't get it. Most of my fellow students sat in silence and winced. It was the last day of the semester, and by now Karns had managed to systematically piss off every one of them with his condescending elitist bullshit.

He would have pontificated longer, but Katherine cut him off. When class ended, she gave us back our term papers. The assignment had been to write a five-thousand-word critique of public art in New York City. It counted as a third of our grade, so I'd spent a lot of time on it. I'd hoped for an A.

But I didn't get it. There was a yellow sticky on the front page. It said, *C+. Matthew, see me after class.*

I sat in a depressed funk while everyone else filed out of the room. Katherine Sanborne finally came around her desk and walked toward me.

"C-plus?" I said. "I thought the paper was a little better than that."

"If you're willing to put in the time, I can give you a chance to improve your grade," she said.

"What do I have to do? I'm not afraid of hard work."

And then Katherine's mischievous gray eyes lit up, and she clicked the lock on the classroom door.

"Take off your pants," she said.

I'd been had.

She stepped out of her skirt. Very graceful. Nice to watch. "If those pants don't come off in five seconds, Mr. Bannon, I'm going to have to give you an incomplete," she said. "By the way, that paper of yours was damn good, but I've come to expect even more from you."

The classroom had a chaise longue that was used for the figure-painting courses, and within seconds Katherine pulled me to it and began caressing, kissing, exploring. Then I was inside her. This was some kind of teacher-student counseling session.

Finally, Katherine put her lips to my ear,

taunting me with kisses and little flicks of her tongue.

"Matthew," she whispered.

"What?"

"A-plus-plus."

Chapter 4

OKAY, LET ME get back to my story about the unexpected treasure trove that I found in locker #925. It was a night I'll never forget, of course. And for the other people in Grand Central Terminal, it was probably their worst nightmare.

I wasn't in New York City on September 11, 2001, but I've lived here long enough to understand the citywide paranoia. *It could happen again.*

New York is, was, and always will be Ground Zero. Code orange is as lax as we get here. I've seen tanks parked on Wall Street, bomb-sniffing dogs in public buildings, and convoys of cop cars barreling into neighborhoods as part of the NYPD's daily anti-terrorism drills.

So, when the post–rush hour lull at Grand Central is shattered by gunshots and followed by two loud explosions, only one thing comes to mind.

Terrorist attack.

In an instant, the collective paranoia was justified. Mass panic ensued.

The screams echoed off the walls of the marble cavern. The first thing I saw was that nobody ducked for cover. Everybody ran—with visions of the crumbling towers replaying in their heads, I'm sure.

And then I couldn't see a thing. Red smoke filled the building.

I've spent a lot of time in war zones, but this was not my responsibility. I wasn't a first responder.

I ran like the rest of them.

And then I saw it in the smoky haze.

A trail of blood.

Instinctively I followed it. And then I saw him.

He was a big bear of a man, slumped against a bank of lockers in a pool of his own blood—from a gaping wound in his neck.

In all the madness, nobody was paying any attention to him. I knelt at his side.

My knee hit something hard. A gun.

"Get doctor. Stop blood." He gurgled out the words in a thick Russian accent.

But there was no time for a doctor. No time for anything.

Before I could say a word, his eyes rolled back in his head and he exhaled a strained breath. He was dead.

His dark blue suit and the floor around him glistened with blood. It coated the door of the bottom locker closest to him. As I looked up, I saw a wide swath of red where he had leaned against the upper locker and slid to the ground.

Locker #925 was covered in bloody hand-prints.

And it was open.

Wide open.

Chapter 5

I COULD THINK of only one reason that a reasonably sane man who was hemorrhaging blood would open a train station locker instead of wildly seeking help. Whatever was inside that locker had to be too valuable to leave behind.

I looked down at the dead Russian. *Was it worth it, Comrade?*

But then, who was I to judge this poor man for choosing locker #925 over calling 911? If I had half a brain, I'd be running out of Grand Central with all my fellow bomb-scared travelers.

But I wanted to know what was inside that locker. No—I *had* to know.

I stood up. By now the red smoke was starting to dissipate and I could take in the pandemonium.

People were stampeding toward the exits, fighting and clawing their way out of the station. Some cops were trying to keep them from getting trampled in the doorways.

Other cops were trying to evacuate the people who refused to leave.

A woman with three suitcases was holding her ground in the middle of the station, insisting that she wasn't going anywhere without her bags.

"Damn it, lady," a ruddy-faced cop screamed, "you can't get a redcap during a terrorist attack."

He grabbed all three bags, and she followed him as he struggled toward an exit.

And then a body came flying through the air and hit the marble floor.

It was a young man, Asian, wearing a busboy's uniform.

Michael Jordan's Steak House is a popular restaurant on the balconies overlooking the main concourse. People were pouring out, shoving their way toward the wide marble staircase at the west side of the station. The busboy must have been caught at the far end of the restaurant and opted for the quick way out. It was about a twenty-foot drop. He stood up on his right leg and started hopping toward the exit.

I thought I'd just experienced the most insane day of my life. What I didn't know then was that after I reached inside that locker, the insanity would only get worse.

I put my hand on the open door and peered in. There was a bag inside. But not just any bag. It was one of those old-timey medical bags that you see in black-and-white movies from back in the days when doctors made house calls.

Maybe the Russian wasn't so dumb after all. Doctor bags are usually crammed with gauze and tape and about twelve hundred cotton balls.

I opened it carefully and looked inside.

My first thought was *Holy shit*.

My second thought was *This is a bag worth dying for.*

Chapter 6

I'D SEEN DIAMONDS before. My mother had one in her engagement ring. My aunt had two in her ears. But my recently shot-up acquaintance, now cooling on the floor of Grand Central, had them all beat. Did you ever enter one of those contests where you have to guess how many jelly beans are in the jar, and there are so many of them, you know you won't even come close? That's how many diamonds were in the Russian's medical bag.

Correction—*my* medical bag. At least for the time being.

When I was growing up, my mom used to tell my sister and me about a leprechaun with a pot of gold at the end of a rainbow. But she never mentioned a Russian Neanderthal with a bag of diamonds at the end of a bloody trail in a train station. Mom also said something about never taking what doesn't belong to you. But to whom did the diamonds actually belong? The dead guy with the gun? I definitely suspected he had taken them from somebody else. My mom meant well, but at a time like this, I had to seriously consider my dad's worldview. Finders keepers.

I could almost hear my dad listing my options. *What are you going to do, Matthew? Leave the diamonds with the dead body and walk away? Or maybe you want to get on the PA system and say, "If anyone at Grand Central lost a bag of diamonds, please meet me on the main concourse"?*

I made a decision, a temporary one, anyway. The diamonds were up for grabs and I was the one who would grab them.

I closed the black bag and snapped the brass latch. My mind started racing. These diamonds could completely change my life.

Little did I know how soon, and how much.

The voice behind me was deep, resonant, and authoritative. "Police. Turn around real slow. Keep your hands where I can see them."

I turned. The voice belonged to a young, very large African-American cop. And just in case his size didn't intimidate me, he was pointing his service revolver at my chest.

Hmm, I thought. *Looks like my life is changing already.*

Chapter 7

THERE WAS A dead guy at my feet, a fortune in diamonds in my hands, and an NYPD uniform pointing his gun at me. Now what happens?

"Officer Kendall," I said, reading his name tag. "I'm really glad you showed up. Thank God. Can you give me a hand here?"

"Who are you? Who is he?" the cop asked.

"I'm Dr. Jason Wood," I said, dredging up a name. "And I have no idea who he is, but I can tell you he's dead."

I knelt down beside the body and tried to appear oblivious of the policeman's gun. "There was nothing I could do. He had expired by the time I got here."

Kendall was young, a beat cop, and this had

to be the most action he'd seen since the Academy. One minute he was probably shooing unlicensed T-shirt vendors off Madison Avenue, and the next he's involved in a bomb attack in the heart of Manhattan.

"Please do me a favor," I said, barely looking up at him. "Would you point that gun somewhere else?"

"Sorry, Doc," he said, holstering the weapon.

I leaned over the dead body like I knew what I was doing. "He must have caught some shrapnel when the bombs went off," I said, stalling. "You know who's behind it?"

"I don't know shit," the cop said. "I was on Forty-sixth Street. The call went out that bombs had gone off at Grand Central. I just got here."

"Just a minute. Hold on. I've got an incoming." I grabbed my cell phone from my pocket and pressed it to my ear. Then I improvised. "Hello, this is Dr. Wood," I said. "I know. I was actually in Grand Central when the bombs went off. I'm still there. I'll get to the ER as soon as I possibly can."

I stood up. "Look, Officer," I said. "There's nothing I can do for this man. But there are people who need my help. I've got to get back down to St. Vincent's. Are the subways running?"

"Shut down," he said.

"All right. I'll walk if I have to."

Kendall's radio came to life then. *"All units, Grand Central Terminal. I have a ten-thirteen. Repeat—ten-thirteen: Officer needs assistance. Multiple looters at Five Borough Jewelry in the Forty-second Street Passageway. Shots fired."*

That's when I found out that an officer in trouble trumps a dead civilian. Kendall didn't hesitate. "I gotta go," he said. "You wait here for the coroner."

He raced off toward the Forty-second Street Passageway. As soon as he was out of sight, I headed in the other direction. As fast as I could.

I cut through the frenzied mass of people in Grand Central. It took maybe five or six minutes to get out to Lexington Avenue, where the insanity was even worse.

With the trains shut down, the street was teeming with commuters who wanted to get as far from midtown Manhattan as possible. And who were fighting over the few yellow cabs that had stopped.

Three men in suits had cornered one driver and were attempting to negotiate their way out of Dodge.

"Scarsdale," one said. "I'll give you three hundred bucks." "Ridgewood, New Jersey," another guy said, and he actually held out a handful of hundreds. "A thousand dollars."

I couldn't believe it. I could fly to Japan for less than that. Jersey won the bidding war. He was about to get in the cab when I grabbed his arm.

"I'm a doctor. I have to get downtown to St. Vincent's Hospital to deal with the victims," I said. "If you're taking the Holland Tunnel, you'll go right past it."

He looked down at my medical bag. "Yeah, yeah, Doc," he said. "Hop in. Let's get out of here."

I got in. The driver locked the doors and began to weave his way through the human traffic jam on Lexington Avenue. St. Vincent's is only a few blocks from my apartment. I was headed home. No charge.

Even if I decide to turn in these diamonds, I thought, *I'm definitely keeping this little black bag.*

Chapter 8

THIRTY MINUTES AFTER Walter Zelvas bled out on the floor of Grand Central, two NYPD detectives pulled up to his apartment building on East 77th Street. Some cops go by the book, some bend the rules. But Detectives John Rice and Nick Benzetti were considerably dirtier than most of the crooks they busted.

They had finished the day shift in Robbery for the Department, and now they were working for Chukov at a much better hourly rate. Their mission was simple. *Find the diamonds.*

The doorman looked away as they entered the building. He knew exactly where they were headed. For fifty bucks he had supplied them with a key to the apartment of that nasty-ass

Russian who had stiffed him at Christmas: Walter Zelvas.

The two cops entered the elevator.

Benzetti stood six feet tall, with slick black hair and an oversize hawk nose protruding from a small, pinched face. Tall, dark, and ugly. In reality, he was wearing six-inch cheater shoes, and his gray hair was slathered with Just For Men hair dye. The ugly came natural.

Rice, six three and bald, didn't need help from a shoe company or a hair dye. But the two cops had one thing in common. They were both terrified.

They had met Zelvas once. And he didn't like them. He didn't care if they were on Chukov's payroll. They were still cops.

They'd sat across the table from him at Chukov's apartment, a bottle of vodka, a loaf of black bread, and a large block of cheese between them.

"Screw me over and I'll kill you," Zelvas had said. "And not with a bullet."

He picked up a stainless-steel slicer and dragged it slowly, menacingly across the top of the cheese. A ten-inch sliver peeled away.

"Do you know how long it takes a man to die if you skin him alive?" Zelvas asked, popping the cheese curl into his mouth. "Six days. Four if you add salt."

Benzetti and Rice stood to the left and right of the door outside apartment 16E, guns drawn. They knew Chukov wanted to ice Zelvas. What they didn't know was that he was already dead.

"If Zelvas is there, we take him out quick," Rice said. "I'll aim for his head. You go for his heart."

Benzetti knelt down, slid the key into the lock, and turned it. With Rice standing over him aiming high left, and his own gun pointed low right, he opened the door. Clear. The two men slowly padded into the living room.

The overstuffed sofa and two massive armchairs were covered in a shiny fabric with black and gold geometric shapes. Walter Zelvas was big and ugly, Benzetti thought, and he had furniture to match.

They scanned the room. Clear.

And then they heard it. A noise. Metallic. It was coming from the bedroom.

The two cops froze.

Whoever was on the other side of the door was too busy to know they were in the apartment. They moved silently, expertly, through the living room and flattened themselves against the wall outside the bedroom door.

From his lead vantage point Rice could see the wall safe. It had just been opened. But not by Zelvas.

He signaled his partner, and the two of them rushed in. "I'm guessing Walter isn't at home," Rice said, pointing his gun at the safecracker.

She looked up. She was drop-dead gorgeous. Midtwenties, dark hair, long legs, wearing ass-hugging jeans and a tight white blouse with the top three buttons undone.

"Shoot her," Benzetti said.

"Back off," the woman said in a voice that seemed to hold no fear. "Do you know who I am? Obviously you don't."

"Don't know, don't care," Benzetti said. "*Shoot her.*"

"Maybe we should find out who she is first," Rice said. "She obviously thinks she's somebody."

"I don't care who she thinks she is," Benzetti said.

"I see, I see," she said. "Good cop, bad cop. You're the two *mudaks* who work for Chukov, Benzetti and Rice. Zelvas warned me about you."

"And you're the woman breaking and entering, then ransacking Walter Zelvas's safe."

"I'm not ransacking. I have the combination. Zelvas gave it to me. As well as a key to his front door."

She was defiant but she was also breathing hard. She was scared.

Benzetti loved watching this one squirm. The nice breasts were an added bonus for him. In a way, it would be a crime against nature to kill her.

"And why would Zelvas give you his front door key plus the combination to his safe?"

"I'm his girlfriend. I'm Natalia."

Rice looked at Benzetti. "Chukov never said anything about Zelvas having a girlfriend."

"So you *do* work for Chukov," Natalia said. "What does he want here? You can tell me. After all, you plan to kill me."

"He sent us to pick up some diamonds," Benzetti said.

"I work for Nathaniel Prince," Natalia said.

"He sent me here for the diamonds, and he's Chukov's boss."

"I thought Chukov was the boss," Benzetti said.

"Chukov?" Natalia said, spitting out the name. "Do you think that boot-licking *dalbaiyob* is smart enough to run an operation like the Diamond Syndicate? Chukov works for Nathaniel Prince, and Nathaniel sent me, so put the guns down, gentlemen, and let me finish what I started. You couldn't open the safe, anyway. I have the combination."

"But we have the guns," Benzetti said. He nodded to Rice. "Cuff her."

Zelvas had a home gym in the bedroom, and Rice handcuffed Natalia's slender right wrist to a two-hundred-pound barbell.

Benzetti reached into the safe and pulled out a black velvet bag. It had some heft to it—at least a couple of kilos. He wondered how many diamonds they could skim off without getting nailed. He dumped the contents on the bed.

No diamonds. Just cheese. A big fat wheel of cheese the size of a birthday cake.

Natalia let out a string of Russian curses.

"Calm the hell down," Benzetti said.

She didn't.

Rice grinned. "I don't speak Russian, but I'm guessing she's really pissed."

Benzetti shrugged. "Hey, she was banging the ugliest guy on the Upper East Side, expecting diamonds, and all she got was a hunk of cheese. Hell, I'd be pissed, too."

Chapter 9

THE TWO COPS left Natalia chained to the barbell and did a quick search of the apartment. After five minutes, Benzetti called it off. "If they're not in the safe, they're not here," he said. "Which one of us breaks the bad news to Chukov?"

They flipped a coin and Benzetti lost. Jesus, he did not want to make this phone call.

Chukov was a two-hundred-fifty-pound powder keg with a half-inch fuse. Benzetti had once seen him smash a beer bottle and drive it into a man's jaw for cheating at poker. And that was over a lousy hundred-dollar pot.

"Cheese?" Chukov screamed. "*Cheese?* You've got to be kidding me."

Benzetti could practically feel the enraged Cossack's spittle through the cell phone. "No diamonds?" Chukov shouted.

"And no Zelvas," Benzetti said.

"Zelvas is dead," Chukov said.

"Zelvas is dead?" Benzetti repeated so that Rice could hear the news. "And you know that how? You're sure of it?"

"He was stealing from us," Chukov said. "I'm in charge of the Syndicate's loss-prevention department. Ten minutes ago I got a confirmation call from the field that Zelvas's thieving days are over."

Benzetti breathed out in relief. "I'm impressed. Where did you find someone who could get the drop on Walter Zelvas? Never mind. Did your man in the field say anything about the diamonds?" Benzetti asked. "If they're not here, I figure Zelvas took them with him."

"If he did, our man didn't see them," Chukov said. "He barely had time to finish Zelvas off when a shitstorm of cops arrived. He was lucky to get away."

"He never saw any diamonds?" Benzetti said.

"That's what he told me. I really don't know,

but I want those diamonds back!" Chukov yelled.

"And so does somebody named Nathaniel Prince," Benzetti said.

That seemed to get the Russian's attention. "What do you know about Nathaniel Prince?"

"Is he your boss?"

"You and Rice work for me," Chukov said. "That's all you need to know."

"Actually, there is one other thing I need to know," Benzetti said. "Who's Natalia? She's around five ten, dark hair, fantastic rack, a very pretty lady."

"How do you know Natalia?" Chukov asked.

"We've got her handcuffed in Zelvas's bedroom. She was opening his safe just as we got here."

"Natalia is Prince's girlfriend."

"*Prince's* girlfriend? She said she was Zelvas's girlfriend."

Chukov laughed. "She gets around."

"What should we do with the lovely Natalia?"

"Two choices," Chukov said. "You can uncuff her, apologize for not knowing who she is, and tell her you're going to do all you can to get the diamonds back for Nathaniel Prince."

"I'm not much for apologies. What's my second choice?"

"Keep her cuffed, rip off her clothes, fuck the living shit out of her—and a few hours later, you'll be happy but dead. Prince will kill you —*gulag-style.*"

Chapter 10

THERE'S SOMETHING SURREAL about sitting in the back of a taxi with a bag full of diamonds. *This can't be happening to me*, I kept telling myself. But it was. I only wished I could open the bag and make sure.

My benefactor from New Jersey didn't even talk to me. He was on his cell with someone in Tokyo, hedging funds or whatever those investor guys do. I'm sure by the time he got to Ridgewood, he'd made more than enough to pay for the thousand-dollar cab ride.

The driver was chatty all the way downtown, filling me in on his own financial plans.

"I can be back at Grand Central in an hour. There's gotta be hundreds of rich guys willing to pop big bucks to get home to the suburbs," he said. "This is the kind of incredible night a cabbie waits for."

So little time. So many desperate stranded souls to gouge. I smiled and hefted my medical bag. Who was I to judge?

He took me to the Emergency entrance at St. Vincent's and left in a hurry. I walked the three blocks to my apartment, looking left, right, and behind me every step of the way.

My apartment is in a five-story brownstone, built back in the early twentieth century, when craftsmanship and integrity were still the hallmarks of the construction industry. The brick is so solid-looking that the tenants call it the Fortress.

I live on the top floor. There's a closed-circuit TV system in the vestibule, and most nights I wave at the camera, and whoever sees me opens their door and gives me a "Hi, Matthew."

But tonight I ran up the five flights, opened my door, double-locked it behind me, and exhaled. I hadn't been arrested or killed and I still had the diamonds. I was safe. For now.

I always feel good about walking into my

apartment, and tonight I felt even better. It's hardly the biggest space in New York, but it feels homey. That's because it's wall-to-wall me. Literally. Every inch of wall space is covered with my paintings. I don't know if I'm any good, but I like my stuff enough to want to look at it all the time.

My cat sauntered in. I got him at the shelter two years ago. He's black and white, with about fifteen shades of gray. His name was Hooper when I adopted him, but I changed it to Hopper, after my favorite painter.

It doesn't matter. He doesn't come no matter what I call him.

"Look what Daddy brought home," I said, showing him the bag of diamonds. He couldn't have cared less, but I had been dying to show somebody.

"Well, *you* might not be interested, but I hear this stuff can be catnip for some women."

I grabbed a beer from the fridge, sat down on the sofa, opened the bag, and let the diamonds trickle through my fingers. I was in *I'm-Rich-Beyond-My-Wildest-Dreams* euphoria when the doorbell rang.

Someone was coming for the diamonds! That had to be it. Shit!

I jumped up, sloshing beer on my pants, and headed for the cabinets where I store my paints, brushes, and a Beretta M9 semiautomatic. I'm an ex-Marine. Whoever was downstairs thought I was just an art student. Advantage: for me.

I gripped the gun and moved over to check the closed-circuit monitor. The cat, just as curious to see who was at my front door at ten minutes after midnight, followed me.

I looked at the screen and breathed a sigh of relief.

"Jeez, Hopper," I said. "One of us is as nervous as a cat."

Chapter 11

AT THE AGE of five I was given my first toy chest. It was a Marine Corps footlocker. While other kids got colorful wooden boxes with their favorite superhero or sports team logo painted on the front, my father decided I should have an olive-drab, steel-reinforced, double-padlock trunk emblazoned with SEMPER FI and steeped in his own personal military history.

I still have it. It's bolted to my bedroom floor. I unlocked it and buried the medical bag with the diamonds under layers of old uniforms and a few souvenirs I brought home from Afghanistan. I shut the lid and made sure it was locked up tight.

Then I went back to the living room, tucked

the gun back in the art cabinet where it belonged, and opened the front door.

And there she was, wearing a dove-gray V-neck sweater that matched her eyes and a just-to-the-knees denim skirt that showed off her legs nicely. Katherine.

"What are you doing here at this hour?" I said. "Besides looking terrific, that is."

She threw her arms around me. "Haven't you heard? There was some kind of terrorist attack at Grand Central," she said, kissing my cheeks, my neck, finally my lips. "I didn't want to be alone tonight."

"Good thinking," I said, pressing her body against mine. "After the railroads, and maybe planes, the next logical terrorist target would be art professors."

She stepped back. "Are you making fun of me, Matthew?"

"Never."

"Will you watch out for me? Keep me company tonight?"

"Uh-huh."

And I meant it. My mother raised me to be an artist, but my father trained me to protect the people I love. When I was growing up, he was more like a drill sergeant than a dad. Once when I was ten, we were hiking in Pike National Forest. One minute we were together and then suddenly he was gone, and I was all alone in the middle of the Colorado wilderness. I had nothing but a hunting knife. No food, no water, no compass. I knew we hadn't separated by accident, either. This was a test. It took me thirty hours to pass it, but I finally found my way home.

I looked into Katherine's eyes. Would I watch over her? Absolutely. I stroked her eyelids, her cheeks, her lips. Then my lips traced the same pattern. Eyelids, cheeks, mouth.

"Can I ask you a question?" she asked when we stopped for a breath.

"Absolutely."

"How did your pants get wet?" She lowered one hand and cupped it between my legs.

"Beer. An unfortunate accident."

"You can't be walking around all wet," she said, unbuckling my belt. Then she unzipped my fly and helped me out of my pants.

The beer had soaked through to my boxers. "Wet also," she said. "And hard, too."

"Can't imagine why," I said.

Within seconds I was naked and then Katherine joined me. I lay on my back and Katherine straddled my hips. I thrust up into her, not hard but firm. She arched her back, dug her knees into my thighs, and pressed down against me. She slowly took in a breath, then just as slowly let it out. She did it again. And again.

The sound of Katherine about to reach a climax is the best part of making love for me, and as her breathing got more frenetic, I matched her until—

Our orgasms came in rolling waves, one after another, slowly subsiding until she let her body fall on top of mine. Then Katherine wrapped her arms around my shoulders and pressed her lips to my ear.

"I'm crazy in love with you," she whispered.

"I love you, too," I said. "Never thought I could love anybody like this. But here we are."

We fell asleep like that.

Not a care in the world.

So incredibly naive.

Chapter 12

VADIM CHUKOV WAS a survivor. When a rival mob captured him, he managed to strangle his captors from the backseat of the car with their own handcuffs. When four prison guards beat him and locked him in solitary confinement, he escaped and lived to kill them and their families. Chukov had been stabbed four times, shot twice, and thrown off a speeding train. He'd be damned if he was going to die from chronic obstructive pulmonary disease.

He sat naked on the ceramic tiles of the steam room, a towel across his lap. His cell phone and a bronchodilator inhaler lay on the towel. Lifelines both.

Chukov had discovered cigarettes when he

was eleven years old. Yava, the full-flavored Russian cancer sticks that gave a young street enforcer for the *Solntsevskaya Bratva* swagger, status, and eventually COPD.

Thirty-five years later, he was a slave to the steam, breathing in the moist heat almost every day to help open his inflamed lungs.

Most of the steam rooms in the city were magnets for fags and yuppies, but the Russian and Turkish Baths on East 10th Street were old school. Real tile, not that fiberglass and acrylic shit they were putting in those new hybrid steam rooms. And no pretty boys. At least not at this hour of the morning. He had the steam room to himself.

Chukov's body was short, thick, and covered with curly black hair and sixteen tattoos. The rose, the tiger, the skulls—every blue line on his body told his history in the Russian Mafia to anyone who knew how to read it.

The cell phone rang. He was waiting for some good news that he could give to Prince. This had better be it. It wasn't.

"Where's my money?" the voice on the other end said.

It was the Ghost.

"Where are my diamonds, you prick?" Chukov came back angrily.

"I don't know what you're talking about," the Ghost said. "All I know is we had a deal. I kept my end of it, you didn't. Walter Zelvas is dead. My money hasn't been transferred to the Caymans."

"Why do you think I hired you to terminate Zelvas?" Chukov said. "He was skimming diamonds from the Syndicate. The diamonds weren't in his apartment, so he must have taken them with him. You were the last to see him alive."

"And if I don't get my money, I'll be the last one to see you alive."

"What's that supposed to mean?" Chukov said.

"It means look to your left."

Chukov turned his head. There was a red dot on the wall. It moved up to the ceiling, made a few *S* turns, danced back to the wall, and then landed on his chest.

He had to clench his sphincter for fear of shitting right there.

"You're here?" Chukov said. "How did you find me here? How did you get in?"

"It's what I get paid to do, remember? So pay me."

"Be reasonable," Chukov said. "Give me time to recover the missing diamonds."

"Not . . . my . . . problem," the Ghost said.

The red dot moved slowly down Chukov's body to the roll of a lifetime of overindulgence around his belly and finally came to rest on the inhaler that sat on his lap.

Chukov was sweating profusely, not all of it from the steam. "Please," he said.

"Lift up your skirt," the Ghost said.

"What?"

"The towel. Lift it up."

Chukov had faced death before. He beat it every time, but not by cringing in fear.

He ripped the towel off and stood up. Naked. Proud. Defiant.

"Fuck you," he bellowed. "Vadim Chukov bows to no man."

The words echoed off the tile walls.

Chapter 13

"WHERE'D YOU DO the seven?" the Ghost said.

"What?"

"I'm not interested in looking at your dick. I can read the tats. According to that star on your knee, you did seven years in prison. I asked you where."

"Butyrka." Chukov spat out the word. "Hellhole. I'd rather have gone to Siberia."

"Put the towel back on and sit your fat ass down."

Chukov wrapped the towel around his waist and sat. "If you can read tattoos, you know that the seven-pointed star on my knee means more than prison time."

"I know. You're a made man in the Russian Mafia."

"I bow to no man."

"I heard you the first time," the Ghost said. "Were you a *pakhan* in the old country?"

Chukov inhaled deeply and filled his lungs with hot steam. "Nathaniel Prince was a *pakhan*. I'm a humble brigadier."

"Brigadier, maybe," the Ghost said. "But not so humble. Not if you choose to violate the *Vorovskoy Zakon*."

Chukov exploded. "Bullshit. I have never violated the Thieves' Code. I've been bound by it my entire life. Even in prison."

"And I say you've desecrated rule number eighteen: *Make good on promises given to other thieves*."

"That means nothing if you steal from me," Chukov said.

"I killed a man for you, but I didn't steal," the Ghost said.

"How do I know you're not lying?"

"You have two choices, Brigadier Chukov," the Ghost said. "You either take my word for it and live by the code, or you don't believe me and die in five seconds."

The red dot made little circles on Chukov's chest.

"*Pyat,*" the Ghost said, counting backward in Russian, "*chetirye . . . tri . . . dva . . . odeen.*"

"I'll pay, I'll pay," Chukov said.

"*Kogda?*"

"You speak Russian?" Chukov said.

"Just the basic stuff you need in my line of work," the Ghost said. "Like *please, thank you,* and *when can I expect my money?*"

"I'll transfer it immediately."

The red dot disappeared from Chukov's chest.

"*Spasibo,*" the Ghost said. "It's been a pleasure doing business with you."

"We're not done," Chukov said. "I have another job for you."

"I'm listening."

"I accept that you didn't take the diamonds," Chukov said. "I want you to find out who did."

"Then kill the *mudak* and return the diamonds to you," the Ghost said. "*Da?*"

"*Da,*" Chukov said, followed by a wet, croupy laugh.

"I want double what you paid me for Zelvas."

Chukov choked on his own laugh. "Double? Are you crazy?"

"It costs more when I have to figure out who the target is," the Ghost said. "Plus, I figure getting back all those diamonds ought to be worth something to you."

"Maybe ten percent more," Chukov said.

"Double," the Ghost said. "Take it or . . ."

The red dot reappeared on Chukov's chest.

". . . leave it."

Chukov took it. "All right. I'll pay double, but only if I get the diamonds back."

"Then we're in business again," the Ghost said.

Chukov looked down at his chest, waiting for the red dot to disappear. It didn't. "You can take the gun off me now," he said.

There was no answer.

Chukov sat there sweating, but the dot didn't move. It took him a full minute until he realized—the dot was never going to move. The laser beam was on autopilot.

Cursing, Chukov stood up and followed the red line through the steam to its source. It wasn't even a gun. It was a cheap key-chain laser pointer resting on a block of wet tile.

The Ghost, of course, was long gone.

Chapter 14

CHUKOV SHOWERED, DRESSED, took a cab home, and begrudgingly transferred the money to pay for eliminating Zelvas.

He poured himself a shot of vodka and downed it, then picked up the phone. He started to dial Nathaniel's number but quickly hung up.

He couldn't face the wrath of Nathaniel Prince without a second shot of vodka.

Times had changed. Forty years ago, Chukov had given the orders and Nathaniel had followed them without question. The two were cousins who grew up in the Sokol Settlement, a working-class neighborhood in Moscow.

Nathaniel was a model student and an

adored only child. His father was a cheese maker, and after school, the boy worked in the family stall at the Leningradsky Market, using his charm and good looks to sell the soft sweet *Tvorog* and *Bryndza* to the tourists and well-to-do shoppers.

Vadim Chukov's father was in prison, and by the age of twelve, Vadim was stealing cars on Arbat Street, where the wealthy parked. Luxury cars often yielded bonuses, such as cameras, watches, or the occasional gun in the glove box, and soon Vadim had a stash of hot merchandise. He showed it to Nathaniel, who had an idea. He would wrap each item in plastic and hide it in a tub of cheese in the family stall. Clued-in customers would ask for a particular batch of cheese, and before long, the smooth-talking Nathaniel was making more money in a few hours than his father made in a week.

Once he got a taste, he wanted more, and he climbed the ranks of the *Bratva* rapidly. He was only twenty-nine when he approached the Diamond Syndicate with the idea that propelled him to the top of the ladder.

The Syndicate trafficked in the illegal

diamonds that had become the currency in war-torn African nations. Rebel armies funded their civil wars and armed conflicts by kidnapping the natives and forcing them to dig out the diamonds buried along the muddy riverbanks. Anyone who refused to cooperate would be mutilated or murdered, so the rivers ran red and the stones came to be called blood diamonds.

Prince came up with a foolproof plan to smuggle blood diamonds into America. Cheese.

He bought a small factory in Marseille where an exquisite Gruyère Fontu was made. When a shipment of blood diamonds arrived from Angola or Sierra Leone, they were cut, dressed, and molded into carefully marked wheels of the heavenly *fromage*.

The cheese was exported to New York, where Zelvas and his crew extracted the stones and sold them to diamond merchants on West 47th Street who cared more about the black-market low prices than the fact that they came from the hands of murderous African warlords.

The plan worked well until Zelvas got greedy. By the time Chukov realized that Zelvas was taking a few stones from every shipment, the man had amassed a fortune.

Now Zelvas was dead, and the diamonds he stole were missing.

Chukov's job was to find them. He downed a third shot of vodka and dialed Nathaniel's number.

"This better be good news, Vadim," Nathaniel said.

"It is," Chukov lied. "Rice and Benzetti are closing in on the diamonds. You should have them back in a few days."

"Rice and Benzetti?" Nathaniel screamed. "You're counting on a couple of crooked cops to bring home a fortune in diamonds?"

"No, no, I've got a dozen other men looking," Chukov said, wheezing. He paused to suck on his bronchodilator. "And I've hired the Ghost to track down whoever stole the diamonds and get rid of him. The Ghost is a legend, Nathaniel. He's the best."

"I'll keep that in mind, Vadim. Because if you don't come up with the diamonds fast, I'll be hiring the Ghost to get rid of you."

He slammed the phone down.

Chukov picked up the vodka bottle and took

a few quick swigs. Then he inhaled another lungful of albuterol from the little canister.

Bastard, he thought. *I've created a monster.*

Chapter 15

THE BRIGHTON BEACH section of Brooklyn is so heavily populated with Russians that its nickname is Little Odessa.

Nathaniel Prince, born and raised in Moscow, refused to live there. His logic: Brighton Beach was a hotbed of crime. And while he wasn't intimidated by the street violence, he didn't want to live where the NYPD had beefed up its manpower.

Instead, he chose Park Slope, a much tonier part of the borough. His neighbors were artists, writers, musicians, and actors. Prince liked that. With all those famous people to gawk at, nobody bothered to look at him. So, for four million dollars, he bought a luxurious hundred-year-old town house and total anonymity.

The master bedroom filled the entire third floor. With its high ceilings, parquet floors, and wood-burning fireplace, it was Nathaniel's haven from the world.

He shared it with Natalia. She stepped out of the bathroom in a crimson silk robe that stopped midthigh. The belt was cinched tight, accentuating her narrow waist and her full, generous breasts.

She smiled at Nathaniel. "Who were you yelling at?" she said.

"Chukov."

"What did poor Vadim do now?"

"Millions of dollars in missing diamonds," Nathaniel said. "Walter Zelvas has screwed us from the grave, and it's all Chukov's fault."

"Not all of it," Natalia said. "I accept some of the blame."

"You? What did you do wrong?" Nathaniel said.

"I thought I had Zelvas under control. He wanted to run off with me," she said. "I never thought he'd leave me and run off with the diamonds."

She unscrewed the top of a jar of Crème de la

Mer. Nathaniel had no idea what was in it, but he had seen the credit-card receipts. Twelve hundred dollars for the tiny pink-and-white jar.

Natalia undid her belt, opened her robe, and began rubbing the outrageously expensive moisturizer into her long, firm, perfectly sculpted legs.

Only ten minutes before, Nathaniel had been between those legs, deep inside her, his face buried between her breasts, his tongue tantalizing her nipples, his brain intoxicated with her perfume. His orgasm, as it always did with Natalia, had left him blissfully happy and totally spent.

But as he watched Natalia slide her hands from her calf to her inner thigh, Nathaniel began to stir. He was still naked under the sheets, and he felt himself growing hard.

Natalia put some more cream on her fingertips and let the robe fall to the ground. Her skin was radiant, still glistening with moisture from the hot shower. She had towel-dried her thick raven-black hair, and it fell in ringlets on her shoulders.

"I'm glad Zelvas is dead," she said as she massaged the creamy emulsion into her breasts and flat stomach. "The thought of having his fat, sweaty body on top of me even one more time makes me sick."

"How do you think it made me feel?" Nathaniel asked.

"I'm sorry," she said. "I had to sleep with him. It was the only way he would trust me enough to tell me he was stealing from you."

Nathaniel grunted.

"Don't be angry," she said, dipping her fingertips into the Crème de la Mer. "You know you are the only man I ever loved."

She walked slowly, seductively, toward him, and sat down on the bed. "You know Zelvas said I should dump you," she said, rubbing the lubricant into the palm of her hand. "He said you were old enough to be my father."

She slipped her hand under the sheet. "Little did he know," she said, "you are."

Chapter 16

IT WAS DARK when Chukov came out of his blackout. *Too much vodka,* he thought. *This is why there is trouble.* Two weeks earlier he had been drinking with Zelvas. They were shit-faced, and Zelvas was bragging about his many kills.

Finally Chukov could stand it no longer. "Any old lady with a gun can kill someone," he said. "Come back and wave your dick when you kill twenty-seven people at one time. That, my friend, is my achievement."

Zelvas belched and the air filled with the stench of the *pelmeni* and sauerkraut they had devoured together two hours before. "Bullshit," he said.

"I swear on my mother's soul. Twenty years

ago my cousin Nathaniel's wife, his son, and his daughter were crossing the street when a taxi came speeding around the corner and hit them. The wife and the little boy were dead before they hit the ground. The daughter was in a critical condition. The driver never stopped."

Zelvas was stunned. "I never knew Nathaniel had a family."

"It was before your time with us. He was a devoted father. For the next six months he sat by his little girl's bedside, singing to her, nursing her back to health. At night I would sit with him and we would talk about revenge."

"He knew who the driver was?" Zelvas asked.

"No. But witnesses saw the blue-and-white taxi. It belonged to the Dmitriov Cab Company," Chukov said. "One morning I took a dozen men, and we stormed the taxi barn as they were all starting their day. Almost every person who worked for Dmitriov was there. Many from the Dmitriov family—sons, brothers, cousins— *family*. I locked them in a storage room, turned on the gas main, covered the floor with petrol, and lit it. One match. Twenty-seven dead."

"I have new respect for you, Comrade,"

Zelvas said. "Whatever happened to Nathaniel's daughter?"

"Natalia?" Chukov said. "She's fine."

Zelvas's admiration turned to shock. "Natalia is Nathaniel's daughter?"

Chukov realized he had just given away the family secret he had sworn to take to his grave. Nathaniel's mistress was his daughter.

"Please swear to me you won't repeat it. He would kill me," Chukov said.

"Don't worry," Zelvas said. "It's too vile to repeat."

Zelvas went home. That night, for the first time since he was a little boy, he sobbed into his pillow. He had slowly stolen a fortune in diamonds from the Syndicate so that one day he could run off with his beloved Natalia.

But now he despised her. He would leave without her. Just him. And the diamonds.

Chapter 17

I WOKE UP with Katherine safely nestled in my arms—and a bag of *presumably* precious gems nestled at my feet. I have to say, I was happy beyond my wildest dreams. I was also rich beyond my wildest dreams. I had only one question: *How rich?*

After Katherine left for the office, I locked the door, opened the footlocker, and dumped the bag of stones on my bed. Hopper was just as curious as I was and jumped on the bed to check out the shiny stones.

I knew as much about diamonds as the cat did, but I could see that they looked to be roughly the same size. No big rocks; no tiny chips. Just countless shiny nuggets, each about the size of a piece of cat kibble. Hopper looked like he had come to the same conclusion, so I tossed him off the bed before he could help himself to a million-dollar breakfast.

I flipped on the TV. The bombing at Grand Central was all over the news. The dead guy had been identified as Walter Zelvas, but there was no mention of the pile of bling on my bed. I did a rough count, picked five diamonds at random, stashed the rest, and took the subway uptown to the Rockefeller Center station.

Fifth Avenue was packed with out-of-towners headed for Radio City Music Hall, St. Patrick's Cathedral, Saks, or any of the many other tourist magnets in the area. Heading west on 47th Street, I entered a completely different world, where Hasidic Jews in long black coats haggled in a language I couldn't understand, making deals on the sidewalk and cementing them with handshakes.

The Diamond District. I'd been here before but never on business.

I walked into the National Jewelers Exchange at 2 West 47th Street. Hundreds of vendors, each with his or her own little booth, were buying and selling gold, silver, fine jewelry, watches, and, of course, diamonds.

Chana Leventhal, a broad woman in her sixties, caught me staring at the diamond rings in her showcase. "You look like a young man in search of an engagement ring," she said.

"Just the opposite," I said. "I just got one returned to me."

"Oy, she dumped you?"

I nodded.

"But she gave you the ring back."

"I think she did," I said. I reached into my pocket and held out one of my five stones. "She only gave me the diamond, and I don't know if she switched the real one for a piece of glass."

"Let me see," Chana said. "I know a professional."

She took the stone before I could answer. "Shmuel," she said to a man sitting at a jeweler's workbench facing away from the counter. "He got jilted. Give a look."

She handed him the diamond and he put a jeweler's loupe in his eye and studied the stone for about twenty seconds. He stood up and walked toward me. He was short, with a neatly trimmed gray beard and the yellowed teeth of a longtime smoker.

He handed me the diamond. "You can relax," he said. "It's kosher. Where did you buy it?"

"Colorado."

He shrugged and looked at his wife.

"You should have come here," she said. "Colorado overcharges."

"What did you pay?" Shmuel said. "Fifteen thousand?"

"Sixteen plus tax," I said.

"*Goniffs,*" he said.

Chana looked at me. "It means 'crooks,' 'robbers.'"

Shmuel shook his head. "It's a decent-quality stone, about a carat, maybe a carat and a quarter, good color, and very slightly included—which means *I* can tell it's not perfect, but you can't. I would have sold it to you with a nice setting for twelve thousand."

"How much would you pay if I wanted to sell it to you?" I asked.

"Half. Six thousand."

"Thank you," I said. "You've been very helpful. I'll think about it."

"Better you should keep it," Chana said. "You're a good-looking young man; you'll find another girl better than the first one. Bring the diamond back and Shmuel will make a nice ring for you."

I thanked them again, walked across the street, and started the process all over again.

I talked to ten diamond dealers so that each of my diamonds got two opinions. The diamonds were all in the one-to-one-and-a-half-carat range and all about the same quality. Nine of the dealers quoted me a price that averaged out to sixty-two hundred dollars. The tenth guy told me my diamond was a fake and offered to take it off my hands for a hundred bucks. I guess there are *goniffs* wherever you go.

I figured there were about twenty-one hundred diamonds in the bag. If I could sell them for sixty-two hundred bucks a pop, I'd wind up with about thirteen million dollars. But I wasn't greedy. I'd happily take less for a quick sale.

I stood on the corner of 47th Street and Sixth Avenue and called Katherine. "I've got great news," I said.

"Tell me, tell me."

"I'm throwing a party. Tonight. Eight o'clock."
"What are you celebrating?"

"I've got thirteen million reasons to celebrate," I said.

"I'm busy," Katherine said. "Give me one."

"I'm in love with the most wonderful woman in the world."

"That's terrific," she said. "I'd love to meet her. I'll see you tonight."

Chapter 18

I COULDN'T TELL people the real reason I was throwing the party, so I e-mailed and texted everybody I wanted to see that night. And a few I didn't want to see. *"School's out. Let's drink. My place."*

I hadn't figured out how to unload the diamonds, so I was still on a student's budget. I bought chicken wings, a six-foot hero, chips, vino, beer, and the cheapest vodka on the shelf.

Katherine showed up at seven to help me set up.

"I have a surprise for you," she said.

I looked at my watch. "If it involves taking our clothes off, I'm definitely in."

"Hold that thought till after the party," she said. "Anyway, since when would having mad, passionate sex be a surprise?"

The onslaught of guests began at ten to eight, and by nine o'clock my apartment was a noisy, boozy, happy mixture of joy, escapism, and release. Most of the people who showed up were friends from Parsons, along with a few of my neighbors from the building.

"Did you invite the three guys who live on the first floor?" Katherine asked.

"You mean the sentries who live in apartment one and guard the building?" I said. "Of course I invited them."

"They're always super-nice to me when I show up," Katherine said. "When they see me, they hold the door and say hi."

"That's about as much as those guys socialize," I said. "They passed on the party, but I love having them live on the ground floor. I haven't had a single Jehovah's Witness stop by since they moved in."

My paintings were all over the apartment, and every few minutes someone would grab my arm and drag me over to one painting or another to talk about it. Sometimes they'd have questions, but mostly they just wanted to give me feedback.

Early in the evening I was getting comments like "I love how you've managed to capture the essence of the urban condition, the sense of isolation and loneliness one can experience in the midst of the asphalt jungle."

But after the alcohol had been flowing for a few hours, the comments were more like, "Dude, your shit is so freaking good. If I had any freaking money, I'd buy all of them."

I had some great friends, and drunk, sober, or anywhere in between, they were fun to hang with. Except Leonard Karns.

Leonard was sitting alone on the sofa, nursing the cheap red wine he'd brought, because "beer is for frat boys and rednecks." He looked amused, like an anthropologist studying a primitive tribe of beer-swilling natives. Everyone ignored him, except Hopper, who jumped up on the sofa to check him out. Karns reached out to pet him, and the cat responded with a nasty hiss and took off.

"Poor Leonard," Katherine whispered. "He seems to be unpopular across all species. Why did you even invite him? He doesn't like you or your paintings."

I smiled. "I know. Having him around keeps me humble."

At ten o'clock the doorbell rang and I checked the closed-circuit monitor. I didn't recognize the guy. He was short and fat—about three hundred pounds—with slicked-back black hair, a small goatee, and no mustache. If I'd ever met this guy before, I'd have remembered him. I didn't.

I'm not usually paranoid about strangers, but I had these diamonds that didn't belong to me, and somebody might be looking for them.

My Louisville Slugger was still standing in the corner next to the front door. With fifty friends and a baseball bat nearby, I figured if he was looking for trouble, I had the edge.

I buzzed him in.

Chapter 19

I HELD THE apartment door open and waited. The fat man was slow and ponderous. He clomped up the stairs, stopping at each landing to catch his breath.

Katherine joined me. "Who's coming?" "Party crasher. Nobody I know."

"A heavyset guy?"

"Fat."

She poked me in the ribs. "Shh, he'll hear you."

"I think he knows he's fat."

She punched me in the shoulder. "Stop."

The fat/heavyset man got to the fourth-floor landing and looked up at us. "Hello, Katherine," he said.

"Hello, Newton," she said. "Take your time."

"Like I have a choice," he said, grabbing the handrail and trudging up the last flight.

"I gather you know him," I said.

"He's my surprise."

The man was red in the face and sweating hard when he got to the top. "Matt, this is Newton," Katherine said. "Newton, this is Matthew Bannon, the brilliant young artist I was telling you about."

"Why does every brilliant young artist I meet have to live at the top of a five-story walk-up?" he said, extending a sweaty sausage-fingered hand.

"Nice to meet you, Mr. Newton."

"Not *Mister*. Just Newton. One name. Like Madonna."

"You look exhausted, Newton," I said as we entered the apartment. "Can I get you something?"

"An oxygen tank would be nice," he said.

"We have beer."

"Even better," he said. "Two cans."

By the time I brought back the beers, Newton had taken off his size 54 jacket. The blue shirt underneath had sweat rings the size of saddlebags under each arm.

"Newton is here to look at your work," Katherine said.

"Great," I said. "I'll give you a tour."

"I work alone," he said. "You stay here with Katherine while I look around."

He popped the top on the first beer and, with a can in each hand, casually began moving his way around the apartment.

"You think he'll like my stuff?" I asked Katherine.

"It doesn't matter if *he* likes it," she said. "He buys art for someone else. A hedge-fund guy. He's got tons of money and no time to shop. Newton shops for him."

"If this guy has so much money, why wouldn't he want a Pablo Picasso or a Willem de Kooning? Why would he want an original Matt Bannon?"

"He has those guys already. He's passionate about discovering young talent."

It took Newton ten minutes to look at my entire life's work. He handed me two empty beer cans and I brought him two more.

"How old are you?" he asked.

"Thirty."

"And you served in the military?"

"Marines."

"He was deployed to the Middle East three times," Katherine added.

"I sensed that from the work," he said.

"What do you think?"

"Bluntly," Newton said, "I think Mr. Bannon has a ways to go, but the raw talent is there." He turned to me. "I think my client will like your work, and I have no doubt he'd be happy to invest in you."

"Invest?" I said.

"I'd like to buy three paintings," he said. "If you're as good as I think you are, not only will my client experience the joy of having them in one of his homes, but years from now an early Matthew Bannon will be worth a lot of money. Win-win."

I couldn't believe it. "Which three early Matthew Bannons would you like to buy?" I said.

"The four people in the subway station, the old man in the bodega, and the woman at the window," he said, pointing at each one as he talked. "How much?"

I had no idea. I looked at Katherine.

"Give us a minute," she said to Newton and pulled me to a corner. "What do you think?"

"I don't know. The canvases cost around fifteen bucks each, and the frames were about thirty. Plus the paint. So my investment on each one is about fifty bucks. I'm a total unknown, so if you could get three, four hundred apiece, that would be huge."

She winked at me and led me over to Newton.

"You're right," she said. "Matthew is raw, he will get better, and at this stage he's an excellent investment. You're smart to get in on the ground floor."

"The fifth floor," Newton said, polishing off his next beer and opening another. "I was so winded climbing those stairs that I wanted to buy the apartment on the third floor and move in. Now stop greasing the skids, Katherine, and tell me how much."

"Two thousand apiece."

"That's a tad steep."

"Five thousand for the three paintings," Katherine said. "That's a thousand for every floor you climbed. And I'd hate to see you go home empty-handed after all that work."

Newton guzzled the last beer. "Deal," he said. "I'll send my crew to pick them up tomorrow."

He shook my hand and left.

I wrapped my arms around Katherine. I could see Karns sitting on the sofa, glaring at the two of us. *Bannon's hugging the teacher. What's up with that?*

"Did you just sell my paintings for five thousand dollars?" I asked.

"Just three of them. You still have plenty left."

I loved this woman so much. I kissed her hard.

Everything in life seemed to be going my way. All I could think was, *This can't possibly last, can it?*

Chapter 20

IT WAS THREE thirty in the morning, and Katherine and I were wrapped in one of those oversize blankets with sleeves. It sounds stupid, but when you're on the roof of your building and you've just made love under the stars, nothing is stupid.

"I was wrong," I said.

She snuggled up closer to me, and I could feel the heat of her body against mine. "About what?"

"When I woke up this morning with you in my arms," I said, "I thought I could never be any happier than I was at that moment. But it's less than twenty-four hours later, and I'm even crazier in love than I was then."

"It probably didn't hurt that I sold three of your paintings," she said.

"You think I love you for your marketing prowess?"

"I don't know," she said. "You're always going on about how you love me, but I don't recall that you've ever mentioned why. Why?"

"Because you're beautiful, you're smart, you're funny, and you're giving me an A in Group Critique."

"Says who? Where'd you hear that one?" She was grinning.

"You mean you're not giving me an A?"

"You deserved an A on your term paper, but I don't post the final grades for another two days," she said and looked a little pouty. "You'll have to wait like everyone else. I don't play favorites. Much."

I kissed her. "Thank you for selling my paintings," I said. "I can't believe you got five grand. I'd have sold them for a lot less."

"I knew that," she said. "And so did Newton."

"He did? Why didn't he negotiate?"

She smiled. "It's all part of the game."

"Since when is art a game?"

"Not art. Commerce. The price of a painting shapes what people think of it. And no matter how sophisticated Newton's boss is, he's not going to be happy hanging something on his wall that costs the same as an Elvis on velvet."

"You're telling me Newton paid top dollar so he could look good to his boss?"

"No," she said. "So you could look good."

I shook my head. "I guess I've got a lot to learn about the art business."

"You're in luck," she said, kissing me. "I'm an art teacher."

We lay there wrapped in each other's arms, gazing up at the stars. I never thought I could feel this good about a woman. Katherine Sanborne had changed my life, and with my medical bag full of diamonds, I was on the verge of changing hers.

"You think all that money will screw us up?" she said.

Shit! She knew about the money. I didn't know how she knew, but she did. It was a punch to the gut. *Deny, deny, deny.*

"What money?" I said lamely.

"You just made your first sale for five

thousand," she said. "It's a pretty impressive way to start your career."

Oh, that money.

I exhaled slowly. "No," I said, "it won't screw us up. Besides, it's only one sale. It could be a fluke."

"No. You're going to resonate with people," she said. "You're honest and it comes through in your work. It's the essence of Realism."

"Thanks," I said.

But she was wrong. I wasn't honest. And I had a bag of somebody else's diamonds in my foot-locker to prove it.

Chapter 21

GRAND CENTRAL TERMINAL is a majestic Beaux-Arts building sitting on forty-eight acres smack in the middle of Manhattan. It's been called the heart of the nation's greatest city, and yet not one of New York City's thirty-five thousand cops has jurisdiction in the terminal.

In a world where bureaucracy trumps geography, Grand Central has been designated the responsibility of the Metropolitan Transportation Authority Police, and MTA cops work for New York State.

"You realize we got no juice here in Grand Central," Rice said as he parked the car in front of a hydrant on 43rd Street.

"I make my own juice," Benzetti said.

"Especially when a bunch of crazy Russians are up our asses. If we don't find the diamonds, they'll just decide that we took them, and they'll ice us the same way they put away Zelvas."

They entered through the Vanderbilt Avenue doors and stood on the West Balcony under a trio of sixty-foot-high arch windows.

"It looks like everything's back to normal," Rice said, looking out over the marble balcony at the vast concourse below.

"Except for the beefed-up security," Benzetti said.

"I know. I counted five Staties when we came through the door," Rice said. "Normally, there's one."

Benzetti grinned. "Nervous times."

"Where are we headed?"

"Central Security Office. Lower level." Benzetti checked his watch. "I got a friend working this shift."

The two cops walked down the sweeping marble staircase, crossed the concourse, passed the circular marble-and-brass information pagoda with its famous four-sided clock, and went down another flight of stairs to the dining concourse.

They made their way through the food court, where Brother Jimmy's, Zaro's, Junior's, and more than a dozen other celebrated New York food institutions had taken up residence underground, then down a ramp till they got to a door that said AUTHORIZED PERSONNEL ONLY.

Benzetti rang a bell and flashed his badge at a camera, and the two of them were buzzed in.

"NYPD," he said to the sullen-faced MTA cop at the front desk. "I'm looking for Sergeant Black."

The cop eyeballed the shield, nodded, checked a directory, and dialed a four-digit number.

"Be right out," the cop mumbled.

Five minutes later, a tall, attractive African-American woman with three stripes on the sleeves of her uniform came out and threw her arms around Benzetti.

"I know this ain't no social call," she said, stepping back from the hug.

"Baby, you know me. I don't need backup for social calls," Benzetti said. "This is my partner, John Rice. John, this is Kylie Black."

They shook hands and Kylie escorted the two

men inside. The grandeur and the classic beauty that made the building an architectural landmark were nowhere to be found in the command center. Whatever charm the space may have had when it was built more than a century ago had been painted or plastered over. What remained was an uninspired sterile cavern with fluorescent lighting, banks of monitors, and rows of people at desks and consoles doing their damnedest to keep an eye on every one of the six hundred thousand people who passed through the terminal every day.

"What can the MTA do for New York's finest," Kylie said, letting her tongue gently glide across her upper lip, "that we haven't done already?"

"I hate to bother you," Benzetti said, "but we need to look at some of *America's Funniest Home Videos* from Tuesday night."

"The bombing?" Black said. "We've already run the tapes for the NYPD, FBI, Immigration, Homeland Security—you name it. We've had everyone looking at that bomb blast except for the fat lady who runs the food stamps program."

"We're not here about the bombing," Benzetti said. "Some reporter from the *Post* was mugged

Tuesday night by some homeless prick who's taking up residence in your lovely train station."

"Mugged?" Kylie said. "First I heard about it. Usually our wretched refuse are pretty well behaved. They come here to sleep and use the toilets. The bus terminal is where you get most of your muggings. Grand Central is the home of the harmless homeless."

"Well, one of your bums ripped off this *Post* reporter's brand-new leather jacket. His wife is a friend of the mayor's wife, and you can guess the rest."

Black shook her head. "NYPD assigns two detectives from Robbery to get a bead on this dude's precious jacket before City Hall shits a brick."

Benzetti shrugged. "Hey, I got two years till I make my twenty. Somebody asks me to do something, I shut up and do whatever makes them happy."

Black smiled broadly. "I'll remember that, Detective Benzetti, next time I can think of something that will make me happy. Come on, I'll set you guys up in a room with the tapes. Knock yourselves out."

Chapter 22

THE TECH WAS gaunt and pasty. His name was R. J. or J. R. Rice and Benzetti didn't pay attention, didn't care. All they wanted was for him to leave.

"You guys know how to navigate this puppy?" the tech asked.

They were sitting in a cramped screening room with a computer, a thirty-inch monitor, and not much else.

"I've got a sixteen-camera surveillance unit at home," Rice said.

"LOL," the tech said, actually laughing out loud. "Well, this will be like going from a Buick Skylark to a Bugatti Veyron."

"They both got four wheels and an engine," Benzetti said.

"LOL," the tech repeated, not laughing this time. "But don't worry, it's idiot-proof." He held up both hands. "Not that I'm saying you guys are idiots."

"LOL," Benzetti said. "Just show us how to work the goddamn Bugatti computer and get out of here."

Ten minutes later the tech left the room, and Rice pulled up the cameras on the main concourse.

"The bomb went off a little after eleven Tuesday night," Benzetti said. "Start the search an hour before."

The images were high-def, and finding Walter Zelvas in the late-night comings and goings of thousands of travelers took less than twenty minutes.

"Freeze it," Benzetti said. "There he is, buying coffee at Starbucks."

They tracked him as he walked into the waiting area, then fast-forwarded as he sat down, got up, checked the monitor, then repeated the process, getting more frustrated each time. "His train is late," Rice said as they watched Zelvas go back to Starbucks.

As the time code approached 11 p.m., Zelvas finished the second cup, crumpled it up, threw it in the trash, crossed the concourse, stopped to have a few words with a porter, and then entered the men's room. Rice froze it again.

"There's the guy the cops described. Beard. Poncho. That's the Talibum—the guy with the bomb. He's following Zelvas into the john."

"That's no bum," Benzetti said. "That's the guy Chukov hired to waste Zelvas. Pick them up on the bathroom camera."

"There are no bathroom cameras," Rice said. "Some crap about civil liberties."

They watched the video at normal speed. Eighty-eight seconds later, Zelvas stumbled out of the men's room, bleeding from the neck and firing his gun backward. Then he disappeared out of the frame.

Seconds later, the man in the poncho stood in the men's-room doorway. He pointed a gun in the direction Zelvas had headed, but first he had to deal with the MTA police.

"This is like watching the Keystone Kops," Rice said as the bearded man handily dispatched a cop with a bucket of soapy water.

The bum grabbed two grenades from under his poncho and pulled the pins, and the screen was engulfed in smoke.

"That bastard is slick," Benzetti said. "See if you can pick him up on another camera."

Rice bounced from one camera to another, but the smoke blocked them all. He hit fast-forward, but by the time the smoke faded, so did the bum. "I can't find him anywhere," Rice said.

"Chukov hired him, so Chukov can find him. Our job is to find the diamonds. Somebody knows where they are."

Rice smacked his forehead. "Duh. Zelvas knows."

"Duh," Benzetti repeated. "Zelvas is dead."

"He's not dead in the video. Hang on."

Rice surfed from camera to camera. "Got him," he said after a few minutes.

They watched Zelvas stagger across the marble floor. He crashed into a bank of lockers, found one on the top row, and opened it.

Rice froze the image and zoomed in on the frame. "Jackpot," he said. "Locker number nine twenty-five. How much you want to bet it's not filled with cheese?"

Chapter 23

RICE UNFROZE THE image, and Zelvas slumped to the floor. A wet circle fanned out from his body, slowly turning the white marble bright red.

And then wisps of smoke crept into the corner of the screen.

"Shit," Benzetti said. "We're going to lose the picture again."

"Relax," Rice said. "He's a good two hundred feet from the blast."

They watched as the smoke cast a pink haze over the picture, then lifted.

"Look at all those people run. They're practically tripping over the poor bastard, and they don't stop to help him," Rice said.

"As far as they're concerned, some terrorist just set off a couple of bombs. It's every man for himself," Benzetti said. "Wait a minute. Here comes Mr. Good Samaritan."

The preppy-looking young man knelt down and tried to comfort Zelvas.

"Who is this guy?" Rice asked.

"Who knows? He looks like some latte-sipping pansy who was running for his life and decided to stop and smell the dead guy."

"Zelvas is telling him something," Rice said.

"Short conversation," Benzetti said, as they watched Zelvas die. "He just cashed in his chips."

"Now what's this guy gonna do?" Rice said.

"If the kid is smart, he'll move his ass out of Grand Central."

But the kid didn't move. He was staring up at the blood-smeared lockers.

"Uh-oh," Rice said. "The monkey sees the banana."

The young man stood up, reached into the open locker, and taking out a small leather bag, looked inside.

"The monkey is about to crap in his pants," Benzetti said.

"He looks like a Boy Scout," Rice said. "Maybe he'll turn it into Lost and Found. I know I would."

Benzetti laughed. "He could be as honest as a full-length mirror, but we all have our price."

The young man shut the bag in a hurry and snapped the latch.

"My instincts tell me this dude just found out what his is."

And then the cop showed up.

"This guy is NYPD," Rice said.

"He must be from the Idiot Squad," Benzetti said. "Why would he pull a gun on a civilian?"

The kid ignored the cop's gun and tended to the dead Russian.

"He's smart," Rice said. "He's using Zelvas's bag as a prop and playing doctor."

"And Officer Dumbass is buying it," Benzetti said as the young cop holstered his gun.

They watched the scenario unfold. Finally the kid dug into his pocket, pulled out his cell phone, and started talking.

"How convenient," Benzetti said. "A phone call."

"It's a ruse," Rice yelled at the cop on the

monitor. "And you're buying it, Officer"—he paused the video and zoomed in on the cop's name tag—"Kendall."

He hit the play button and watched as Kendall listened to his radio. The call was brief but it seemed to energize the cop.

"Oh, crap," Benzetti said. "I think I know how this movie is going to end."

Kendall spent a few more seconds with the kid, then took off toward the Forty-second Street Passageway. The kid waited another ten seconds, then cut and ran in the other direction.

"Track him," Benzetti said.

Rice followed the action from camera to camera as the kid made his way to the Lexington Avenue exit. The final camera caught the drama outside as three men haggled over a cab and the kid bummed a ride with the winner.

Rice froze the frame. "The hack number is six J four two," he said, writing it down. "I'll call the TLC and hunt down the driver."

"I wouldn't get my hopes up," Benzetti said. "It'll probably be some towelhead who won't remember anything because he was too busy gouging people that night."

Rice hit play, and the cab, the kid, and the leather bag with the diamonds were gone.

"He wasn't carrying any luggage," Rice said. "So he's either a regular commuter or he works in one of the shops here at Grand Central. I'll pull a screen shot of his face. We can find this guy."

"And when we do, I will personally put a bullet through his head and bring the diamonds back to Chukov," Benzetti said.

"Y'know," Rice said, grinning, "there really ought to be a finder's fee for something like that."

"There will be," Benzetti said. "A fistful of diamonds."

"Two fistfuls," Rice said.

A close-up of the young man filled the thirty-inch screen, and Rice froze the image. "And if the Russians notice that any stones are missing," Rice said, "we can just blame it on Pretty Boy."

Benzetti nodded. "LOL, baby. L.O. Fucking L."

Book Two

THE CHASE

Chapter 24

NATHANIEL PRINCE SAT on his bed, his eyes fixed on the cordless phone beside him.

"You can't make it ring by staring at it," Natalia said.

"Chukov should have called hours ago," Prince said.

"Then call him."

"It's not my job to follow that incompetent prick around with a broom and a dustpan," Prince said. "Chukov is the underling. He's the one who should be calling me."

Natalia looked at her watch. "It's getting late. Pretty soon he'll be too drunk to dial."

Prince couldn't argue with the logic. He picked up the phone and pushed a single button. Chukov didn't answer until the fourth ring.

"Nathaniel, I was just going to call you," Chukov said. "I have good news. We zeroed in on the guy who has our diamonds."

"It's about time," Prince said.

"I e-mailed you his picture."

"His picture? I want his head delivered to my front door with his balls stuffed in his mouth," Prince screamed. "Who is he?"

"He's just some asshole kid who was at the right place at the right time. Zelvas stashed the diamonds in a locker at Grand Central. This guy found them and took off."

"You told me the diamonds were in Zelvas's safe," Prince said. "Why did he move them to a locker in a train station?"

Because Natalia knew the combination, and Zelvas didn't trust a whore who would bed down with her own father, Chukov thought.

"I don't know, Nathaniel," he said.

"What do we know about the guy who has the diamonds? What's his name?"

"We don't know his name yet," Chukov said, "but he probably either works at Grand Central or is a regular commuter. Somebody has to know who he is. We definitely will find him."

"Who's *we*?"

"Me, Rice, Benzetti, and the Ghost," Chukov said.

"Not enough," Prince said. "I want more people on it."

"I have a dozen of my men . . ."

Prince cut Chukov off before he could finish. "I don't want foot soldiers. I want a professional. A hunter. A killer."

"The Ghost is a professional . . ."

"He's one man," Prince said. "The Syndicate is going to blame me for the missing diamonds. I don't care how good this Ghost guy is. He can't be everywhere. I need insurance, backup. Somebody smart. Somebody we've worked with before. What about the German?"

"Krall?"

"That's the one."

"I don't know," Chukov said. "These killers for hire are like prima donnas. They don't like to be in competition with someone else. They want an exclusive contract."

"I don't care what they want," Prince said.

"They're mercenaries. I pay, I make the rules. I want you to find the bastard who took my diamonds, and I want his fingers chopped off, one by one. And if Krall doesn't want to do it, find somebody who will."

Prince hung up the phone and went to his computer. He printed out the picture of the man who had stolen his millions. He showed it to Natalia. "You know this *muzhik*?" he asked.

She studied the picture. "I'd definitely remember him if I saw him. He's cute," she said, toying with Prince.

"He won't be so cute when I'm finished with him."

"Don't be jealous," she said. "I think you're cuter." She dropped the picture to the floor and kissed him lightly on the mouth, letting her lips linger.

He kissed her in return. Not so lightly.

She unbuttoned his shirt, slowly, button by button.

He unbuttoned her black silk blouse the same way. Then he cupped her breasts.

It was a ritual they had performed many times before. Undressing one another slowly, tantalizing and teasing each other. But this time Nathaniel couldn't wait.

He pulled down her slacks, then her panties and got behind Natalia as she leaned forward over his heavy oak desk. He dropped his trousers, planted his hands on her ass, angled her into position, and entered her.

It had been twenty years since the taxi mowed down his wife and son and left his little girl for dead. They had forged a bond since that tragedy. And as Natalia grew into a beautiful girl, the bond became a physical and emotional union, a fierce, unstoppable love that had erupted the summer she was seventeen. For the next decade their love had flourished without guilt, without regret, and without shame. If it was forbidden and wrong, then so be it. It was their lives, their choice to make.

It was a give-and-take relationship, but tonight Nathaniel Prince needed to take more than he could give. His body was racing to climax and he couldn't wait for Natalia. He came violently, repeatedly, panting, exhaling her name like a prayer.

She called out to him in Russian—just as she

had called out to him every day and every night as he sat by her in the hospital, watching her fight for her life.

"Papa, Papa."

Chapter 25

MARTA KRALL WAS as beautiful as she was intelligent, as intelligent as she was deadly. She was nearly six feet tall, with white-blond hair, a former model who could make a man's heart beat faster just by walking into a room. But for the right amount of money she could make a man's heart stop. Permanently.

Chukov had tracked Krall down in Los Angeles. Eight hours later, she entered his apartment, wearing Marc Jacobs pleated black leather jodhpurs and a Derek Lam dark gray cashmere cowl-neck sweater. Her hair was cropped close to her face, framing perfect features and flawless skin that most men and many women longed to touch.

She sat down and stared at Chukov.

An ice sculpture, he thought. *Cold to the very core. The perfect killer.*

"I read in the *New York Times* that Walter Zelvas was found dead in the Grand Central fiasco," she said.

"Yes," Chukov said. "He decided to take early retirement."

"You should have called me," she said. "Then his retirement party might not have been front-page news."

"It was a rush job. He was planning to leave town."

"More likely he was planning to leave the hemisphere," Krall said. "Why was he running?"

"He was stealing from the Syndicate, and we found out about it."

"I see. And since you're in the diamond business, I'm guessing he wasn't pilfering office supplies."

"Very observant," Chukov said. "And now I want to recover everything he stole."

"Thanks, but no thanks," she said. "I don't do lost and found. Call me when you have something more challenging and interesting. Wet work is best for me."

"Here," Chukov said, handing her a photo of a preppy-looking young man standing next to a locker. "Get this guy as wet as you want."

Marta studied the picture. "Sexy guy," she said. "I almost hate to kill him. Not really, but a little. I'd prefer to play with him first, though."

"Just find out what he did with my diamonds. Can you do that?"

"With one hand tied behind my back," she said, staring at the Russian with sea-green eyes. "And both hands tied behind his."

They negotiated her price, a high one.

"One question," Marta said. "Who am I in competition with? And if you lie to me, I'll know it, and I'll be on the first flight back to L.A. Or Hamburg."

"It's not a competition," Chukov said. "I got two local dickhead cops who work for me, and one professional."

"Who?"

"The Ghost."

Marta kept her icy exterior, but inside she was roiling. She had never met the Ghost, but she despised him. People talked about him like he was a god.

"The Ghost," she said casually. "I've heard he's pretty good."

Chukov laughed. "*Pretty good?* They say he's the only assassin who will go to heaven. Satan would be too nervous having him around."

"If he's so good, why do you need me?"

"Because my boss wants a backup."

She stood up. "I'm nobody's backup. Get somebody else to suck hind tit."

Chukov knew he'd handled her wrong. He watched as she headed toward the door. Prince would kill him if he lost her.

"Wait," he said. "Forget about what my boss wants. I want you because I think the Ghost might know more about the missing diamonds than he lets on, and I'll pay you double if you'll do me the honor of killing him."

Krall looked surprised. Nothing would make her happier than to eliminate the Ghost. And now someone was willing to pay her to do it.

She reached out and shook Chukov's hand. "I accept."

Chukov had surprised himself by his impulsiveness. But then he lowered his eyes to his chest. He could still see the red dot boring into his skin, into his flesh, trying to tear a hole in his dignity.

He had no regrets about his sudden decision. The Ghost must die.

Vadim Chukov bows to no man.

Chapter 26

MARTA KRALL TOOK a cab to 42nd Street and Sixth Avenue and bought a turkey, avocado, and bacon sandwich at the 'wichcraft kiosk in Bryant Park. She found a quiet table under a London plane tree in the northern promenade and called Etienne Gravois in France.

He wasn't happy to hear from her. He never was. Marta had saved Etienne's life, and he had been paying for it ever since.

Etienne was a compulsive gambler who made the mistake of borrowing twenty thousand euros from an Algerian drug dealer and failing to pay it back. Marta was hired to kill him. Instead, she paid off his debt. Etienne was much more valuable to her alive. He worked in computer records for Interpol.

"*Bonjour,* Etienne," Marta said. "I e-mailed you a photo of a young man."

"I've left the office for the evening," he said.

"Then go back."

"I'm meeting my wife for dinner. It's her birthday."

"Please give her my best. And tell her that in a few days I, too, will be meeting her. Only by then she'll be your widow."

"I'll go back to the office."

"The photo was taken at Grand Central Terminal in New York City a few days ago," she said. "I want to know who the man is and where to find him."

"Do you know anything about this man?" Etienne asked.

"No. That's your job, Monsieur Gravois. You sold your worthless soul to the devil. Now go back to your computer and get the devil what she wants."

"Yes."

She gave him a phone number. "How long?"

"If he has a criminal record, maybe two hours. If I have to dig deeper, a little longer."

"Don't waste time. I need it now."

"I understand."

"One more question, Etienne. Do you have anything new on the Ghost?"

"No." He laughed.

"What's funny?"

"Nothing, nothing. It's just that half the police agencies around the world are looking for the Ghost. Now you, too."

"Well, if you get anything on him, I hope you don't make the mistake of calling any of them first. *Comprenez-vous,* Etienne?"

"*Oui.*"

She hung up.

Marta Krall rarely smiled. All those years of posing for fashion photographers had drained the joy from her. Her eyes were cold and malevolent-looking. Her face could not hide the evil in her heart.

But that was before Chukov hired her to kill the Ghost. She opened her bag and took out a pocket mirror.

Just as she suspected. She was smiling now.

Chapter 27

MARTA WAS CONFIDENT that Gravois would identify the handsome guy in the photo. His life depended on it. As for tracking down the Ghost, she had a better resource. And he was right here in New York City: Ira.

She took a cab down to lower Manhattan and got off on Canal Street, where the air was thick with the fumes of the hundreds of trucks and a few scattered cars that crawled their way into the Holland Tunnel heading for Jersey.

She walked from Canal to Laight, then along West to Watts, and finally, positive that no one was tailing her, past the sprawling UPS truck garage to a soot-gray brick building on Washington Street.

The building was a little piece of old New York gone to seed. Six stories; six doorbells. She pushed the only one that had a name on it—ACME INDUSTRIES.

A voice answered. "Sorry, we're closed."

"I'm told that you're open late for your premier customers," Marta said.

The voice came back. "What level premier customer?"

"Titanium."

She was buzzed in. She walked past the elevator and took the stairs. On the second-floor landing she saw a rat gnawing on a moldy bagel. He didn't move, just glared at her and bared his teeth until she passed.

Ira's door was on the fourth floor. Another buzzer and she was inside the loft. It was three thousand square feet, every inch of which was covered. There were rows of mismatched tables holding electronic equipment, and a kitchen area where Marta could see two more rats scavenging on a countertop. There was a bed littered with food containers, beer cans, and porn magazines. Stacks of computer manuals piled waist-high were parked next to an overflowing garbage can.

A path wide enough for a wheelchair wound its way through the chaos. The man in the chair was somewhere between thirty and fifty, grossly overweight, and seemingly uninterested in personal hygiene. He had an open bag of Cool Ranch Doritos on his lap and a two-liter bottle of Pepsi on the computer stand next to him.

"I'm Ira," he said. "Sorry if I smell a little gamey. We don't get many social calls, and getting in and out of the tub is a bitch."

"No problem," Marta said. "I'm Giselle."

"Who sent you, Giselle?"

"A friend."

"My best reference," Ira said. "If I ever meet this Mr. A. Friend, I'd love to buy him a beer. What can I do for you?"

"I've got a husband who can't keep his dick in his pants, but if you can't get in and out of a tub, I doubt you can do anything for me. My problem requires someone with a lot more muscle."

"We have a division of labor at Acme Industries," Ira said. "Brains and brawn. I'm brains."

"I hate to disappoint you, Ira," Marta said, "but I already have brains. What I'm looking for is someone strong enough to toss a hundred and ten pounds of shit off a roof."

"I'm guessing the husband with the wandering dick weighs more than one ten," Ira said, "but I wouldn't be surprised if he had a hard-bodied little mistress about that size."

"Well, *I* was surprised, Ira. And now I'm going to surprise them. Yes or no, is this something you know how to handle?"

"Absolutely. Do you want your husband roughed up as well?"

Marta laughed. "I could rough the dumb bastard up. I could also bash his head in with a cast-iron skillet when he's sleeping. But I'd rather see the look on his face when he finds out that his little office-manager–slash-whore did a swan dive off a building."

"No problem. I have several candidates who can handle the job."

"I don't want several. I want one. The best man you have."

"I can give you second best," Ira said. "But my number-one man doesn't do matrimonial."

"What the hell is that supposed to mean?"

"He gets top dollar for hunting down hard-core dirtbags. He doesn't believe in killing some pretty little thing just because she's banging your old man."

"A killer with a conscience. How noble. What's his name—Don Quixote?"

"They call him the Ghost."

"And you're sure he's good?" Marta said.

"Nobody better."

"Excellent," Marta said. "He sounds like just the man I've been looking for."

Chapter 28

"I THINK I WOULD really like to meet this Ghost fellow," Marta said. "Tell me about him."

Ira stroked the stubble-covered rolls of fat that were his chins. "Let's see, what can I tell you about the Ghost?" he said. "He likes candlelit dinners, long walks on the beach, outdoor concerts at Tanglewood, and doing the *New York Times* Sunday crossword puzzle in bed with a smart, sensuous woman. Someone like you, *Giselle*."

He shoved a handful of Doritos in his mouth.

Marta stiffened. "What the hell are you talking about?"

"C'mon, Marta, do you think I'm stupid?" Ira said, Cool Ranch crumbs blowing out of his mouth. "I have a database of millions of voice-prints, and I have yours from half a dozen phone calls. Somebody buzzes me from downstairs, I check the voice for a match. I'm flattered you would visit. My clients usually come here, but my operatives almost never come to the office. It's dull as hell around here on Take Your Daughter to Work Day. What do you want with the Ghost?"

"We're working on the same job."

"What job?" Ira said. "Zelvas is dead. Finished."

"Not finished," Marta said. "The diamonds that Zelvas stole from the Syndicate got stolen from him."

"I know," Ira said. "Chukov sent me a picture of some guy nabbing the stones out of a locker. I passed it along to the Ghost. You want a copy of that?"

"I have it. Chukov hired me as backup. Sorry about trying to con you, but since the Ghost and I are on the same side, I thought you could connect us."

"I couldn't even if I wanted to," he said. "He contacts me. But it's a pleasure to meet you in person. Forgive me if I don't stand up."

"Did you ever meet the Ghost in person?" Marta asked.

"No, ma'am. He's got a policy. Nobody gets to see him. That way, nobody knows what he looks like."

She unsnapped the clasp on her black leather Bottega Veneta shoulder bag and removed her Glock 38 semiautomatic. The light .45-caliber pistol fit comfortably in her hand, and its ten-round magazine gave her a soul-satisfying feeling of power.

"Funny thing," she said, pointing the gun squarely at Ira's sagging chest. "I have the same policy."

He stared at her, much less afraid than she expected. "Oh, come on, Marta. Do you really think I'd rat you out?"

"Would you?"

"Never. How do you think I've been able to do this all these years? I keep secrets. Yours, his, everybody's."

"I believe that," she said. "But I also believe that you might part with a few of his secrets if I let you live."

"You call this living?" he said, spitting out a

bitter laugh. "Eating, drinking, and jerking off in this shit hole—that's not a life. The only thing that keeps me from slitting my own throat is the danger. Working with assassins, executioners, butchers. I'm a conduit to the death squad. That's my life. You want to put me out of my misery? Go ahead. You're not the first one to pull a gun on me."

"Maybe not. But I'm the first one who will pull the trigger."

She pressed the muzzle of the gun hard against his sternum.

"It might be an ugly life, Ira," she said, "but it's the only one you've got. Do you want to live?"

The bravado drained from his face. "Yes," he said. "Given the choice . . ."

"You hear anything—*anything*—that will lead me to the Ghost, you call me."

She handed him a card with a cell number on it.

"I'll call," he said. "I swear." His body began to shake, and the bag of chips fell from his lap and spilled on the floor.

"Careful," Marta said, lowering the gun. "You don't want to mess up the place."

Chapter 29

I THOUGHT THAT what I was about to do would blow Katherine's mind. At least I hoped it would. I dialed her cell number.

"What's up?" she said. Two words, but just hearing her voice got me going. We were still at that stage in our relationship, and I hoped it wouldn't end.

"It's payback time," I told her. "You had a surprise for me. Now I have one for you."

"Cool. What is it?"

"What it is," I said, "is a *surprise* . . . as in I'm not telling you anything over the phone."

"Can you at least give me a hint?"

I was sitting on my bed with Walter Zelvas's medical bag at my side. I ran my fingers over the pebble-grain leather.

"Okay, one hint," I said. "It sparkles."

"Sparkling surprises are my favorite," she said. "When do I get to see it?"

"Immediately, if possible. Where are you?"

"I'm just wrapping up at the Whitney. I need about a half hour."

"I'll meet you at the Amity and buy you lunch," I said.

"Deal. Love you," she said.

"You're going to love me even more when you see this surprise," I said, hanging up before she could ask for another hint.

Five minutes later, I was on the subway headed uptown on the number 6 local. I sat next to an elderly woman who took one look at my medical bag and told me how wonderful it was that there were still doctors who made house calls.

At 42nd Street I switched to the express, got off at 86th Street, and walked to the New Amity diner at 84th and Madison. I opened the door and immediately felt like a rock star.

"Mottchew," Gus called from the back of the diner. "Mottchew Bannon. Good to see you, my friend."

The owner, Steve, two other waiters, and the short-order cook behind the grill all gave me a big welcome.

As Greek diners go, this one is the absolute best. The food is good, the prices are affordable, and the service is fantastic. Gus was about sixty, with thinning silver hair, a ready smile, and an endearing accent. He was from Greece, or as he called it, *Grrrriss*. I didn't know much about him, but I got the feeling he'd had quite an interesting life in the old country.

He pointed to a booth, and before my butt hit the vinyl, he delivered my usual mug of half-regular, half-decaf coffee and a small pitcher of skim milk.

"Long time ago, I had one like this," he said, eyeing my medical bag.

"Were you a doctor back in Athens?" I asked.

He shrugged. "You have a doctor bag. Are you a doctor?" he said, avoiding my question and adding to the mystery of his past. "Is the pretty lady coming today?"

"The lady is here," Katherine said as she breezed in and plopped down on the other side of the booth. "She's not feeling pretty, but she's definitely thirsty."

Gus brought Katherine her usual: a large glass of water, no ice, slice of lemon, and a straw. We ordered sandwiches—one turkey and tomato, one tuna melt—to be split in the kitchen so we could share.

"So, what's the occasion?" she said. "What did I do to deserve a surprise?"

"It's just my little way of thanking you for giving me an A for the semester."

"I haven't posted the grades yet, so your surprise sounds more like a bribe," she said. "And Katherine Sanborne does not accept bribes."

She took a long sip of her water. "But in your case, I'll make an exception. Don't keep me in suspense any longer. Where is it?"

I put the medical bag on top of the table.

"That's it?" she said.

"You look disappointed," I said.

"You said the surprise sparkles, so I was expecting one of those little robin's-egg-blue boxes from Tiffany's," she said.

"Who knows?" I said. "Maybe Tiffany's changed their packaging."

"I guess there's only one way to find out," she said.

She unclasped the brass latch and opened the bag.

I held my breath.

Chapter 30

KATHERINE REACHED IN and pulled out a bundle of postcards that I had tied with a red ribbon.

"The Louvre, the Eiffel Tower, the Arc de Triomphe, Notre Dame Cathedral," she said as she thumbed through the cards. "I'm beginning to sense a theme here."

"There's more," I said. "Keep going."

She took out a bottle of wine.

"Georges Duboeuf Beaujolais Nouveau," she said. "Is this what sparkles?"

"No. It's flat and cheap. On sale for seven bucks," I said. "I spared no expense."

"This is fun," she said. "Like a treasure hunt."

She reached in and took out two baguettes and a wedge of Brie. "Are we going on a picnic?"

"Yes," I said.

"Where?"

"Keep digging," I said.

She reached in and pulled out two e-tickets that I had printed from my computer an hour before.

And then she shrieked. "Paris? We're going to Paris?"

She looked around and realized that half the people in the diner were watching us. "We're going to Paris," she said, in case any of them hadn't heard her the first time.

Several people applauded.

"I don't know what to pack," she said. "When are we going?"

I pointed at the e-ticket.

She looked at it and shrieked again. "Tonight? Are you crazy?"

"Yes," I said. "About you."

"I can't go tonight."

"Sure you can," I said. "We'll travel light and buy what we need along the way. People who buy cheap last-minute tickets on the Internet are usually poor and flexible. I figure we qualify as both."

She was dumbfounded and over the moon at the same time. "I only have eight hours to get ready. I don't know what to do," she said.

Two middle-aged women were sitting at a table across from us. One of them leaned over and said, "Honey, if you don't go to Paris with this gorgeous guy, I will."

"I'm going, I'm going," Katherine said. "This is the most fantastic, most romantic, most extravagant gift I've ever gotten."

Gus arrived with our lunch and took a look at the wine, the cheese, and the French bread. "That looks better than a tuna melt," he said. "You want I should wrap up these sandwiches to go? You can have them for lunch tomorrow."

"No can do, Gus," I said. "Tomorrow the two of us are having lunch in the City of Light. I hear it really sparkles."

Chapter 31

RICE AND BENZETTI tracked down the cabbie who picked up Bagboy, their code name for the young guy with the bag full of diamonds.

"You remember this guy?" Rice asked, showing the driver the surveillance photo.

"No. Should I?"

"You had him in your cab the night of the bomb blast at Grand Central."

He took a second look at the picture. "Oh, yeah, I remember. Crazy night. I picked up a fare who wanted to go to Jersey. This dude tagged along for the ride."

"Where in Jersey did you take him?" Benzetti asked.

"He didn't go the whole way. He's a doc. I

dropped him at St. Vincent's Hospital downtown. And it was a free ride. No charge. Them kind of nights bring out the Good Samaritan in me."

"Yeah, you got *philanthropist* written all over your face," Benzetti said.

The two cops spent the next few hours hitting the shops, restaurants, and ticket windows at Grand Central, hoping to find someone who could ID Bagboy.

Whoever he was, he wasn't a regular. Nobody recognized him.

"Let's talk to the uniform who pulled the gun on him," Benzetti said.

"His name's Ruben Kendall," Rice said. "He's over at the Seventeenth."

"I don't want to make a house call," Benzetti said. "Too many people know us there and will ask why we're nosing around. See if you can get him to meet us on the outside."

Rice called the Seventeenth Precinct and got Kendall on the phone.

"Officer Kendall, this is Detective John Rice. Nice job the other night at Grand Central."

"Um, thanks. What can I do for you?"

"I'm trying to wrap up some paperwork on

that whole bomb thing," Rice said. "Got time for a few quick questions?"

"Sure. Come on over to the precinct."

"If my partner and I set foot inside the Seventeenth, we'll run into at least a dozen guys who will want to catch up and schmooze about the old days," Rice said, faking a chuckle. "Would you mind popping outside? We're in a black Chevy Tahoe around the corner at Fiftieth and Third."

"No problem. I'll be right there."

At six four, two hundred and forty pounds, Officer Ruben Kendall was an intimidating presence. But his baby face and warm brown eyes transformed the tiger into a pussycat.

The two detectives got out of their car and introduced themselves. Rice handed him the surveillance photo. "You recognize this guy?"

The cop took a quick look. "That's the doc from the other night at Grand Central."

Benzetti jumped in. "How'd you know he was a doc?"

Kendall hesitated. He knew a loaded question when he heard one.

"He . . . he told me," Kendall said.

"He *told* you?" Benzetti said.

Kendall put a hand across his eyes and slid it down his face. "I never got around to checking his ID. It was a madhouse. It was like nothing they teach you at the Academy."

"I went to the Academy," Benzetti said, "and I distinctly remember being told, if you see a guy standing over a dead body, check his ID."

"Hey, man, people were insane, trying to get out of the station, and then I got a ten-thirteen call," Kendall said. "'Multiple looters. Officer needs assistance.' This guy wasn't a threat. I took off."

"Listen, kid, nobody expects you to check IDs during a terrorist attack," Rice said, putting a hand on Kendall's shoulder and oozing Good Cop from every pore. "So the guy said he was a doc. What else can you tell us about him?"

The cop pulled a pad from his pocket. "I remember he said he worked at St. Vincent's," Kendall said as he flipped through the pages. "He gave me his name and I wrote it—here it is. Jason Wood. Dr. Jason Wood. Does that help?"

"If it's his real name, it'll make our job easier," Rice said.

"And if it's a phony, what happens to me?"

"Meter-maid patrol," Benzetti said.

"Don't pay any attention to him," Rice said. "He goes by the book, but we all make mistakes."

"Is he going to write me up?"

"I'm not going to let him," Rice said. "Nick, listen to me. We're not turning this kid in. You made plenty of mistakes when you were a rookie."

Benzetti shrugged. "Fine. But I don't want to get nailed for not turning him in. So this conversation never happened. You never even met us. You got that, kid?"

"Yes, sir. It never happened. Thanks. Thanks a lot."

"Get out of here."

Kendall turned fast and headed back to the precinct house.

"Dumb bastard," Benzetti said. "Call St. Vincent's."

"Why bother? Fifty bucks says they never heard of Dr. Jason Wood."

"I wouldn't bet fifty cents on it," Benzetti said. "But you might as well go through the motions."

They got back in the car, and Rice called the

hospital. Two minutes later he hung up. "Never heard of him," he said. "Now what do we do?"

Benzetti didn't answer. He was too busy mind-humping a tall, leggy blonde who was walking down Third Avenue. "Take a look at that," he said.

"Dream on, Beans. If that woman ever saw you with your shoes off, she'd laugh herself into a coma."

They watched as the woman walked toward the car.

Benzetti rolled down his window.

"What are you doing?" Rice said.

"She's great from the front. I want to get a good look at her ass as she walks past."

But the woman didn't walk past. She stopped, reached inside the window, grabbed Benzetti's tie, and yanked hard, smacking his head against the car door.

"You're Chukov's Boys in Blue, right?" she said. "I've been looking for you."

Chapter 32

BENZETTI YOWLED IN pain. He fumbled for his gun, but before he could get it, there was a muzzle of a Glock pistol in his mouth.

Rice went for his gun.

"Unless his head is made of Kevlar, the bullet will go right through him," the blonde said. "Then right through you. One shot. Two dead cops."

Rice froze. "Is Chukov giving you a bonus if you kill us both with one bullet?"

"Kill you? The thought never crossed my mind." She smiled, beautiful and evil at the same time. "Chukov hired me to work with you. I'm Marta, your new best friend."

"If I were you, I'd work on my first-impression

skills. If we're friends, why is that gun in my partner's mouth?"

"Because he was drooling over me like a dog in a meat market. I wasn't hired to give your greaseball partner a hard-on." She jiggled the gun in Benzetti's mouth. "You got that, Romeo?"

He grunted a yes.

Marta slid the gun from his lips, but kept it pointed at him. "Nice to meet you," she said.

"Yeah, a real joy," Benzetti said, rubbing his head where it had smashed into the top of the car door.

"What have you got on this guy who walked off with Chukov's diamonds?"

"Nobody we talked to at Grand Central recognized him," Rice said. "A rookie beat cop saw him bending over Zelvas's body, but the kid conned him into thinking he was a doctor. As soon as the cop got distracted, Bagboy split for the exit and hopped a cab. The last person to see him was the cabbie who dropped him at St. Vincent's Hospital."

"But he's not a doctor, so how does that help us find him?" Marta said.

"The guy just stumbled on a fortune in

diamonds," Benzetti said. "Where's the first place he'd want to go? Home. He wouldn't give the cabbie his real address, so he plays out the doctor ruse and asks to be taken to a hospital in his neighborhood. St. Vincent's is on West Twelfth Street, which means it's a good bet he lives within a five-to-ten-block radius."

"That's a big territory," Marta said.

"Give me a break," Benzetti said. "I just eliminated four boroughs and most of Manhattan."

"What if he got to St. Vincent's and caught another cab?" Marta said. "What if he jumped on the subway to Brooklyn?"

"Look, I'm a cop. I can't handle all the what-ifs. I follow the leads I got, and if I run into a dead end, I try something else. It's called leg work."

"Leg work takes time, which is something you two useless losers don't have. So you better come up with something smarter than standing on the corner of West Twelfth Street with your hands in your pockets, waiting for some guy to walk by with a bag full of diamonds."

She wagged the gun in his face. "Do I have to add *or else?*"

"We get the point," Benzetti said. "We'll find the diamonds."

"I doubt it," Marta said. "But if you do . . . every last one of them goes back to Chukov. Got it?"

"Got it," Benzetti said.

"I'll have my eye on you two, so be careful, boys. This is your last warning."

She put the gun in her shoulder bag and headed down the street without a care in the world, window-shopping of all things.

Chapter 33

"SHE'S RIGHT," RICE SAID. "We don't have a lot of time left to find those diamonds. First Chukov warns us, now she does."

"So, what are you suggesting? Give me a plan."

"We go public. Get the surveillance shot of Bagboy out to the press."

"Are you crazy?" Benzetti said. "This isn't even our case. The bombing at Grand Central belongs to Homeland Security. We're trying to find a bag of blood diamonds stolen from ruthless killers, and we're trying to do it on the down low. If we go public, we'll have Feds all over us."

"I understand that. So we go to the press and we don't say anything about Grand Central.

We're just two cops looking for a suspect. We can say he's wanted in connection with whatever we want. We can say he's a person of interest in an ongoing murder or robbery investigation. Doesn't matter. But we don't give the TIPS phone number. We just give out our direct lines and we handle the incoming. What do you say?"

Benzetti nodded. "Let me think about it."

Rice exploded. "How about putting a gun in your mouth while you're thinking? Damn it, Nick, that blond bitch was even crazier than Chukov. She said she's keeping an eye on us, and from the way she got the jump on us, I believe her. I don't care about walking away with a fistful of diamonds. I got two kids. I want to walk away with my life."

"Okay," Benzetti said. "We'll go public. I got a guy over at New York One. It's not CNN, but they do twenty-four-hour, 'round-the-clock news—and it's all local. We'll tell them they have an exclusive for a day. They'll flash this poor bastard's picture and our phone numbers every six minutes until we find him and kill him."

Chapter 34

"IS KATHERINE ONE IN a couple hundred million or what?" I asked. "Can you even begin to think of another woman who would meet me for lunch and then a few hours later drop everything and jump on a plane to Paris?"

No answer.

"Okay, okay, maybe a lot of women would drop everything to go to Paris. But name one besides Katherine who would go with me."

No answer.

"What's the matter?" I said. "Cat got your tongue?"

At that point, my somewhat bored audience finally responded with a loud meow.

We were in the apartment. Just me and

Hopper. He was licking himself and I was packing. I was so hyped that I needed to talk, and I must have been interesting, because he seemed willing to lick, listen, and watch me pack.

"According to my father, there are two ways to pack," I explained to the cat. "The Marine way and the wrong way. First rule: travel light. Unless you're flying to the moon, you can buy anything you didn't bring. If you know what you're doing, you can go around the world with one bag."

My one bag was a well-traveled Red Oxx Sky Train, the world's most efficient carry-on. I opened it up and then started bundle-wrapping. It's an old military trick that saves space and avoids creases. It's also a great way to hide things in plain sight.

You lay your clothes out flat, one on top of the other, biggest stuff on the bottom. At the top of the pile, you put a central core object. Mine is always an organizer pouch filled with socks and underwear. Then you carefully fold your clothes over the core, one by one, until you have a compact little bundle. Once you master the technique, you'll never pack any other way.

I had done it hundreds of times, but this time,

my central core was the medical bag and my socks filled with diamonds. "I know it's risky, smuggling these into a foreign country," I told Hopper. "If I get caught by French customs, I could wind up in jail. Even worse, if anyone finds out I'm the guy who has Mr. Zelvas's diamonds, I could wind up dead. If that happens, Hopper, my neutered little friend, you'll have to stay at the cat sitters' forever. But it's worth the risk. If I can sell these, I'll be in fat city. Even if I get half of the thirteen million they're supposed to be worth, I'll still be pretty much set for life."

I got another meow.

"You're right. *We'll* be set for life. You, me, Katherine, and maybe a couple of rug rats. Don't get excited, I'm not talking about actual rodents, I mean—"

The doorbell rang, and I checked the monitor.

"It's Katherine," I told Hopper. I zipped up the Sky Train and buzzed her in.

She came bounding up the stairs, wearing jeans, a navy sweater, and a New York Yankees baseball cap.

"This is all I brought," she said, dropping a soft-sided canvas carry-on bag to the floor.

"Boy, when I said *travel light,* you really took me seriously," I said.

"Everything is washable," she said. "Plus, I'm hoping you rented one of those Paris hotel rooms where clothing is optional."

I turned to the cat. "What did I tell you? She's one in a million."

I wrapped my arms around Katherine's slim waist and pulled her close. Her breath was warm and sweet. Her lips were soft and seductive.

This was joy. This was all I ever needed. I had my art, I had the woman I wanted to be with for the rest of my life, and if things went according to my makeshift plan, I was about to have all the money I'd ever need.

Nothing could stop me now.

Chapter 35

"HIS NAME IS BANNON," Gravois said. "Matthew Bannon."

Marta didn't have to write it down. It was seared in her mind. "What took you so long, Etienne?" she said. "Please don't tell me you decided to meet your wife for dinner after all."

"No, no, I didn't meet my wife."

"If I find out you did, I'll kill her and make you watch."

"I swear I went straight back to the office, but my boss was still there. He knew it was my wife's birthday and wanted to know why I came back. I told him we had a fight. Then I had to wait for him to go home."

"Why?"

"He hovers," Gravois said. "What was I supposed to do? Tell him I came back to break into confidential police files and download data for some assassin's next target?"

Marta lit a cigarette. She was, as always, in a no-smoking hotel room. They were always so much cleaner than the rooms that allowed smoking. Most smokers were pigs. Not her.

She inhaled deeply and watched the smoke billow into the air slowly. She took a second drag so that Gravois could suffer in silence for at least a minute.

"All right," she finally said, "I'll take your word for it. Now tell me about this Matthew Bannon."

"He's not in the criminal database," Gravois said. "I picked him up through his military records. He's an American, served in the Marines."

"Combat-trained?"

"Very. He did a tour in Iraq and two in Afghanistan."

"Where is he now?"

"New York. He's a student."

"A student?" Marta said. "How old is he?"

"Thirty. He's a master's candidate in Fine Arts at Parsons in Manhattan."

"A combat-trained Marine studying Fine Arts? He sounds conflicted."

"There was nothing in his military records about psychological problems," Etienne said.

"Relax, Etienne. I was only making a joke."

"Oh," the Frenchman said, laughing. "Yes. Very funny."

"Where can I find Mr. Bannon?"

"His apartment is on Perry Street," he said, and gave her the number. "Parsons is a few blocks away on West Thirteenth."

Marta smiled. And St. Vincent's Hospital is on West Twelfth. Maybe that dumb cop wasn't so dumb after all.

"I can e-mail you a complete dossier with his address, phone number, military records, and his school transcript," Etienne said.

"All that's missing is his obituary," Marta said.

Etienne laughed loud and hard.

"I wasn't joking," Marta said.

"I'm sorry. The German sense of humor is so different from the French."

"Yes," Marta said. "We're not funny."

Etienne held his breath, trying to guess whether to laugh or not. "It's late, Marta," he said. "Do you need anything else?"

"Not tonight. Why don't you go home and wish your wife a happy birthday," she said.

"*Merci*."

"And many more," Marta added. "But that, of course, will be entirely up to you."

She hung up the phone.

Chapter 36

MARTA HAD A rule when on a job: Never leave an impression that can't be forgotten, controlled, or erased. Part of that meant never taking a taxi to a contract killing. Cab drivers remembered too much. She walked from the hotel to Times Square, then blended into the evening rush hour and caught the downtown number 1 train to Sheridan Square.

Once out of the rush-hour mob, she had to watch her movements. Her determined stride turned into a casual saunter. She strolled along Christopher Street, gawking at store windows, looking more like a sightseer than a murderer on a mission. She headed north on Bleecker, where the street was wider and the stores and restaurants not nearly as funky.

At the corner of Bleecker and Perry, she stopped to look in the window of Ralph Lauren, checking the glass's reflection for tails. Those moron cops might follow her, looking for payback. But she was clear, so she headed west on Perry, a tree-lined residential street dotted with classic West Village brownstones and town houses.

She walked slowly past Matthew Bannon's building, then doubled back and walked past it again. Five stories. Bannon's apartment was on the top floor. Compared with some of the other buildings, this one looked secure. But she'd faced tougher.

She climbed the six steps and tried the front door. Open. She stepped into the vestibule, where the security kicked up a notch—a closed-circuit camera and a heavy brass plate protecting the inner door from being jimmied.

The doorbells were clearly labeled. She pressed apartment 5, BANNON.

There was no answer, but then the inner door was opened.

A man came through, African American, early

thirties, about six foot six, with a thick bull neck and a square head that was shaved clean. He barely looked at her, just pulled the inner door shut and quickly left the building.

She rang Bannon's bell a second time. Still no answer. She rang all the bells. Someone would buzz her in and she'd wait for Bannon in his apartment.

She held the thumb latch on the inner door and waited for the buzzer. Through the glass, she could see the door to apartment 1 open. A man stepped out—blond buzz cut, baby blue eyes, wearing faded jeans and a gray muscle shirt that left no room for the imagination.

He smiled and opened the front door.

"Can I help you, ma'am?"

A gentleman, Marta decided. And from what she knew of American accents, his was not from New York. He was from one of the southern states. Alabama, or maybe Mississippi.

"I'm looking for Matthew Bannon," she said.

"He's not here," the southern gentleman said. "But surely you must have figured that out when he didn't answer the second time you rang. Now, are you gonna keep ringing all the bells till you find someone dumb enough to let you in? Because we don't rent to stupid people. So, take a hike, Blondie."

Marta's Bottega Veneta bag was hanging from her shoulder. She pressed it to her side with her upper arm until she could feel the Glock against her ribs.

Her face remained icy calm. "I'm one of his teachers at Parsons," she said. "Can you tell me where to find him? I have his final paper. I wanted to give him his grade."

The man from apartment 1 relaxed a little. "Oh, so you're an art teacher."

Marta gave him her most seductive smile. She had been on the cover of German *Vogue* four times. This guy would be easy. "Yes," she said. "I'm Professor Mueller."

"So, then, Professor," he said, still filling the doorway, "how do you feel the Dadaist movement affected the growth of postmodernism in twentieth-century America?"

"Fuck you," Marta snapped.

"Yeah," he said, "that's pretty much how I feel about Dada. But I'm a big fan of those dogs playing poker. Now, get out of here."

Marta hated quick hits. This one wasn't researched, wasn't planned, but the Russians were in a hurry to find Bannon. If she was going to be waiting for him in his apartment when he got home, she'd have to kill the asshole blocking the door.

She ran through the scenario in her head. *Turn toward the outer door, take the gun from my bag, spin around, shoot him between the eyes, drag his body inside, clean up, go up to the fifth floor, and wait for Bannon.* The guy in the muscle shirt would be collateral damage. Tough luck, pal. You asked for it.

She turned to the front door, one hand on the clasp of her black bag. And then she saw him.

The first guy, the one with the shaved head, who looked like he was in a hurry to go some-place, hadn't gone anywhere. He was standing outside sucking on a cigarette.

She removed her hand from the leather bag. Killing one person was manageable. Killing two was messy. Too messy for Marta.

She opened the front door, and the black guy with the cigarette grunted a polite but detached New York hello. The white guy followed her out of the building and stood at the top of the front steps.

"Happy trails, Professor," he said.

She walked down the steps and onto Perry Street.

She'd be back. To kill Matthew Bannon and the redneck bastard from apartment 1.

Chapter 37

GETTING THROUGH AIRPORT security at JFK turned out to be a snap. For me. I breezed through with my multimillion-dollar carry-on.

Katherine, on the other hand, got caught red-handed, carrying a five-ounce tube of toothpaste into a three-ounce world.

She was stopped by a TSA screener—a chunky Hispanic woman wearing a government-issue white shirt, black pants, blue latex gloves, a gold badge, and a name tag that said MORALES.

"I'm going to have to confiscate this," the screener said, pointing at the toothpaste.

"I know the three-ounce rule," Katherine said. "And yes, this is a five-ounce tube. But it's more than half empty. There's maybe only two ounces left."

"I appreciate that, Miss," Morales said, "but you really *don't* know the rule. All liquids, gels, and aerosols must be in three-ounce or smaller *containers*. Larger containers that are half-full or toothpaste tubes that are rolled up are not allowed on the aircraft."

"You're joking," Katherine said.

"Miss, we do not joke here."

"For God's sake," Katherine said, "what do you think I'm going to do with half a tube of toothpaste? Blo—?"

I clamped my hand on Katherine's mouth before she could say the four words that would land us both in jail—*blow up the plane.*

Katherine pulled away. "Matt, what the hell are you doing?" she barked as two more security screeners stepped in and flanked us on both sides.

"I'll tell you what he's doing, Miss," Morales said. "He's saving your ass. Now, unless you want to miss your flight to Paris, you'd be smart to toss that toothpaste in that bin and be on your merry way."

I squeezed Katherine's arm gently. "Please," I said. "I promise I'll buy you toothpaste in Paris."

"This is Tom's of Maine," she said. "They won't have it in Paris."

"I'll buy you French toothpaste. They make the best in the world."

"This one is called Tom's Wicked Fresh and it's all natural and it keeps my breath fresh for hours. It's the only one I use."

I leaned close to her and whispered in her ear. "You may find this hard to believe, but we are about five seconds from being arrested, strip-searched, and thrown in jail for the night. I've never asked you to do anything for me on blind faith, but I'm asking you now. Please, please, please, give the nice lady your toothpaste, don't utter another word, and I promise you that tomorrow morning we will be checking into our hotel, racing up to our room, peeling off our clothes, snuggling under the sheets, and I will kiss you over and over and over, even if your breath smells like a Paris sewer. Please?"

She tossed the toothpaste in the bin.

"Have a nice flight," Morales said.

"Thank you," I said, bowing my head. "Thank you."

Morales smiled. She knew what I was thanking her for.

I only wished I could have told her that she might have saved the world from Tom's toothpaste but she missed the guy who was leaving the country with a bag full of diamonds he stole from a dead Russian.

Chapter 38

"LET'S FIND A bar," I said as I propelled Katherine as far from security as I could. "I need a drink."

We found a little place close to our gate that served burgers and beer. I had one of each. Katherine didn't want either, so she decided to backtrack to the Starbucks we had seen as we walked through the terminal.

I sat at a small table, munching my burger, which was not hot, sipping my beer, which was not cold, and staring at the LCD flat-screen TV over the bar. It was tuned to a local news station. The sound was muted, and I was too far away to read the closed captioning.

I was just starting to unwind from the

toothpaste incident when I gagged so badly I almost puked my burger and beer all over the table. I wasn't choking on the mediocre airport cuisine. What made me want to throw up was what I saw on the television screen.

Me.

Me at Grand Central, holding a black medical bag with a bank of lockers behind me.

"Holy shit," I said.

"Holy shit, what?" Katherine said, sitting down at the table with a grande cappuccino and a blueberry muffin.

She sat facing away from the television.

"Holy shit, I need another beer," I said, jumping up and heading for the bar. I got there just in time to read the tail end of the closed captioning: . . . *wanted for robbery.* They flashed a phone number.

And then they cut to a commercial.

I looked around the bar to see how many other people had caught it. A dozen, maybe more. What else do people sitting around an airport bar do but stare at the TV? Hopefully they wouldn't look up at me.

I tucked my chin down, put one hand over

my eyes, and studied the floor tiles as I walked back to the table where Katherine was sitting.

"Where's your beer?" she said.

"I changed my mind," I said. "You know what I really need?"

"No."

"A hat."

I lifted the somewhat faded, definitely broken-in Yankees cap off her head. I put it on mine. It didn't fit.

"It's way too small for your big head," she said.

"Well, let's buy one that fits," I said.

"As soon as I finish," she said, picking up her muffin and biting it.

So we sat and talked. And then it happened again. My picture flashed on the TV screen.

I didn't try to read the closed captioning. I just kept my head down until Katherine polished off her cappuccino. Then we walked over to Hudson News. Katherine checked out the magazines, and I went to the gift shop.

I was about to buy a Yankees baseball cap when I saw the berets. *Absolument*, I thought. *Très français and a much better disguise.* They had two colors—brown or red. I settled on brown.

I moved over to the sunglasses rack and picked out a pair of mirror-lens wraparounds.

Then I found Katherine. "What do you think?"

She laughed out loud. "What happened to the baseball hat?"

"I'm an artist. We're going to France. I definitely need a beret. And sunglasses," I said, putting on my shades. "Is this perfect or what?"

"Or what," said Katherine. But she was grinning.

Chapter 39

DINNER WAS SERVED about an hour into the flight to Paris. "At long last," I said. "Fine French cooking. Maybe we should eat and critique our dinners."

I had the beef goulash; Katherine opted for the herbed chicken.

"Bland, dry, overcooked," she said after a few bites. "One star, and that's only because I'm an easy marker. How about you?"

"Four stars," I said.

Katherine threw me a look.

"I think it's the ambience," I said, kissing the back of her neck. "And the company, of course."

As soon as the trays were cleared, we turned out the overhead lights and raised the armrest between our seats, and Katherine curled up against me, wrapped in a blanket and my arms.

She zonked out in minutes. I couldn't sleep.

I loved this woman. What was I dragging her into?

If that toothpaste incident had escalated one more notch, Katherine's behavior might have branded us as troublemakers, but my carry-on bag would absolutely have landed us both in jail.

What was I thinking? What had I gotten her involved in? Was I crazy? The questions were bouncing around in my brain like a beach ball at a rock concert.

Somewhere along the way I fell asleep, and I didn't wake up till we were on our final approach to Orly airport. Looking out the window, we could see the lush vineyards and tiny red-roofed farmhouses that dotted the French countryside.

"I can't believe you're actually taking me to Paris," Katherine said, still snuggled up against me.

"Believe it," I said. Then I kissed her.

She pulled away fast. "Matt, no. I have horrible morning breath."

"Are you kidding?" I said. "Your breath smells Wicked Fresh."

She punched me in the shoulder. "Matthew! You are so totally lying." God, I loved this woman.

The plane parked on the tarmac, and one of those big mobile lounges off-loaded the passengers and drove us to the terminal. All around me people were speaking French. The signs, the sounds, even the music piping through the PA, were French.

I took off my sunglasses and my beret. I was thousands of miles away from New York, where my picture was being flashed on a TV screen every ten minutes. I felt safe. Nobody would be looking for me here.

Chapter 40

THE ARTIST KNOWN as Leonard Karns had a nearly pathological crush on Katherine Sanborne, and that was just one of the reasons he hated that muscle-bound, no-talent Matthew Bannon. Bannon and the professor were an item. No doubt about that. But now Karns had a way to get back at both of them.

God, he despised Bannon and Sanborne. For one thing, they were into Realism, even into portraits. Karns *hated* portraits. "If that's all you're going to do," he said one day in his Group Critique class, "you might as well work at a carnival." One girl left the room in tears.

Karns was a Big Bang! artist. Big Bang! was the new, hip abstract painting for the twenty-first century. Big Bang! surged with energy and exploded with color. The imagery emanated from computer technology, quantum physics, genetics, and other complex contemporary issues. That, as far as Leonard Karns was concerned, was art.

Losers like Matthew Bannon were stuck in time, painting variations on pictures that had been done years ago and sucked even back then.

Karns was sitting in his pathetic apartment, thinking about Bannon, when his picture suddenly flashed on his TV, and the announcer said he was wanted for robbery.

And there was a reward.

He dialed the number on the TV screen and got a recording. A Detective Rice told him to leave his information and said that his call would be returned as soon as possible.

"I know the guy you're looking for," Karns said into the machine. "The robbery suspect. I saw his picture on TV. He goes to art school with me. I also know where he lives. Call me."

Karns gave his name and phone number. He was about to hang up when he had to add a delicious afterthought. "Plus, the guy is a total fraud as an artist."

Chapter 41

SOONER OR LATER I figured Katherine would ask the one question I was hoping to avoid. It turned out to be sooner. We were still in the airport, and I had stopped at a currency-exchange window to trade dollars for euros. Katherine handed me some cash from her wallet.

"That's okay," I said. "I got it."

She laughed. "What do you mean *you* got it? You're not paying for both of us. Absolutely not. No way, Matthew."

"Sure I am," I said. "I invited you to join me in Paris. My treat."

"Hey, Matt, I invited you to join me at Parsons," she said. "I don't remember springing for your tuition."

"This is different. It's a date. Happens to be in Paris. Guy pays."

"Not if he's a struggling artist."

"Don't worry about it," I said, trying not to make this a macho thing, which it wasn't. Well, maybe it was. "I recently came into some money."

"Oh, Matt, I hope you're not spending the money you got for your paintings," she said.

"No," I said, keeping it playful. "This is different. Trust me, okay?"

"You came into some money?" she said. "How come you never mentioned it before? What money is this?"

"It's too crazy," I said. "I figured you wouldn't believe me."

"Try me," she said.

I shrugged. "Okay. I found a big bag of diamonds in a train station."

"And I'm having tea with the queen of England," she said.

"Hey, if you invite me along, I'll pay."

She wrapped both arms around me. "You are the most generous, lovable, adorable man I ever met," she said. "But you're a terrible liar. If you found a bag of diamonds, you'd give it back."

She kissed me long and hard, and the subject of how I could afford the vacation was dropped. At least for now.

We breezed through customs—I guess the French don't have diamond-sniffing dogs. We were both too tired to even think of hopping on a bus and saving money, so we headed for the taxi rank and got into a sleek, comfortable black Peugeot.

The driver was a robust man with a gray beard and a broad smile. "You are going to where?" he said.

"The Hotel Bac Saint-Germain," I said. "You know where it is?"

"*Oui, monsieur,*" he said. "You are very in luck. It is the only hotel in all of Paris I know where to find."

Katherine and I both laughed.

"You speak English, *and* you're funny," I said.

"English is not so necessary. But to drive a taxi you must have big sense of humor," he said as he guided the car toward a ramp that said A106.

"Where are we staying?" Katherine asked me.

"It's a little hotel I found online. It's on the

Left Bank, in the Quartier Saint-Germain-des-Prés, which is the hippest, coolest section in all of Paris."

"And about to get hipper and cooler," she said.

The driver laughed. "You two cool hipsters are art lovers?" he said.

"*Oui*," Katherine said.

"The district where you are staying, there are art galleries on every street corner," he said. "And many cafés, and beautiful shops, and crazy, wonderful people."

"That's why we're here," I said. "We heard you had room for two more crazies."

"You like Aznavour?" he asked, sliding a CD into the sound system.

"Who doesn't?" I said.

And then the seductive voice of Charles Aznavour filled the cab.

If you're not in love when you get to Paris, you will be when you leave. If you're already in love, it only gets better.

Katherine curled up in my arms, with her head on my chest, and for the rest of the ride, we were serenaded by the sexiest tenor in all of France, possibly in the world.

"Are your eyes open or closed?" Katherine whispered to me at one point.

"Open."

"Mine, too," she said.

Why would anyone close his eyes in Paris? I thought. Wherever you look, everything is just so incredibly romantic. Even being stuck in traffic. With a woman like Katherine.

Chapter 42

THE HOTEL WAS colorful, modern, and cheap —only 110 euros a night. Our room wasn't ready when we checked in, so a bellman escorted us to a cozy little restaurant on the seventh-floor terrace, where we enjoyed steaming cups of frothy café au lait, flaky buttery croissants, strawberry jam, fresh fruit, yogurt, and a magnificent view of the entire district.

Forty minutes later the bellman returned and took us to our room. He set down the bags, and I tipped him, hung the NE PAS DÉRANGER sign on the doorknob, and locked the door.

Katherine and I hadn't been alone since she came by my apartment an eternity ago, and we couldn't wait to get our hands on each other.

Within seconds, our clothes were strewn on the floor and we were under smooth, cool sheets.

The sex was a little fast, but the afterglow lasted much longer. We talked, then drifted off to sleep. Katherine woke me three hours later, and again we made love, this time slowly and tenderly, then took a long, hot shower together and headed out to explore Paris.

"Where to first?" I said. "I can think of a dozen places I want to go. Right off the top of my head."

"Lunch," Katherine said. "But you have to let me buy."

"Lunch?" I said. "Okay, sure."

"Good. We have a one-thirty reservation."

"We do?"

"I decided to stick with the surprise theme of our vacation."

We caught a taxi. "Le Jules Verne restaurant," she told the driver. Ten minutes later he dropped us off at the base of the Eiffel Tower. We walked under the tower to a yellow awning, where we were greeted by a smiling maître d'.

"Sanborne," Katherine said. "We have a reservation for two."

"I called from New York," Katherine told me as the maître d' checked his book. "It's kind of popular. I was hoping to get a dinner rez, but that was impossible."

We took a private elevator to a magnificent room that was suspended from the steel latticework of the Eiffel Tower. It afforded us a spectacular panoramic view of the city below.

A tuxedoed host escorted us to a table near the center of the room.

"There's a six-week wait for a window table," Katherine explained.

"I hope that's not an apology for this one. I'm floored."

It was the most fantastic lunch I had ever had. And the most expensive. I almost choked when I looked at the prices on the menu.

"Don't worry about it," Katherine said. "If you can spend all your 'newfound diamonds' on everything else, the least I can do is buy lunch."

We were sipping champagne when the waiter brought a small, intricately decorated chocolate cake with a single candle in the center to the couple sitting at the next table. White-haired, well-dressed, and from the way they held hands across the table, very much in love, they had to be in their eighties.

The woman blew out the candle.

"Happy birthday," Katherine said.

"*Merci, no,*" the old woman said. "It is our anniversary."

"Congratulations," I said. "How many years?"

The man smiled. "One-half," he said. "Émilie and I have been dating for six months."

The City of Love was living up to its reputation.

After lunch we went to the École Nationale Supérieure des Beaux-Arts. It was Katherine's idea. It's the French national art school, where we could wander the halls, looking at works in progress by students.

"It's just like Parsons," Katherine said.

"Almost," I answered. "Except for the fact that Monet, Degas, Moreau, and Delacroix didn't go to Parsons."

"True," she said. "But Jasper Johns, Edward Hopper, and Norman Rockwell did."

I winced. "As they say in Paris, *touché, mademoiselle.*"

"As they say in New York, gotcha, dude."

After that, we hit the Louvre, along with about fifteen thousand other people. We didn't see them all, but that's how many the guidebook said show up on a daily basis. It could take a week to see all four hundred thousand pieces of art that are in the Louvre. We decided to spend two hours focused on a handful of works by Michelangelo, Raphael, and other Italian masters.

Then we did a one-eighty and took another taxi to the Galerie Mona Lisa. The average tourist wouldn't know about it, but the elderly couple in the restaurant had tipped us off to it. It was jam-packed with works by contemporary artists. There was no single medium, no unifying school of thought, just great art from people who were still very much alive.

"One day you could be hanging here," Katherine said.

"And the best part is, I don't have to be dead to get in."

We left the Galerie and were strolling along the Boulevard Saint-Germain when we took a random left turn on Rue de Buci and stumbled on Cacao et Chocolat.

The store was a work of art in itself, and every

bit of it was edible. We sat in a booth while a petite waitress served us the thickest, richest cocoa I'd ever tasted. Then we fed each other chocolate truffles from a silver tray.

"I'll be in a sugar coma in about five minutes," Katherine said as she licked a bit of *chocolat noir* from my fingertips. "But what a way to go."

Leaving the chocolate shop, we found our way to Le Bon Marché, a French department store that makes Bloomingdale's look like a flea market. Katherine insisted she didn't want anything, so I bought myself some Christian Maquer lingerie in Katherine's size.

We weren't ready to call it a night yet, so we walked past our hotel and across the river to the Jardin des Tuileries. Then we strolled hand in hand back to our hotel, and Katherine tried on the incredibly sexy sheer black camisole, and minutes later I removed it.

We turned out the lights, opened the blinds, and let the moonlight pour into the room as we made sweet, sweet love.

Chapter 43

NY1 RAN BAGBOY'S picture a dozen times. They'd have run it a lot more except for the crane collapse on 57th Street. One entire section came crashing down on a crosstown bus, killing three and injuring fourteen, including a pregnant woman. In keeping with the age-old tradition "if it bleeds, it leads," the station abandoned Bagboy and focused on the crane disaster around the clock.

Even so, there were ninety-one tips waiting for Rice and Benzetti in the morning. They separated them into three batches. Solids, Possibles, and Nut Jobs.

Leonard Karns sounded like a Solid until they got to the part of the message where he said the guy he wanted to turn in was a "total fraud as an artist." He sounded like someone with an ax to grind, which dropped his tip to a Possible. Then, just before Karns hung up, Benzetti could hear him cackling hysterically, as though he'd just escaped from the flight deck at Bellevue.

Nut Job, he decided.

It took the two detectives a full day to track down and question all the callers in the Solid and Possible folders.

"So far I got squat," Rice said. "What have you got?"

Benzetti looked at his call sheet. "I got one lonely old lady who was angling to get me to come over for tea, three angry chicks hoping to pin a robbery on their ex-boyfriends, and a whole bunch of bullshit artists and hustlers trying to peddle bogus information to score the reward."

"We might as well start calling the crazies," Rice said.

He dialed Leonard Karns's number.

"It's about time," Karns said as soon as Rice identified himself. "I called in the tip a day and a half ago."

"You and a lot of other people," Rice said.

"You said something on your message about this guy being an artist."

"He'd like to think so," Karns said. "I was in one of his art classes at Parsons and his paintings are shit, but he's banging the professor, so he's getting a straight A all the way."

Rice was only half listening. He was about to write this numbskull off when he heard the one word that sparked his adrenaline.

Parsons.

"Mr. Karns, sir, please refresh my memory," Rice said, his tone now reeking of respect and deference. "Where exactly is Parsons?"

"West Thirteenth Street."

A block from where Bagboy took the taxi from Grand Central. *Bingo!*

"So, then, what's this lousy artist's name?" Rice asked.

"Not so fast," Karns said. "First let's talk about the reward."

The reward, of course, was pure fiction, but Rice and Benzetti had decided that without it, no one would even bother calling.

"Like it said on TV, the reward is twenty-five grand. And you get to remain anonymous."

"Screw anonymous," Karns said. "I want credit for turning the cops onto this phony."

"No problem," Rice said. "We'll invite you to the press conference."

Press conference. NY1. "Now you're talking," Karns said.

"Do you know where he is?" Rice asked casually. "His name would be helpful, but if you tell us exactly where he is, the reward can go even higher."

"I know who he's with, and she's easy to find," Karns said.

"Who would that be?"

"Like they say in the movies, Detective," Karns said, "show me the money. You're not getting my valuable information over the phone. You show up with some kind of NYPD legal document that says I get paid if I help you catch him. Then I'll tell you his name and how to find him."

"Fair enough, sir," Rice said. "We'll send over our person in charge of rewards."

"And what's his name?" Karns asked.

"It's a female," Rice said. "Her name is Detective Krall."

Chapter 44

"I GOT HIM," Rice told Benzetti as soon as he hung up. "I think this total asshole Leonard Karns actually knows where our Bagboy is."

"Let's go pay him a visit," Benzetti said. "Right now."

"Not us," Rice said. "Did you forget about the butch German who shoved the gun in your mouth?"

"She caught me by surprise. You thought she was *butch*?"

"Marta Krall is a pro, and she's expensive. She'd whack two cops like us and not even break a sweat. We found Karns. Now he's her problem."

"Fine," Benzetti said. "You deal with Marta. I hope I never see her again."

Rice called Krall's cell. "We've got a lead on the guy with the diamonds," he said.

"You know who he is?" Krall said, and sounded absolutely astonished.

"No."

"You know where he lives?"

"No."

"I know his name, and I've been staking out his apartment for two and a half days," she said. "So much for your police work, your vaunted NYPD protocols."

"Listen," Rice said. "My partner and I are just trying to hold up our end of the deal. But if you've got the guy, you don't need us. So good-bye."

"Wait. I don't actually *have* the guy," Krall said. "Not yet. But he'll be back sooner or later."

"Well, if you don't feel like waiting for later, I've got the name and address of someone who knows how to find him."

Chapter 45

MARTA KRALL CHECKED her Breitling Starliner and rang the doorbell to Leonard Karns's apartment. One thirty-three in the afternoon. The building was drab, dilapidated, and depressingly quiet. Karns buzzed her in, and she took the stairs to apartment B4.

A short, fat lump in gray sweatpants and an olive-drab T-shirt that said ART IS RESISTANCE stood in the doorway.

"You Detective Krall?" he asked.

She smiled and nodded. Then she pointed to her throat and whispered, "Laryngitis." She liked acting and had unsuccessfully attempted a transition from modeling to movies back in Germany.

"That sucks," he said. "But no problem. I

know what you're here to find out."

Marta smiled again. *Good boy.*

She stepped into the apartment, and he shut the door. It was stuffy and smelled of burnt coffee. There was art all over the walls. Undoubtedly his. She stopped to look at one of the paintings and gave him a big thumbs-up.

"It's called *Improbabilities Number Six*," he said.

"Nice," she whispered. It was true. She genuinely liked *Improbabilities Number 6*. It was powerful, meticulous, urban chic—nothing like the loser who painted it.

Marta tapped her hand to her heart to show how much she loved it. Karns's eyes settled on her chest as he mumbled a shy thank-you.

Marta took the picture of the man she was trying to find and handed it to Karns.

"You're going to give me the paperwork for the reward, right?" he said.

She waved him off with an *of course I will* gesture, and sat down on the sofa. She pulled her skirt up a little so he could get a good look at her legs. She took out a pad and pencil and sat waiting for him to speak.

"The guy you're looking for is Matthew Bannon," Karns said. "He's in one of my classes at Parsons. Since you like my work, you'd hate his. He's all technique. But he's dead inside. No originality."

Marta nodded and tried to communicate that she understood this idiot.

"Who did he rob, anyway?" Karns said.

Marta turned to a clean page on her pad and wrote *Where can I find him?*

"Believe it or not, he's been shacking up with the professor of our Group Critique class. Her name is Katherine Sanborne. She's an asshole, just like he is. Talk about a conflict of mediocrity."

He watched her write it down. "No, that's not how she spells it," he said.

He took the pad and wrote Katherine Sanborne in clear block letters. Marta wrote the words *Where is she* above the name and added a question mark after it.

"Just a sec," Karns said. He scrambled over to his desk, opened a center drawer, and pulled out a packet of papers that were held together by two brass brads.

"This is the faculty directory," he explained.

"They don't exactly give it out to students. I happened to get my hands on a copy. You never know when you might want to get in touch with one of your professors."

Or stalk her. Marta gave him another thumbs-up for his ingenuity.

He opened it to Katherine's name in the directory. There were penciled doodles all around it. Karns had obviously spent time staring at it. Below Sanborne's name were her address, home phone, cell phone, and e-mail. That was all Marta needed.

"And you think that zis Sanborne woman will be wiz Bannon?" Marta said loud and clear.

"Definitely," Karns said. "Hey, how did you get your voice back like that?"

"I *sink* it's a miracle," Marta said.

Karns looked totally confused. "Are you German?" he said.

"What's the difference?" Marta said as she crossed her legs like sharp scissors.

He never even saw the Glock. He was staring at Marta's thighs, lightly licking his lips, as she pulled the trigger and blew most of his head off.

A few minutes later, Marta Krall casually

walked down the steps and checked her watch as she left the building. She'd taken something to remember Leonard Karns by. *Improbabilities Number 6.*

Chapter 46

LIKE A LOT of young women who move to Manhattan, Katherine Sanborne couldn't afford to live in a building with a doorman. So she invested in three heavy-duty locks for her front door. And none for her windows. As she had said to her concerned parents, "Who's going to climb five stories up the side of the building? Spider-Man?"

Marta Krall didn't have to climb up. She took the elevator to the roof, rappelled ten feet down, and went through the unlocked window. It took less than thirty seconds.

The apartment looked like it had been hit by Hurricane Katherine. Dresser drawers were open, and there were piles of clean clothes on the bed and the floor. Katherine had obviously packed and left in a hurry.

Marta was familiar with the scenario. Her target was on the run and he had invited his girlfriend to run with him.

But where were they going?

The first clue lay on Katherine's four-by-five-foot dining room table: a red ribbon and a handful of postcards with pictures of the Eiffel Tower, the Arc de Triomphe, and other Paris landmarks.

There was also a bottle of French wine on the table.

Instinctively, Marta opened the refrigerator. It was single-girl-in-the-city sparse. But there, alongside the nonfat yogurt and the Coke Zero, were two baguettes and a chunk of creamy-rich 60-percent-butterfat Brie.

All part of Bannon's romantic invitation, Marta decided.

Katherine's computer was sitting on her desk. Marta booted it up. No password required, because, once again, the prevailing thought process was *I don't have anything worth stealing, and even if I did, how could anyone get into my apartment?*

Marta opened Katherine's e-mail in-box. The last message was from Beth Sanborne.

Kat,

Can't believe you and Matthew are going to Paris on the spur of the moment. Oh, to be young and in love. Send us the flight number and the name of the hotel. I don't care how old you are. Mothers need to know.

Love,

Mom and Dad

Marta checked the sent mail. Katherine's response had the flight details, and she'd followed up with *Don't know the hotel yet. Will text you from Paris.*

She shut down the computer and called Etienne Gravois at Interpol.

"This Matthew Bannon you found for me is on his way to Paris," she said. "He's traveling with another American, Katherine Sanborne. They should have landed at Orly the day before yesterday. I need a confirmation."

"Hold on," Gravois said. Twenty seconds later he was back. "They cleared passport control

Saturday, no problem. He's a student. Should they have flagged him?"

"No, he's not a terrorist," Marta said. "Just a small nuisance I have to deal with."

"Yes," Gravois said. "I know how efficient you can be with nuisances."

"And don't ever forget it," Krall said. "Where are they staying?"

"The Bac Saint-Germain."

"Is that a decent hotel?"

"It's not the George Cinq, but it's clean and it's in the Quartier Saint-Germain-des-Prés, which is very vibrant, very artsy. It's quite nice."

"Good," Marta said. "I'd hate to stay in a dump."

Chapter 47

MARTA WAS HUNGRY. She softened the bread and cheese in Katherine's microwave, found a corkscrew for the wine, and ate a late lunch. While she was eating, she called Chukov.

"I know who has your diamonds and where they are," she said.

"Who? Where?" Chukov made no attempt to hide his anxiety.

"A man named Matthew Bannon has them. He's in Paris."

"Paris?"

"Yes, he and his girlfriend are on the run," Marta said. "But he has no idea I'm running after him. I'll get a flight tonight and be there tomorrow."

"Fly coach," Chukov said.

"Marta Krall doesn't travel in coach."

"All right, all right, but don't stay at some thousand-dollar-a-night hotel. This whole thing has cost us a fortune already."

"Relax," she said, enjoying listening to him whine about a few dollars when there were millions at stake. "I'll be staying in the same hotel as Bannon and his lady friend, in the Quartier Saint-Germain-des-Prés. And despite the fact that I've been told it's very vibrant and very artsy, I won't be staying long."

"What's the name of the hotel?" Chukov said.

"Why do you ask? Are you going to send champagne to my room? Or are you planning to call your friend the Ghost to back me up?"

"I am not calling the Ghost," Chukov said, trying to sound indignant at the suggestion. "I told you I want you to kill the Ghost. As far as I'm concerned, we still have an agreement. Unless you've decided to back out."

"Not at all," Marta said. "But information has a way of leaking, and if I tell you where I'm staying, the Ghost might find me before I find him. I'll call you from Paris," she said and ended the call.

Marta left Katherine's apartment through the front door.

Chukov immediately called the Ghost. "The man you're looking for is named Matthew Bannon. He and his girlfriend are in Paris. Their hotel is somewhere in the Quartier Saint-Germain-des-Prés. Can you find him?"

"Yes."

"I hope so," Chukov said. "So far it looks like I'm the one doing all the work."

He hung up. The noose was tightening around the neck of the young man who had his diamonds. And now Chukov had two assassins competing to track him down. Once he had the diamonds back, he'd be happy to pay Marta Krall for killing the Ghost.

He smiled to himself. *In an ideal world,* he thought, *they would kill each other.*

Chapter 48

KATHERINE WAS SITTING up in bed when I got back to the room.

"*Bonjour,* sleepyhead," I said as I sat down beside her.

She was wearing a pale pink nightshirt made of the softest, silkiest cotton I ever touched. The neckline had a tiny little bow in the center, totally nonfunctional but definitely adorable.

I gave her a quick kiss.

"*Bonjour* yourself," she said. "It's way too early in the morning to be this chipper. What have you been up to?"

"I woke up at six, went for a walk, grabbed some coffee, and then had a long, serious talk with the concierge."

"About what?"

"Dinner. I had him make us a reservation at a nice little restaurant he recommended. It's called Antico Martini."

"It sounds Italian."

"It should," I said. "It's in Venice."

"Venice? Italy? We're going to Venice for dinner?"

"That would be crazy," I said. "So I had the concierge book us a hotel for a couple of nights."

"But . . . but . . ." She was dumbfounded, and I hated to admit it, but I was having fun dumbfounding her. "But we just got here."

"Hey, I'm feeling adventurous. We've already made love in one romantic city. Let's do it again in another."

"Just like that?" she said.

"Why not?" I said. "Didn't we leave New York *just like that?* Come on, our flight leaves at ten fifteen."

I got up, took my bag out of the closet, and started packing.

"I can't believe it," she said. She grabbed a pillow and threw it at me. "You are not only drop-dead amazing to look at, fantastic in bed, and wildly spontaneous, but you are also ridiculously romantic. Who cares if you're going to be a poor struggling artist all your life?"

"Who cares?" I said. "I care." I threw the pillow back at her.

She hugged the pillow to her chest. "I love you," she said.

"You talking to me or the pillow?"

"Our plane leaves at ten fifteen?" she said.

"Yup."

She looked at her watch. "It's only seven oh five, and I'm a real fast packer."

She lifted the pink nightshirt up over her head, tossed it on the floor, and slipped under the covers.

"I love you," she repeated. "And I'm not talking to the pillow."

Chapter 49

MARTA KRALL CAUGHT the 7 p.m. Delta flight out of JFK. She had only one small suitcase, and despite the fact that there was plenty of room in first class to bring it on board, she checked it.

She touched down at Charles de Gaulle airport at 8:45 the next morning and went to the baggage carousel, where she was reunited with her bag.

She cleared customs, then found the nearest ladies' room. She locked the stall door, sat on the toilet, and opened her bag. Her hair dryer was in the black drawstring case, exactly as she had packed it.

It wasn't a working dryer. It was built for her by a mold maker in Holland. She used a paper clip to push a recessed button on the grip. The dryer popped open. Inside were the pieces of her Glock, each one held in place by a steel clasp.

It took only three minutes to assemble the gun.

Forty minutes later, she was in the lobby of the Hotel Bac Saint-Germain.

The front desk clerk was young, slender, and extremely beleaguered.

"No, *madame*. No one else has complained about the water pressure," she told the guest on the other end of the phone. Her voice was calm, but her body language said otherwise. "Of course. I'll send the engineer back to your room immediately. Yes. I know. Room three one four. *Merci*."

She hung up and smiled at Marta. "*Bonjour, madame*. May I help you?"

"I'd like a room," Marta said. "Preferably on the same floor as my friends Matthew Bannon and Katherine Sanborne."

The clerk's long bloodred fingernails clicked lightly on her keyboard. "I'm afraid you just missed them," she said.

"Out sightseeing, I'm sure," Marta said. "Do

you happen to know when they'll be back?"

"They're not expected back. They checked out this morning."

Marta stood at the front desk, cool and composed on the outside, boiling over on the inside.

"How strange," she said calmly. "I guess I can FedEx the paperwork I was going to discuss with them. Did they leave the address of their next stop?"

"No, but I saw Monsieur Bannon talking with the concierge a couple of hours ago. He might be able to help you."

The front desk phone rang, and after checking the caller ID, the clerk turned back to Marta. "Now, what size room are you looking for? They *all* have excellent water pressure."

"You're busy," Marta said. "Why don't you deal with room three fourteen, and I'll see if the concierge knows where to find my friends."

Marta walked across the lobby as the front desk clerk reluctantly picked up the phone.

The concierge was tall and trim and had thick, dark hair that was slicked back. He wore a well-tailored gray uniform with black piping and two crossed gold keys—the *clefs d'or*—on each lapel. He was currently engaged with a Japanese couple, and the language barrier made the slow communication process painful to watch.

After several minutes, he paused to nod to Marta. "Sorry to keep you waiting," he said.

She didn't know if he was just being polite or trying to let the couple know that there were other people who needed his attention, too. But he looked up several times and smiled at Marta.

Another five minutes passed before the concierge handed the couple a map, a packet of brochures, and a printout of their itinerary for the day. They thanked him profusely with head bows and several euros.

"*Mademoiselle*, I am Laurent," he said, offering up his name quickly. "Sorry to keep you waiting. How can I be of service?"

She leaned forward and rested her hands on his desk so he could get a good look at her breasts. He didn't seem all that interested. *Ah, the French*. She loved them.

"I was supposed to meet my friends here, but there seems to have been some miscommunication," she said, lowering her voice to a whisper. "According to the front desk, they checked out this morning. I'm wondering if you know where they went."

"These mix-ups happen all the time," he said with a smile that showed a mouthful of perfectly straight, professionally whitened teeth. "What are their names?"

"Matthew Bannon and Katherine Sanborne."

His lips tightened and the smile disappeared. He sat broom-up-his-ass straight in his chair. One second he looked like he was ready to invite himself up to her room, and the next he was transformed into the quintessentially cold, uncaring, unhelpful Parisian.

"I'm sorry, *mademoiselle*," Laurent said, "but I have no forwarding address for your friends."

It was clear he was lying through his cosmetically enhanced, pearly white teeth.

The question was why.

Chapter 50

"LAURENT," MARTA SAID sweetly. "Of course you know where they went. This may help jog your memory." She slid fifty euros across his desk.

He ignored the money. "Whether I know or do not know is not relevant. The privacy of our guests is of utmost concern, and I'm not at liberty to say anything. Hotel policy."

The cash bribe didn't work. Marta leaned across his desk, her breasts almost out of their nest. "You can tell me," she purred. "And you can surely imagine how grateful I would be."

The concierge leaned in toward her and wagged a finger in her direction. "*Mademoiselle,* I absolutely cannot divulge any—"

Marta grabbed his finger and held it tight.

"I guess you're not the breast man I thought you were," she said. "How do you feel about fingers?"

His eyes widened, but he tried to maintain his composure. "What do you mean?"

"I mean," she said, pressing hard on the top of his knuckle joint with her thumb and squeezing the rest of the digit with viselike strength, "how much do you care about your fingers?"

"This is ridiculous," Laurent said. "Surely, you can't be threaten—"

She snapped his finger in two, and the crack of Laurent's bone was followed by a piercing scream.

Marta covered it up immediately with a shriek of her own and began laughing hysterically. The harried desk clerk was still on the phone with the dissatisfied guest and barely turned to see what the noise was about.

Marta let go of the concierge's broken finger and grabbed on to his pinkie. "You've got nine left," she said. "So let me ask you again. How much do you care about your fingers?"

Tears were streaming down the concierge's

face. Excruciating pain and paralyzing fear trumped hotel policy.

"I made reservations for Monsieur Bannon this morning," he whimpered. "A flight to Venice and dinner at the Antico Martini at eight tonight."

"What hotel?"

"The Danieli."

"One more question," Marta said. "Why didn't you tell me this before? You don't strike me as a man who would be a slave to hotel policy."

"Monsieur Bannon gave me a hundred euros to be discreet about where he was going."

Or where he was taking Chukov's diamonds, Marta thought.

She released Laurent's pinkie. His hands flew to his chest and he tucked them safely under his armpits.

He stood there cowering as Marta picked up the fifty euros she had put on his desk. She slipped the money into her purse, then slowly turned and left the hotel.

What a merry little chase this was turning out to be. Marta Krall absolutely loved it.

Chapter 51

IT WAS 4:30 A.M. in New York City when Chukov's phone rang. The voice on the other end was female and the accent German. Marta Krall didn't have to identify herself.

"He's in my sights," she said.

"Where are you?"

"I'm in a taxi on my way to Charles de Gaulle airport."

"*To* the airport?" Chukov said. "Aren't you on your way *from* the airport into the city?"

"I did that while you were sleeping. I went to his hotel. He checked out this morning."

"Checked out—where did he go?"

"Venice. He booked a room at the Hotel Danieli."

"The Danieli?" Chukov screamed. "Do you know how much that costs?"

Marta laughed. "I'm sure he doesn't care. He's spending your money."

Chukov was apoplectic. "That's a five-star hotel! I want five bullets in his head—one for every star." He grabbed the inhaler from his night table and sucked on it.

Marta closed her eyes and savored the sound of the fat Russian gasping for air.

"Five bullets won't be easy," she said. "One shot with my forty-five-caliber Glock and his head will explode like a mush melon."

"Then put the other four bullets in his worthless dick," Chukov wheezed. "But first get the diamonds."

"If he still has them," she said. "He was in Paris for twenty-four hours. He could have sold them."

"No," Chukov said. "What idiot would sell diamonds in Paris? And never in Venice. He's not stupid. He'll go to Antwerp or Amsterdam or even Tel Aviv."

"No, he won't," Marta said. "Venice will be Matthew Bannon's final stop. I promise you that."

Chapter 52

CHUKOV TURNED UP the hot water in the shower full blast. He stood on the bathroom floor for ten minutes inhaling the steam, sipping his morning vodka, and trying to figure out his next move.

He dressed, ignoring the Bowflex and the rest of the exercise equipment he regularly bought from late-night infomercials, some of the pieces still in their boxes.

Then he called the Ghost. "Do you still have your thumb up your ass in Paris?" he asked.

"No," the Ghost said. "My ass is currently in Venice, sitting in a very comfortable chair in a premium deluxe room at the Hotel Danieli."

Chukov was stunned. "You're at the Danieli

already? How did you find out Bannon was in Venice?"

"It's what I do," the Ghost said. "The better question is, How the hell did you know? It's five in the morning in New York. Who called you?"

Chukov took another swig of his vodka. Time to put his plan in motion. "Marta Krall. Do you know her?"

"Only by reputation," the Ghost said. "She's slow, she's stupid, but she's beautiful, so she has no trouble convincing lonely men like you to pay her fat fees and first-class travel. And then, more often than not, she botches the job."

Chukov laughed. The Ghost was just like the rest of them. He didn't like competition. "Maybe you're right," he said. "Or maybe you can buy Fraulein Krall a celebratory drink after she's found the diamonds and killed Bannon. She's the one who's been doing all the heavy lifting."

"Are you firing me?" the Ghost said.

"Why would I fire you?" Chukov said. "Two assassins are always better than one. But just a reminder—only one of you gets paid."

Chapter 53

THE GHOST HUNG up on Chukov.

He looked around the room. It was exquisite —highly polished antique furniture, lush draperies made from the finest Venetian fabrics, a luxurious handcrafted marble bathroom, all counterpointed with state-of-the-art electronics, including a forty-two-inch flat-screen LCD television, high-speed Internet, and a relaxing Jacuzzi.

The Danieli was expensive but well worth it. Especially with Chukov footing the bill. *And now,* the Ghost thought, *it turns out he's hired a backup.*

Krall. Despite what he had said to Chukov, the Ghost knew Marta Krall was anything but slow and stupid. Contract killing was more than her profession, it was her passion. She was the queen of the slow death.

She had once put eighteen bullets into an undercover DEA agent over the course of three days. The man died from shock and blood loss four times, but Krall revived him each time with a makeshift crash cart to keep the party going. The Jamaican drug lord whose operation had been infiltrated by the narc happily paid a premium for the additional pain and suffering.

The Ghost stood up and looked out the window at the lagoon directly below. The view was spectacular. Venice was incomparable—a thriving cultural center surrounded by water. He only wished he had the time to stay and enjoy it.

He stretched out on the brocade silk spread that covered the king-size bed and stared up at the crystal chandelier.

He closed his eyes and tried to think like Marta Krall would think. Where was she? What was her next move? How could he stay one step ahead of her?

The door to the room burst open with a bang. Before he could move, a woman bounded into the room, leaped onto the bed, and pinned him down.

And then she kissed him. Hard.

"Jesus, Katherine," he said. "You scared the living shit out of me." He wrapped his arms around her and kissed her again.

"I tried your cell, but it went straight to voice mail," Katherine said. "Who were you on the phone with?"

"The Antico Martini," he said. "I was just confirming our dinner reservation. I want to make sure it's extra special."

"I don't care where we eat," she said, "as long as it's just the two of us. You're a real catch, Matthew Bannon. I wouldn't be surprised if another woman came after you."

"What woman would possibly want to come after me?" Matthew asked, smiling at the irony.

"Sweetie, you look a little pale. Are you sure you're okay?" she said.

"I'm fine," he said quickly. "Just a little tired. It's a lot of hard work being a tourist."

"Okay," Katherine said. "But you had me worried. You look like you've seen a ghost."

Book Three

THE DIAMONDS

Chapter 54

I SWORE THAT everything I was going to tell you would be true. It has been. I actually did serve in the Marines. I am an art student at Parsons in New York City. And I'm definitely in love with my professor Katherine Sanborne. But I did leave a few things out. Such as—

I'm a hired killer.

It's not exactly something I signed up for on Career Day at my high school. My father was a Marine, and I more or less decided to follow in his footsteps—at least for four years. The night I got out, my dad took me for a beer.

I knew he wasn't too happy about my going to New York to become an artist, and I figured he was going to try to talk me out of it.

"So, what did you learn in the corps?" he asked.

"Nothing that you hadn't already taught me," I told him and smiled. "Is that what you're fishing for?"

"Don't be a wiseass," my father said. "I'm trying to be serious here. The Marines taught you a lot. I just asked what you *learned*."

I wasn't sure where he was going with this, but he was definitely very serious.

"I guess I learned how to push myself to my limit," I said. "Even farther than you pushed me. I learned the meaning of a lot of words that were just concepts when I was a kid—*loyalty, bravery, friendship, selflessness*."

He nodded. "What else?"

"I learned how to survive," I said. "And that means I had to learn how to kill. I did it for my country, but I doubt it's a skill I can put on my résumé when I'm looking for something to help me pay for school in New York."

"Don't be so sure."

We were sitting at a corner table in a little bar tucked away in the back room of the North Fork Diner in Hotchkiss, Colorado. My father took a long tug on his beer and set the bottle down.

"I've been waiting for the right time to tell you this, Matt."

I could feel my chest tighten. *Tell me what?* I didn't like the look on his face.

"For as long as you can remember, you've seen me travel around the world from one corporate headquarters to another as a security consultant. Well, that's not exactly true," he said. "I do fly all over the world, but I'm not a consultant. I kill people, Matthew. Bad people. But I kill them all the same."

I was in shock. Complete. There was a buzzing sound suddenly in both my ears. My chest felt hot on the inside.

"You murder people?" I said. "For money?"

"I *eliminate* scum—the dregs of our world. Most of them are killers themselves. Some just order the murders of others. It doesn't make it any more righteous that I target only folks who deserve to die. But you know what? I sleep okay at night. I don't have a problem with it. Do you, Matthew?"

I did, actually. "And you think, what? That that's what I should be doing? Killing bad people?"

"Not *should* be doing," he said. "*Could* be doing. It's just an option you have. I saw your service record. I held your shooting medals. You're one of the best-trained Marines to come out of Parris Island."

"Dad, fighting for this country is a lot different from being an assassin for hire."

"Is it?" he said. "Badasses are badasses, aren't they? I think so. Seems perfectly logical to me."

"I don't know about your logic there, Dad."

But I'm pretty sure the seed was planted inside that barroom in Colorado.

A few months after I talked to my father, I took my first job, and I've been following in his footsteps ever since. I think of myself as the ghost of my father. That's how I got my name.

I remember the last question I asked my dad the night he told me about his secret life. "Does Mom know?"

He nodded. "I didn't tell her at first, but I knew I had to sooner or later. You can't live a lie with someone you love. She could have walked out on me. She could have told me to give it up. But your mother stuck with me and never brought it up again. *Rarely* brought it up again, I should say. Occasionally she does. When she wants something she considers worthwhile—like tuition if you decide to go to art school."

And now it was my turn. It was time to share my secret with Katherine.

I went to the closet and opened the room safe. I got out the doctor bag filled with diamonds. I sat down on the bed next to her.

"Katherine," I said, "I've got something to tell you."

Chapter 55

KATHERINE LOOKED AT the bag. "Dr. Matthew's magic medical bag," she said. "Is there another surprise in there?"

"Kind of."

"Well, you gave me Brie and baguettes when we went to France. What's in there now that we're in Italy? Chianti and cannolis?"

"No. Remember I told you I found a bag full of diamonds at the train station?"

"How could I forget?" she said. "The first thing I thought when we set foot in this incredible room was, I hope you brought enough diamonds."

"But you don't think the diamonds really exist," I said.

She rolled her eyes, put her hand to her chin,

and shook her head slowly from side to side. I think it's something she learned in professor school. It's a way of letting a student know he is completely wrong without broadcasting it to the entire classroom.

I dipped my hand into the bag. The diamonds were loose now. I had taken them out of my socks so I could show them to Katherine in all their dramatic glory. I scooped up a fistful just as Professor Sanborne decided to let me know how preposterous my story was.

"Matthew, you know I love you," she said. "But love is not blind or stupid, and that whole cock-and-bull story about finding diamonds in a train station is ridiculous. I don't care how you can afford to pay for this vacation, but I'd feel a whole lot better if you finally decided to tell me the truth."

What the hell? I thought. I dropped the whole fistful of diamonds on the bed.

"Behold the sparkling truth," I said.

Katherine shrieked. "Oh, my God!"

Then I opened the medical bag wide and held it so she could get a good look at the other thirty or forty fistfuls.

This time she jumped off the bed and the *oh, my God*s came in a flurry. Then she sat back down. "Are they real?"

"Very."

"My God, Matthew, they must be worth—I don't know—millions."

"So I'm told."

"Are they yours?" she asked.

"They are now. In fact, they're ours. This is the key to a whole new life."

I gave her the watered-down version of how I found them in Grand Central. *Bomb goes off. I stumble on Zelvas. He dies. I take the diamonds.*

"What are you going to do with them?" she asked.

"Sell them. Depending on what I can negotiate, I figure I can get seven to ten million."

She let loose another string of about half a dozen *oh, my God*s.

"But what about that man who got killed at Grand Central?" she said. "Maybe he's got a wife, kids. I don't even know what I'm saying, Matthew . . ."

"Trust me," I said, "Walter Zelvas had nobody. No wife, no kids, nobody."

I inhaled. It was time to tell Katherine the whole truth about myself and hope she didn't walk out when she heard it.

"Katherine," I said, "there's one more little fact about me you really should know. That man Walter Zelvas who had the bag of diamonds. . . . I'm the one who—"

Bam! A loud cracking sound and the door to our hotel room flew open. And there she was— Marta Krall standing in our doorway with a large-bore gun in her hand.

Pointed at me, then at Katherine, then back at me.

"Where do I start?" she said.

Chapter 56

"MR. BANNON, I presume," she continued.

Katherine had gasped at the sight of the gun—who wouldn't?—but now she bombarded me with questions. "Who is this woman? How does she know your name? What does she want? *Matthew?*"

Krall answered the important question for me.

"Some of what I want is right there," she said, pointing the gun at the handful of diamonds on the bed. "And I'll bet the rest is in that black bag—isn't it, Ms. Sanborne?"

A shiver ran through Katherine's body at the sound of her name. She whispered in my ear. "Give her the diamonds. Okay, Matthew?"

Krall heard every word. "Spoken like a woman who doesn't want to die young. I can respect that."

If Marta Krall had known I was the Ghost, she'd have shot me the second she entered the room. She already had what she came for—Chukov's diamonds. But Krall wasn't just a killer, she was a sadistic killer. Thinking I was Matthew Bannon, art student, she figured she could take her time. She wasn't satisfied just to recover the diamonds. I had made her work hard to find them. She wanted to play with me now.

"So, tell me, Mr. Bannon," Krall said, "are you sleeping with all your professors or just the pretty ones?" Then she went after Katherine. "I hope he was good in bed, because your affair is going to cost you your life."

The talking was a big mistake. Those extra few seconds were what I needed. I pushed Katherine to the floor and flung the medical bag at Marta.

She got off a shot, but the bullet went inches wide and suddenly diamonds were raining all over the room. The distraction gave me a second and I barreled into Krall. Her gun fired again, the bullet smashing into the LCD TV, glass shattering in a spectacular fashion. I threw my body at Marta Krall, and her gun went flying.

I rolled, but she dived on top of me and began punching my face. She could really punch, too. I head-butted my way past a hail of fists and sharp elbows and rammed my skull into her perfect nose. She grunted like a man, toppled backward, and, still stunned, staggered to her feet. I sprang up and the two of us were standing face-to-face. No guns. *Mano a mano*, so to speak.

I aimed a right jab at her beautiful face. She ducked, and I drove a left hook into her stomach. She doubled over, gasping. I charged and hit her again with my full body weight.

I'm pretty sure she expected to crash into the wall behind her, but that's not what I had in mind. There was no wall behind her. Just an oversize, multi-paned, arched window, and from what I could see from my vantage point, nothing behind it but blue sky.

"*Ooooo-rah!*" I screamed, and Krall went flying through the handcrafted Venetian glass window. Arms flailing, she dropped like a stone to the street below.

I was sure the fall would kill her. But she never hit the sidewalk. Venice isn't famous for its sidewalks. She hit the water. I picked her gun up off the floor, leaned out the window, and scanned the canal.

At least fifteen seconds passed before Marta came up to the surface, sputtering. I could've shot her, but I didn't do it.

Not in front of Katherine.

Chapter 57

KATHERINE WHISPERED ACROSS the room. "Is she dead?"

"Unfortunately not," I said.

"Matthew, I can't believe it. She tried to kill us. We have to call the police."

"No, Katherine. That's one thing we can't do," I said.

"What are you talking about? Of course we call the police. That woman is insane. She knows about your diamonds. She knows our names. What if she comes back?"

"Listen to me," I said. I put my hands on her cheeks. Her eyes were filled with fear. "Sweetheart, we don't have a lot of time, and I hate to play the do-you-love-me card, but do you love me?"

"Of course. Yes. Always."

"Do you trust me?"

She hesitated.

"Let me rephrase the question. I didn't ask if you understand everything that has happened in the past three days, but do you trust me enough to believe that whatever I ask you to do in the next few minutes will be because I love you madly and will do anything to keep you safe?"

"Absolutely," she said. No hesitation, and with a hint of a smile.

"We don't have to call the police," I said, "because in a few minutes this place will be crawling with cops. If we're still here, they'll arrest us."

"Why? We're innocent."

"Even if these cops speak perfect English, there's no way they're going to believe a word we say. There's a bullet hole in our TV, a body went flying through our window, and there are millions of dollars' worth of diamonds scattered around our room, which—oh, by the way, Officer, just happens to be totally trashed. We have exactly two minutes to grab whatever we can and get out. Trust me. Please."

I hit the floor and started scraping diamonds off the rug and tossing them into the medical bag. A second later Katherine was scooping them off the bedspread.

The desk, the dresser, and two chairs had been knocked over, and I stood them upright. Then I moved the rest of the furniture so we could get whatever had rolled underneath.

"Ninety seconds and we pop smoke," I said.

"Pop smoke?" Katherine asked.

"It's Marine-speak for get the hell out of this hotel room before we wind up doing some serious time in an Italian prison."

We crawled on the floor, scavenging among the broken glass, shattered furniture, and overturned room-service cart, grabbing as many loose stones as we could find.

A minute later I pulled the plug. "Time's up," I said. "You have thirty seconds to throw your clothes in a bag or leave them behind."

At the two-minute mark I grabbed Katherine by the arm and pulled her toward the door.

"Over there," Katherine said, pointing to a corner. "Is that diamonds or broken glass?"

They were diamonds, and my trained sniper's

eye could spot at least half a dozen spots where the sparkle was definitely not glass. But we didn't have time to get them all.

"Leave them. They'll be a nice tip for the maid," I said, looking around our formerly glorious room. "Believe me, she'll have earned it."

Chapter 58

THE BEST WAY I can describe what was going on in the lobby of the Danieli was discreet commotion. The manager of the hotel, several of his assistants, four desk clerks, and a couple of bellmen were scurrying about—some of them communicating by radio in hushed voices. But I could hear the overtones of panic.

I caught the words *al quinto piano* repeated several times—"on the fifth floor"—referring to the location from which Marta Krall had just taken her swan dive. Members of the hotel staff were on their way to the room with the broken window. I figured la Polizia di Venezia couldn't be far behind.

The chaos worked in our favor. Katherine and

I strolled casually through the lobby and out the front door with our bags. Had anyone been paying attention, it might have been noticed that we hadn't bothered to check out. But everyone was far too busy to notice a chatty couple who were debating whether to visit the Peggy Guggenheim collection at the Museo d'Arte Moderna or spend a few hours at the Gallerie dell'Accademia.

If this were New York City, we'd have jumped in a cab and tear-assed down the Grand Central Parkway straight to JFK. But there aren't a lot of high-speed getaway options in Venice. A gondola would have been romantic but not too smart.

There was a water taxi parked in front of the hotel and we got in.

It was a ten-seater. We were the only two passengers.

"Railway station," I said. "Venezia Santa Lucia."

"*Cinque minuti,*" the driver said, not moving the boat. He pointed to the eight empty seats.

"What's going on?" Katherine said. "Why aren't we moving?"

"He wants to wait five minutes till he gets more passengers."

I could see cops storming into the hotel. Katherine and I had registered in our own names, so it wouldn't be long before the local police were looking for us. When they didn't find us, they'd widen the search. We had to get out of Italy before our pictures were posted at every border crossing.

"Waiting is not an option," I told Katherine.

She clasped her hands together and looked to the heavens. "God, my boyfriend's been a little crazy lately," she said. "Please don't let him ask me to swim."

I kissed her on the forehead and turned to the water-taxi driver. *"Siamo in ritardo per il nostro treno,"* I said.

Katherine looked at me.

"I told him we were late for our train."

The driver shrugged. *"Gli Americani sono sempre in ritardo,"* he said.

"He says we're always late. *Quanto?"* I said. "How much?"

"Novantacinque euro."

"Ninety-five euros. How much for *tutto?"* I said. "The whole damn boat. *Immediatamente!"*

"Seicento."

I dug into my pocket and peeled off three two-hundred-euro notes. The engine turned over as soon as the bills left my hand.

"*Siete Americani?*" our taxi driver said as we cut through the water past the Palazzo Ducale.

"No, we're not," I said.

He shrugged again. He had all the money he was going to get out of me. No small talk required.

Katherine leaned into my chest and I wrapped my arm around her. "Just in case you were wondering," she said, "I'm petrified."

"I'm sorry," I said. "This isn't exactly what I had planned."

"Don't apologize," she said. "Paris was amazing. Venice is inspiring. Except for that blond bitch who shot at us, it's been a heck of a vacation."

I kissed her.

"Where are we going now?" she asked.

"Amsterdam."

"What's there?" she said.

"Beautiful canals, great nightlife, and incredible art—the Rijksmuseum has all the Dutch masters. Rembrandt, van Gogh, Vermeer —you'll love it."

She stared at me. Her gray eyes were steely now. "Matt, cut the travelogue bullshit. The Italian police are looking for us, and instead of racing back to New York, we're on our way to a museum in the Netherlands? What happened to *Trust me?*" she said. "So let me repeat the question. What's in Amsterdam?"

I leaned in close and whispered in her ear, "People who buy diamonds."

Chapter 59

IT TOOK FIFTEEN minutes to get to the train station. I was eager to come clean to Katherine, but just in case our six-hundred-euro captain had a better handle on English than he had let on, we just sat and enjoyed the view.

The next train to Milan was leaving in forty-five minutes. From there we could catch the overnight train to Amsterdam. Flying would take only two hours, but that meant going through airport security, and I had decided to hang on to Marta Krall's gun.

I bought two first-class train tickets to Milan and reserved a sleeper car for the second leg of the trip.

We sat down to wait at a little coffee bar. I

ordered a cappuccino. Katherine had a *caffè con panna*, which is basically espresso topped with sweet whipped cream.

"Do you remember what we were talking about in our hotel room before we were so rudely interrupted?" I said.

"Do I remember? First you nearly gave me a heart attack when you showed me what was inside your little doctor kit, then you said something like—but wait, that's not all. You were going to tell me another big secret, when the door crashed in." She sipped her espresso. "Are you going to tell me now?"

I nodded. "Walter Zelvas—the guy who got killed at Grand Central—was a professional killer," I said. "He worked for the Russian mob. Among other things, they run a global diamond-smuggling operation, and Zelvas was taking off with a bag full of diamonds that he stole from them. They found out, and they hired another hit man to kill him. Zelvas didn't die from a bomb blast. He was professionally terminated."

She put her hand to her mouth. "You're . . . you're telling me the truth, aren't you?"

"Yes. I swear."

"But how do you know? How did you find out?"

"I'm the person . . . they hired to kill Zelvas."

Her body started to shake. "No. No. No. It can't be possible. No."

"Katherine, first of all, it's true," I said. "I can't expect you to understand, but I love you too much to keep it from you. And after what happened in our hotel room, you have to know. That woman's name is Marta Krall. The people who hired me to kill Zelvas hired her to kill me and get their diamonds back."

"This can't be happening," Katherine whispered. She was staring at the floor now, not at me. She couldn't look me in the eye.

"I think I know what you're going through," I said. "The night I got out of the Marines, my father told me that he'd been a professional hit man. He made it sound almost all right. Logical. He only killed bad people, he said. It was like being an executioner in a prison—a really well-paid executioner. He wanted me to think about doing it, too. At first I wouldn't even consider it. But eventually he turned me. I kill evil men like Walter Zelvas. And the money I get paid lets me follow my dream—it lets me paint."

Katherine was in shock. Her face looked tortured. Tears were streaming down her cheeks. "I can't believe it. You kill people? For money? And your father was doing it before you?" She paused, and then she hit me with the same question I had asked my father. "Did he ever tell your mother?"

"Yes," I said. "He said it took her years to get used to it."

"Well, I'm not your mother," she said, sobbing. "Goodbye, Matthew."

She stood up, grabbed her bag, and started walking.

I jumped up and followed her. "Where are you going?"

"Away from you. There's a bus that goes to the Venice airport. I'm buying a ticket and flying to New York. I'm going home. Don't follow me. Don't call me. Ever."

I ran after her, took her by the shoulders, and spun her around. "Please, Katherine. Don't leave."

I stared into her eyes, but the eyes that looked back at me were empty, lifeless. My mind told me to let her go. She would be safer in New York. But my chest was heaving, my heart was breaking, and the emotions I've always managed to keep bottled up inside began spilling out.

"You know how much I love you?" I said, my voice cracking. "Please don't leave. I'll change. I'll do whatever I have to do."

"Take your hands off me," Katherine said. "Or I'll scream."

My hands dropped to my sides. "Katherine, what I do . . . what I did . . . it's a job, like being in the Marine Corps was a job. But it's not who I am. You know the real me. Nothing is more important to me than our relationship."

"You're wrong, Matthew. I never knew the real you. And our relationship has been built on a mountain of lies. Goodbye."

She turned and walked off.

I stood and watched her disappear into the crowd, feeling something I can't remember ever feeling before.

Abandoned.

Chapter 60

THE TRIP ACROSS the northern Italian country-side took almost three hours. The train stopped at Padua, Vincenza, Verona, and other cities steeped in the history of the Venetian Republic, but without Katherine to appreciate them with me, I barely looked.

It was 7 p.m. when we pulled into Milan, and I had forty-five minutes to stretch my legs before the sixteen-hour train ride to Amsterdam.

Milano Centrale is one of the most beautiful railway stations in the world, but it reminded me of Grand Central Terminal, and that reminded me of the night I found the diamonds. And of course finding the diamonds is what led to losing Katherine.

I was miserable. I pulled out my cell phone and dialed the only person I knew who could understand what I was going through.

It was 11 a.m. in Colorado, and my father picked up on the first ring. "How you doing, boy?" he said.

"Been better," I said. "I made the mistake of taking my girlfriend on a business trip and it didn't go well."

"I'm guessing she found out what business you're in, and she's none too happy about it," he said.

"You're pretty smart for an old jarhead."

"Don't have to be smart if you're experienced," he said.

"So lay some experience on me. I could use a little of that fatherly wisdom you enjoy beating me over the head with."

"That's the thing about us Devil Dogs. We never did get much subtlety training," he said. "But I'll give it a shot. I got three questions for you."

"Let's hear them."

"First question," he said. "Do you love her?"

"Of course I do. More than anything."

"In that case, fatherly wisdom won't do it," he said. "Matthew, I could teach you how to shoot, how to live as a man, how to soldier, but when it comes to love I'm as dumb as the next guy, who's as dumb as the guy next to him. Kind of like dominoes. Men are dumber than dirt when it comes to love."

"So it's hopeless."

"No. You just have to learn to understand how women think."

"I'm listening."

"Okay. Good. Second question, then," he said. "How many pairs of your shoes did Jett chew up before you got her to quit?"

I smiled. Jett was my favorite hunting dog, but she had a taste for shoes, especially the ones that smelled like me. "About a dozen."

"But you didn't get rid of her after she ruined two pairs. Or four pairs. Or ten."

"Hell, no, I loved her, and I was determined to train her."

"That's how women think," he said. "They love us, and they're determined to train us."

Now he had me laughing. "So what you're saying is I just need to be housebroken."

"According to your mom, we all do," he said. "Last question. This business trip you're on— what's the degree of difficulty?"

"It was supposed to be a slam dunk, which is why I brought Katherine along," I said. "But I have this aggressive competitor who would like to put me out of business. Permanently."

"In that case, it's time to beat you over the head with some professional advice. Snap out of it, boy. Put that girl out of your mind and focus on your business a hundred and ten percent. You can't afford to be pining away like a lovesick puppy when you've got chips on the table. You hear that?"

"Yes, sir."

He was right. As soon as Marta Krall found some dry clothes and a new gun, she'd come after me again. Being in a funk could get me killed.

"So, here's the wrap-up, boy," my father said. "You're a man, so Katherine expects you to be as dumb as the rest of us. She's a woman, so she's hardwired to fix you, which means you're going to get at least one more chance at redemption. Most important, if you don't watch your ass on this trip, there ain't ever gonna be any grandkids.

And if that happens, your mama will blame it all on me."

"Good advice, Dad," I said. "I owe you one."

"You can pay me back right now," he said. "I know exactly where you are."

I figured he would. The stationmaster's announcements in the background were a dead giveaway.

"I've been there a dozen times," he said. "There's an old nun, Sister Philomena, sitting outside track seven. She used to be a mail drop for me. Put a hundred bucks, or whatever that new Italian money is, in her basket. Tell her it's from Colorado."

"Will do."

"I don't want to know where you're going, but is there anybody you want me to give your regards to?" he said.

That was code for I do want to know where you're going, but don't say it on the phone. Spell it out for me.

"Yeah, say hi to Adam, Mom, and Sarah," I said. *AMS*. Airport code for Amsterdam.

"Safe travels," he said.

"Thanks. I love you, Dad."

"Semper fi, boy."

My father is old school. That's as close as he ever gets to *I love you*.

Chapter 61

JUST AS MY father had said, there was an ancient nun outside track 7. She sat on a folding chair with her head bowed, but she looked up to thank anyone who tossed a coin in her basket.

I dropped in a one-hundred-euro note. Her head came up fast. *"Grazie mille."*

"It's from Colorado," I said.

"Ah, Signor Colorado. Nice man." She studied my face carefully. "You are the young Colorado, sì?"

"I'm his son," I said.

She beamed and touched a bony blue-veined hand to her heart, much the way I imagined she would have if she'd been in the maternity ward thirty years ago when my father announced, "It's a boy."

"Where are you going?" she said.

I hesitated. "I'd rather not say, Sister."

She lowered her head and peered at me over rimless glasses. She smiled, amused at my lack of trust. The deepset, watery eyes and crinkled-paper skin put her somewhere north of eighty, but her teeth could not have been more than a few years old. Straight, white porcelain dentures that were so perfect, I imagined they could only have been the generous gift of a devout Catholic dentist.

"It's okay," she said. "You can tell me. I will pray for you to Saint Christopher."

I trusted my father, so I trusted her. "Amsterdam," I said.

She took my hand, closed her eyes, and mumbled a prayer. Then she opened her eyes, flashed another dazzling smile, and said, *Vai con Dio.*

I said good-bye, not sure if my father was paying her back for past kindnesses or buying me some travel insurance.

I got my answer when I arrived in Amsterdam.

The train ride had been uneventful, but as soon as I stepped up to the taxi stand at the station, a man called out, "Colorado."

I turned, ready to fight.

The man held up both hands. "I'm a friend of Sister Philomena's," he said. "You don't want to take a taxi. They remember every passenger and write down every destination. I remember nothing."

My father had been long retired, but his network was still open for business.

My driver's name was Harold, and my ride was a spacious black Citroën that still smelled factory fresh.

Harold was a professional. He asked no questions and spoke only when spoken to. He negotiated expertly through the midday traffic, and after driving me to the Zeedijk neighborhood, he handed me a business card that had nothing on it but a phone number.

"Anytime," he said. "Day or night."

I reached for my wallet, but he wouldn't take my money.

I got out of the car and did a slow three-sixty, scanning the area. I hadn't been tailed. I silently thanked my father and watched as the wheelman he had sent turned the car around and disappeared into traffic.

Chapter 62

THE ZEEDIJK REMINDED me of Times Square in New York—part trendy, part seedy. I checked into the Bodburg, a hotel on Beursstraat that was also a little of both.

The Bodburg should have been called the Bedbug. The elevator was out of order, the fire hose in the hall leaked, there were rat droppings in my room, and my only window looked out onto a sex shop. It was the ultimate comedown after the Danieli. But it was perfect. Hardly the kind of place you'd go if you were looking for a guy with a bag of diamonds.

Now all I had to do was sell them. Matthew Bannon might not know how to unload millions of dollars' worth of blood diamonds, but the

Ghost did. And my main contact was right here in Amsterdam.

When you think of organized crime in the European Union, the Italians overshadow everyone. But there are plenty of well-oiled smuggling operations in Holland. The Dutch play such a big role in transporting legal goods across the continent that crossing the line to smuggling is an easy step.

I knew most of the players by reputation, and I decided that the best possible buyer in the country was Diederik de Smet. I had two reasons. One, he had the money to handle the kind of volume I was selling. And two, he hated the Russians. A year ago, de Smet had been running a cell-phone hacking operation that was so profitable, the Russian mob couldn't resist trying to move in on it.

The Dutch pushed back, and it escalated into a blood feud with a nasty body count on both sides, so I knew I didn't have to worry about de Smet ratting me out to the Diamond Syndicate. I did have to worry about him, though. His street name was *de slang*—"the Snake"—and word had it he was as treacherous as a king cobra.

I had a meeting scheduled with him for tomorrow afternoon. But first I needed some sleep.

I locked my door, pulled down the window shade, got down on the floor, sliced open the underside of the box spring, and shoved my bag of diamonds in between the coils. Then I stretched out on the bed, not even bothering to undress first. The mattress was lumpy, and I felt good knowing that one of those lumps was going to bring me millions.

I woke up at 9 p.m., showered, got dressed, and felt almost human. I went downstairs and asked the guy at the front desk where to eat.

"The Grasshopper around the corner on Oudebrugsteeg," he said. "They're a steak restaurant, a sports bar, and a cannabis café. They've got a little something for everyone."

I strolled over and opted for a rib eye and a baked potato at Evita, the Grasshopper's Argentinean steak house on the third floor. The food was good, but it triggered the memory of the night Katherine and I shared a porterhouse at Peter Luger to celebrate my getting into Parsons.

Dinner was a lonely affair, and by the time I

finished, I was feeling pretty damn sorry for myself. I knew I should get back to my room and keep one eye on the diamonds and the other peeled for Marta Krall, but sometimes, no matter how hard trouble is beating down on you, you just don't give a shit. So despite my better judgment, I went downstairs for coffee and some weed.

Technically, selling marijuana is illegal in Amsterdam, but it's not punishable, so the law isn't enforced. Most of the coffeehouses that sell it follow some basic rules, like no hard drugs and no selling to kids. The espresso was mediocre, but the weed was primo. After my first few hits, I wanted Katherine to be with me something fierce.

I figured she was back in New York now, and I wondered if she missed me as much as I missed her.

And then I started wondering if my father was right. Would she give me another chance? And what did I have to do to earn it?

I hadn't smoked grass since I got out of the Marines, and this stuff was powerful. It sneaked up on me, and before I knew it, I was half-baked.

I desperately wanted to call Katherine, but I knew I'd regret it in the morning. So I did what any lovesick, stoned-out artist would do.

I took a pen out of my pocket and began sketching her face on a place mat.

Chapter 63

I HAD ROUGHED out the portrait of Katherine when a group of about a dozen college kids piled in. They were loud, American, and drunk. A few of them pushed tables together while one guy with a wispy blond beard and a Duke University Blue Devils T-shirt leaned over my shoulder.

"Whatcha drawing, dude?" he said.

"Looks like I'm drawing a crowd," I said.

My cannabis-infused wit escaped him. "How much to do a picture of me?" he said.

"No charge if you'll pose nude," I said.

He gave me the finger and joined his friends.

The waitress brought me another double espresso and a bottle of beer.

"I didn't order these," I said.

"They're my treat," she said. "Would you like to drink them outside, where you don't have to put up with these dickheads?"

"Thanks," I said and took a swig of the beer. It was definitely the better of the two beverages.

"We artists have to stick together," she said. "My name is Anna."

"Matthew."

She picked up my coffee and carried it outside. The entire three-story building was bathed in an eerie green light. "The owner loves it," Anna said, "because it's the color of grasshoppers. Pretty ugly, right?"

"Not to another grasshopper," I said.

There were at least forty tables, all empty. Anna set me up in the corner farthest from the noise and only ten feet from the canal. A street lamp cast a soft yellow light on the table. Anna excused herself, then returned a few seconds later with about twenty clean white paper place mats.

"We're all out of sketch pads," she said.

"Thanks again."

She looked at my drawing of Katherine. "She's pretty. Who is she?"

"Nobody," I said. "I'm over her."

"I get off work in an hour. You want to come up to my apartment, look at some of my paintings, drink some wine?"

Anna had a lithe, athletic body, blue eyes, blond hair pulled back in a ponytail, and a heavenly smile. So it took me a solid five seconds to answer the question. "Thanks," I said, "but I'm kind of tired."

Anna was not the kind of woman men say no to, so she looked a little surprised when I turned her down. But she shrugged and laughed it off.

She took another look at the sketch of Katherine. "You're not as over her as you might think." She turned around and walked back inside to deal with the rowdy college guys.

I took a long pull on the beer, picked up my pen, and started to work on a second drawing.

"I guess that's the last I'll be seeing of table service tonight," I said as Katherine's face began to emerge from the page. "I know you don't approve of my job, but at least give me some credit for not jumping into some other woman's bed."

The sketch came to life quickly. I don't know if it was the pot or the pain I felt from losing her, but it was the best drawing of Katherine I'd ever done.

Sometimes the difference between a piece of art and a piece of crap is the artist's ability to know when to stop. I worked furiously. And then I set my pen down. I had labored over hundreds of sketches of Katherine since we met, but this one had poured out of me in minutes. It was not only finished, it was inspired.

I sat back and stared at her face. I wanted her in my life forever. I promised myself I would do whatever it took to get her back.

And then I felt the cold steel on the back of my neck.

"It looks like Ms. Sanborne doesn't like this life you lead, does she, Mr. Bannon?" a female voice with a thick German accent said. "Don't worry, you still have me."

I sat there frozen.

"The party is over, pretty boy," Krall said. "Now, tell me, where are Mr. Chukov's diamonds?"

My assassin's playbook of options ran through my head. I'd been in life-or-death situations before. There's always a way out.

But at the moment I couldn't come up with a single one. I was that stoned.

Chapter 64

"I'LL REPEAT THE QUESTION," Marta said, digging the muzzle of the gun into the back of my neck. "Where are the diamonds?"

"I'm stoned," I said, "not stupid. If I tell you where they are, you'll kill me."

"You're right, but if you give me the diamonds, it will be quick and painless. One bullet," she said, pressing the gun directly below my medulla oblongata.

"What happens if I don't give you the diamonds?"

"You'll still die fast," Marta said, and I could sense a note of delight creep into her cold, robotic delivery. "But Katherine Sanborne won't be so lucky."

Hearing Katherine's name was a jolt to my system.

"She had nothing to do with this," I said. "I took the diamonds. She didn't even know about them until ten minutes before you showed up. Keep her out of it."

"And when I say a slow death," Krall said, "I'm not talking about ten minutes."

Krall was the Marquis de Sade of assassins. For many of her targets, death was only the beginning. When their hearts stopped, she'd rip the cord out of a lamp, plug it into a wall socket, and jump-start the victims back into consciousness. Then she would slowly torture and kill them again. She was sicker than Zelvas. And now she was threatening to kill Katherine over the course of days, maybe weeks.

My mental faculties had been dulled, but my adrenal gland started firing on all cylinders. I could feel the adrenaline rush as my body went into fight-or-flight mode.

I am invincible, I thought.

My brain shook off the effects of the marijuana and I forced myself to think in straight lines—somewhat straight, anyway. Maybe a little crooked. Marta Krall had a gun, but I had one small advantage. She still had no idea who I really was. If she knew I was the Ghost, I'd be dead already. I'd gotten the best of her in Venice, but she probably figured that was my Marine training. I was an amateur who got lucky. It wouldn't happen again. I had to convince her she was right.

"I'll take you to the diamonds," I said. "Please don't hurt my girlfriend. You have to promise."

"You have my word," she lied through her perfectly white teeth.

"I . . . I . . . I hid them." My body started to tremble and my head shook from side to side. The trick was to look petrified and not to let her catch me scanning the area for a weapon, anything I could use against her.

But she was one step ahead of me. "Pick up the beer bottle," she said, "and lower it to the ground. *Slowly.*"

"Yes, ma'am." I did exactly what she asked.

"Where did you hide them?"

"Bus station. A locker."

"Give me the key."

"Sorry," I said. "I hid that, too. It's in my hotel room."

"Take me to it."

"Promise me you won't hurt Katherine," I begged.

"I already promised," she said, disgusted with me. This was not what she expected from a guy who had thrown her out of a fifth-story window. She relaxed. The gun was no longer pressed to the back of my neck. She stepped around to face me.

I froze just looking at her—a deer in her headlights. My body language told her exactly what I wanted her to think—*you won.*

"Not so brave now, are you? *Are you?*"

I shook my head. "No. Not so brave. Not brave at all."

"You're nothing but a dickless wonder, Matthew Bannon. Let's go," she said.

I started to walk, but then stopped. "My picture. Please."

"What?" she said.

"My picture. Katherine. I can't leave it here," I sniveled, acting stoned. "Can't leave it."

By now Krall was sick of me and ready to do whatever it took to get me to the bus station. "Take the fucking picture," she said.

I turned, teetered unsteadily toward the table. I picked up my sketch of Katherine. Then I let out a moan. "Oh, no. Oh, God."

"What now?" she said.

I lowered my head. "I pissed my pants."

"You're absolutely disgusting," she said. "Turn around. Let me see you."

I turned, and her eyes dropped to my crotch for an instant. I grabbed the Rapidograph pen from the table, and plunged the steel tip directly into the gel of Marta Krall's right eye. She gasped, and I forced it deeper—into her brain. Her long legs went out from under her. She collapsed into me but I let her fall.

I think she was dead before she even hit the ground. Her green eyes looked up at me. No movement. Nothing. Dead killer eyes.

I scanned the patio quickly. It was still empty. There were no witnesses to what had just happened here.

I couldn't help thinking—I'm damn good at this, killing bad guys. *Even stoned.*

Chapter 65

WHAT HAPPENED NEXT proved that I was definitely still stoned. I stood Marta Krall upright and put her arm around my neck. Her head drooped and her right eye socket was still leaking blood. "I wish I had one of those pirate eye patches," I muttered as I slipped my sunglasses on her.

I sat her down in a chair and picked up my sketches and her gun—a J-frame Smith & Wesson snubnose. Then I lifted her up again.

"Here we go, sweetie," I said. "I'm going to find a nice place for you to sleep it off."

The canal was only a few feet away, but I didn't have anything to weigh her down with. "Besides," I said to her, "I already had the fun of tossing you in the drink on our first date."

We started walking along Beursstraat, which was teeming with nightlife.

Three guys in Holy Cross sweatshirts were standing outside an Internet café, saw us, and immediately started laughing their asses off.

"Somebody's not going to get laid tonight," one of them called to me.

"Hey, buddy," the second one yelled. "You're supposed to get them drunk, not put them in a coma."

I played along. "She's a blind date," I said. "She wasn't blind when I met her, but she is now."

That cracked them up, too.

"Where'd you meet her?" the third one asked.

"At an Alcoholics Anonymous meeting," I said.

They whooped more laughter, and I kept walking. Marta and I were the entertainment of the moment, and people stopped what they were doing to stare at us. Not everybody said something, but those who did had a wisecrack. Nobody suspected she was dead.

Marta and I turned onto a dark side street that

was lined with parked cars on both sides.

"Oh, look, honey, here's our car," I said, grabbing the door handle on a silver Vauxhall Corsa. It was locked.

I moved on to a second car. Locked. Same with the third.

The fourth one was a faded red Volkswagen van. I was able to open the door—after I smashed the side window with Marta's gun.

I laid her flat on the backseat and retrieved my sunglasses. She stared vacantly at the roof of the van, her right eye a whole lot more vacant than the left.

"Thank you for a memorable evening, Marta," I said, "but I'm afraid this is our last date."

I shut the car door and headed back to my hotel to sleep off my buzz. I needed my wits about me tomorrow.

I had diamonds to sell.

Chapter 66

I CHECKED OUT of the Bodburg Hotel at 6 a.m. and relocated to a quiet little bed-and-breakfast on Geldersekade in the heart of Amsterdam's Chinatown. I had about eight hours to get ready for my face-to-face with Diederik de Smet.

But first I had to change my face.

Too many people were looking for Matthew Bannon.

The homeless-man disguise I used when I was stalking Zelvas was simple enough to do on my own, but this time I needed a total transformation that would stand up to close scrutiny.

I've used the services of a dozen different makeup artists around the world, and one of the best was right here in Amsterdam—a Cuban expatriate named Domingo Famosa.

Domingo had worked for Dirección de Inteligencia, the main intelligence agency of the Castro government. His job was to create special-effects makeup, sometimes for the DI agents, and sometimes for the face and body doubles who stepped in for Fidel when the assassination threat level on El Jefe was high.

I took a cab to Domingo's studio on Waalsteeg.

He was in his late sixties and had a severe speech impediment that was reputed to have been caused by having his tongue seared with a red-hot poker. It's not clear whether the punishment was at the hands of the enemy or his own people, but whoever did it made their point. In the six hours I spent in the makeup chair, Domingo never uttered a word.

He gelled my hair flat, glued on a bald cap, and covered my face with wet plaster bandages. Once it hardened into a mask he removed it from me, added Plasticine, and sculpted fifty years of lines and wrinkles into the face.

He made a second mold and filled it with hot gelatin, creating a flexible prosthetic that he applied to my face with surgical glue.

For the next hour he artfully applied makeup, giving me the uneven skin tone and the telltale age spots of an eighty-year-old man.

Finally, he added contact lenses to create old-man rings around my irises and topped off the look with a gray wig.

I looked in the mirror. Young Matthew Bannon was gone. I was staring at my grandfather.

"That's frightening," I said.

He nodded, then led me to a walk-in closet and pulled out a three-piece charcoal-gray suit.

"Prosperous, but conservative," I said. "I'll take it."

He finished off my wardrobe with a white shirt, a conservative blue-and-gray-striped tie, and black-leather wingtips.

I got dressed and stood in front of a full-length mirror, adjusting my posture by dropping my shoulders and bending my head and upper back forward.

Domingo was behind me. I turned around. "I want to thank you, young fellow," I said in my new gravelly voice. "You are a true artist and I am grateful for your services."

He grinned.

I stood there for a beat and made little sucking noises through my teeth—my grandfather's trademark. "So, Señor Famosa, what do you think?" I said.

The grin got wider. He raised his right hand, made a gun out of his thumb and forefinger, aimed it straight at me, and pulled the imaginary trigger.

I took it as a sign of approval. Still, it was unnerving coming from someone who had spent his career disguising guys to take a bullet for Castro.

Chapter 67

DIEDERIK DE SMET had been charming over the phone. "If the quality is good, and you're selling at a reasonable price," he said, "I'd be happy to buy your merchandise."

From what I had heard about the Snake, I knew he'd be even happier to steal my merchandise. And he had the organization to do it.

De Smet set the meeting for 2 p.m. at the Café Karpershoek, the oldest bar in Amsterdam. It's directly across from Centraal Station, so it's usually crowded with tourists who are eager to drink down the Heineken and soak up the atmosphere.

It's also a big draw for the locals, because the café has a hard-and-fast no-music policy, which makes it a perfect place for anyone interested in a pint, a snack, and a serious conversation.

I walked through the door at exactly 2 p.m. and took a red silk pocket square from my jacket and mopped my brow. A man at a corner table stood up. I recognized him immediately. His face had been on the front page of the papers many times, but his ass had never been in jail.

I walked over and shook his hand. "I'm Yitzchak Ziffer," I said, adding an Eastern European Jewish accent to my aged voice.

"Diederik de Smet. A pleasure to meet you."

"What a charming place," I said, scanning the room. "The dark wood, the brass fixtures, the artwork . . ."

Two men at a far table and two more at the bar were watching my every move.

"What a rich history this establishment must have," I continued.

"It was built in sixteen oh six," he said.

"Ah, it's good to find something that's older than I am," I said.

We laughed and sat down, and he poured two beers from a pitcher on the table.

"How come we've never done business before,

Mr. Ziffer?" he said.

"I'm from New York," I said. "I worked in the Diamond District. I retired fifteen years ago, but I'm helping a friend. He came into some lovely stones unexpectedly, and he doesn't know anything about the art of negotiating."

De Smet smiled. He was about forty-five and had a hawk nose, thin lips, perfect teeth, and enough gel in his thick black hair to wax a bowling alley.

"I heard something about a young man who recently came into quite a few lovely stones," he said. "Can I see them?"

"These are but a small sample," I said, handing him a velvet pouch that held about thirty diamonds.

He rolled them through his fingers, then put a jeweler's loupe in his eye and studied about ten of them.

"Lovely, indeed," he said. "Good color, slightly included. Where are the rest?"

I handed him photos I had taken before leaving New York. All the diamonds sat in a glass container on a scale.

"Very impressive," de Smet said. "There are

rumors circulating that these might have belonged to my competitor."

"They belong to my client," I said. "Would you rather I sell them to your competitor?"

"You couldn't," he said, his toothy grin turning into a sneer. "And if you tried, they would kill you. Word travels, Mr. Ziffer. The Russians are looking for some stolen diamonds."

I stood up. "I came to Amsterdam looking for a buyer, Mr. de Smet. Obviously you're not him."

"Sit," he said.

I didn't. "I've wasted enough time as it is," I said.

"Please," he said. "Sit."

I sat.

"I didn't mean to offend you, Mr. Ziffer," he said, "but you know what they say—let the buyer beware."

"Beware of what?" I said. "Have I given you reason not to trust me?"

"Mr. Ziffer, I wouldn't trust you if you were my Dutch uncle. But if all your diamonds are as good as they look, I'll take them off your hands for five million American dollars."

"I'm an inadequate photographer, Mr. de

Smet. These diamonds are better than they look, and they're worth thirteen."

He didn't blink.

I sipped my beer. "But in the interest of a quick sale, I will accept ten."

"Six," he snapped back.

I shook my head. "My client won't be happy with anything less than nine."

"Your client will be happy if the Russians don't find him and connect his balls to a car battery. Final offer—seven million dollars."

"I'm at nine, you're at seven," I said. "Let's meet at eight million."

"Let's not. Seven million. Take it or leave it. Either way, the beer is on me."

"You're practically stealing them," I said. "But I never had a problem with stealing. I'll take it. Can we do the transfer tonight? You can pay me in euro banknotes. I don't know what the equivalent of seven million American weighs, but at my age I don't think I'll be able to lift it."

Actually I knew exactly what it weighed. Seven million in hundred-dollar bills would tip the scales at one hundred and fifty-four pounds— too much to carry at any age. The same amount in five-hundred-euro notes was only twenty-six pounds.

De Smet shrugged. Dollars, euros—he didn't care. He was probably planning to hand over the money, take the diamonds, and then take the money back.

"Tonight is fine with me," he said. "There's a bar on Rembrandtplein where we can do business in total privacy."

I shook my head. "It's not only the buyer who must beware," I said. "I'd rather go somewhere not so private. How about the two of us take a nice romantic moonlight dinner cruise along the canal. I'll be on the boat that leaves the Prins Hendrikkade dock at seven-thirty. Bring the money. And come alone."

"Of course," he said. "You as well."

"The cruise lasts two hours. When we get back to the dock, I will be at the front of the queue and get off first. You, my friend, will be at the very back of the line. By the time you will get off, I'll be gone, and you won't be tempted to follow me. Is that condition acceptable?"

"No problem," de Smet answered. "All I want are the diamonds."

Chapter 68

I STEPPED OUTSIDE the Café Karpershoek, and the two men who were watching me from the bar followed. The Ghost could have lost them in half a minute, but it wouldn't have been smart for old Mr. Ziffer to shake them like a pro. I'd have to make them think they lost me.

I walked across the street to the cab stand at Centraal Station. I got into the first taxi and told the driver to take me to the InterContinental Amstel Hotel.

"Drive slowly," I said. "I want to enjoy the view."

De Smet's boys caught the cab behind me and had no trouble keeping up.

I knew the Amstel well. I had stayed there the

last time I had a job in Amsterdam. It's a beautifully restored landmark building—a grand old palace that sits majestically in the heart of the city, overlooking the Amstel River. It's the essence of Dutch charm, elegance, and efficiency.

The cab stopped at the entrance, and a burly uniformed doorman with a handlebar mustache opened the door. I recognized him immediately.

"Rutger," I said as he helped me out of the taxi. "My favorite doorman. Do you remember me from last summer? Yitzchak Ziffer. You took excellent care of me. Good to see you again."

I put a hundred-euro note in his hand, and his eyes popped. He had no idea who I was, but that didn't slow him down.

"So excellent to see you again, Mr. Ziffer," he said. "Welcome back. Do you have bags?"

"No, I checked in last night. But if it's not too much trouble, I need one small favor."

He slipped the money deftly into his pocket as he helped me to the red-carpeted stairs. "Mr. Ziffer, whatever you need."

"As you know, I'm an author, and I'm here for another book signing," I said. "But some of my fans are more like stalkers. Do you see those two men who just got out of that taxi?"

He looked discreetly over at de Smet's men. "Yes, sir. Are they annoying you?"

"They mean well," I said, "but sometimes this famous-author business can be exhausting. Could you just delay them at the door for a few seconds so I can get upstairs to my room to take a nap without being accosted by any more autograph hounds?"

"You'd be surprised how long I can delay them," Rutger said.

"You've always been so kind," I said, toddling slowly up the stairs. "That is why I stay here."

I walked through the front door as de Smet's men were approaching the stairs. I caught a glimpse of Rutger spreading his arms wide and stopping them in their tracks. "Gentlemen," he said. "Are you registered guests?"

"Out of my way," the first thug said, shoving him hard.

But it's not easy pushing a two-hundred-and-fifty-pound doorstop out of the way. Rutger pushed back.

The thug threw a punch. I darted into the lobby and looked back. Rutger was bleeding from the nose. But he wasn't down. He wrapped both his arms around the attacker and started blowing his whistle.

A second doorman, two bellmen, and a parking valet jumped into the fray, and suddenly all the palatial grandeur and European civility of the Amstel Hotel had disintegrated into a brawl.

I didn't stick around to see how it turned out. De Smet's men wouldn't be held back for long. I bolted across the marble floor of the lobby to the rear door and exited into the hotel garden.

From there I ran along the riverbank, turned right on Sarphatistraat, and caught a cab back to my little bed-and-breakfast in Chinatown.

I looked out the rear window as the Amstel faded into the distance.

Someday I'd like to come back here, I thought. I'll bring Katherine. And a serious tip for Rutger the doorman.

Chapter 69

DIEDERIK DE SMET was more treacherous than I had expected. I knew he would have me tailed, but the fact that his men beat up the doorman at the Amstel meant they had been ordered not to lose me. Their instructions had probably been to follow me to my room and grab the diamonds. So much for honor among thieves.

I took a cab to the Prins Hendrikkade dock at five-thirty—two hours before departure.

The excursion was a dinner cruise, so people were encouraged to come early—and buy lots of drinks. I bought a ticket and went on board. The entire dining area was enclosed in glass. Several couples had already commandeered the primo window-seat tables.

I spotted a tiny table right next to the swinging kitchen door, where the clatter of pots and pans and the constant waiter traffic would take most of the romance out of a dinner cruise.

It was perfect for me—in the corner, with a clear view of the dock, the gangplank, and the entire dining room.

I ordered a club soda from the bar and took a stroll around the boat. Most of it was under glass, but there was some deck space for people who wanted to fill their lungs with the fresh night air.

None of de Smet's men had shown up yet. I was betting that two of them were still hanging out at the Amstel, waiting for me to come down from my room.

At 7:15 I spotted de Smet on the dock. He was wearing black jeans and a black leather jacket and had a black duffel bag slung over his shoulder. I had no doubt that he would show me the money. But I was pretty sure he didn't plan for me to get off the boat with it.

He bought a ticket but didn't board yet.

A minute later, two of his men from the Café Karpershoek arrived. They bought tickets and stood a few yards away from de Smet, pretending not to know him, having a smoke and a chat.

Finally, the two punks who had followed me to the Amstel showed up. They didn't buy tickets. One of them picked up a brochure and tried to look fascinated by it. Four brutes with a passion for dinner cruises? The rest of the passengers were all boy-girl couples. How dumb did de Smet think I was?

At 7:20 de Smet gave the signal, and his two hulks came on board. They stood at the front of the dining room and began eye-searching the tables. As soon as one of them spotted me, he gestured to the other, who dialed his cell phone. I watched as de Smet took the call, smiled, and came on board.

Chapter 70

AT 7:30 ON THE DOT, the boat pulled away from the dock, and de Smet slithered into the dining room. He caught my eye, then headed directly for my table, all smiles.

"Yitzchak," he said, shaking my hand.

"Diederik," I responded. We were obviously now on a first-name basis.

He looked around the room. "This is an inspired place to meet," he said. "Crowded, but nobody will bother us, and we can enjoy a nice leisurely dinner while we do business."

You're so full of shit, I thought. "I'm so glad you like it," I said.

"How did you come to think of it?" he asked.

"My late wife and I took this same dinner

cruise along the canals fifty years ago," I said. "I'm only in Amsterdam for a brief time, and I couldn't leave without coming back here."

"A sentimental diamond merchant," he said.

"Guilty as charged," I said.

It was partly true. In an uncharacteristic fit of sentimentality I had transferred the diamonds to a small Adidas sports sack. Zelvas's doctor bag had changed my life, and I wanted to hang on to it as a memento.

"But I'm also practical," I said. "Let's get down to business."

I set the bag of diamonds on the table.

De Smet took it, then passed his much larger duffel to me. I opened it and looked inside. It was filled with purple five-hundred-euro banknotes.

"Would you like to count it?" de Smet asked.

"Yes," I said, and stood up. "I'll be back in a few minutes. That should give you time to inspect the stones. I won't be far."

The men's lavatory was at the opposite end of the dining room but still easy to see from where de Smet was sitting. He didn't plan on letting me out of his sight. I took the bag into the lav and locked myself in a stall.

I had no plans to count the money. Now that de Smet had the diamonds in his hands, I wouldn't have time. I set the duffel bag on the floor and climbed over the divider into the empty stall next to it. I stepped onto the toilet lid and crouched down.

Twenty seconds later, through the crack between the stall door and the wall, I saw de Smet's two heavies walk in.

They looked at the two stalls, ignored the one that appeared empty, and leveled their guns at the one with the locked door and the duffel bag on the floor.

They pumped half a dozen suppressed rounds right where they expected me to be sitting counting the money.

One of them kicked open the stall door. I bet he was real surprised to find it empty. But I never got to see his face.

I stood up on the toilet lid in the adjacent stall and fired a bullet straight down into his skull. Then I shot his partner.

I jumped down and retrieved the duffel bag, which was sticky with blood. I stepped over the bodies and walked to the bathroom door. I opened it a crack. I could see de Smet sitting at his table, waiting for his men to bring back his seven million.

I pulled out my cell and quickly sent a text. I had a partner—and we had a plan.

Then I bolted through the bathroom door and ran for the deck.

De Smet saw me. He jumped up and followed in a big hurry.

Most people were in the dining room, but there were a few couples strolling along the deck, oohing and aahing at the illuminated bridges and the brightly lit houses along the canal.

I crashed into them, knocking down one poor guy. De Smet was right behind me, the bag of diamonds in one hand, a gun in the other.

He began firing on the run, not even bothering to aim.

Glass shattered and wood splintered. My fellow passengers screamed and ducked for cover.

I raced down the deck like a broken-field runner dodging tacklers, only I was avoiding bullets.

De Smet was right behind me. "You're way

out of your league, old man," he yelled. "Give me the bag."

"And then what? Are you going to throw me over the side?" I said as I climbed onto the rail on the port side of the boat. "Why don't I save you the trouble?"

And I jumped overboard.

I landed on a pile of rafts that a friend of mine named Kino had tied together to break my fall. I had just texted him from the bathroom. He was my partner for this getaway.

"Well, look who dropped in," he said as he gunned the engine and a sleek Stingray Cuddy/Cruiser barreled down the canal.

Within seconds, the lights of the cruise ship and the outraged screams and wild gunshots coming from de Smet faded into the distance.

"How'd it go?" Kino yelled over the roar of the three-hundred-horsepower dual prop.

"I got paid; he got what he paid for," I said. "Seems incredibly fair to me."

"Sounds like a perfect evening," Kino said.

"It was, but then it got wet. Very wet," I said.

Kino shrugged. "Shit happens."

"Yeah, it does," I said.

I reminded myself not to explain it quite that way to Katherine when—that was, *if*—I ever saw her again.

Chapter 71

WHAT CAN I say about Kino? My buddy is an ex-Marine who left the service with a chest full of medals, got engaged to the daughter of a millionaire real-estate developer in Hong Kong, and could have spent the rest of his life in Fat City. But he missed getting shot at.

So Kino went back into combat, and over the next eight years got wounded five times, each one for a different foreign government.

I've never met anyone happier about his work.

He's five foot four and a hundred and fifty pounds of solid muscle—though he swears that at least five pounds of it is shrapnel.

"You won't have to bury me when I die," he

always says. "Just take me to a salvage yard."

He's worked in dozens of hot spots around the world but decided to live in Holland because "it's the most tolerant damn country on the whole damn planet."

As soon as the cruise ship was out of sight, he slowed the Stingray down to a safe, respectable canal speed.

There was a compact little sleeping cabin below the deck, where I shucked my clothes, peeled off my old-man face, and washed up. My Red Oxx Sky Train bag with my clothes was waiting for me, and I put on jeans, a clean shirt, sneakers, and a Windbreaker.

I went back up on deck. Kino had pulled into a dock and was tying the boat down.

"Abandon ship," he said.

I grabbed my Red Oxx and the duffel bag, and we walked to his car.

"Where to?" he asked.

"There's a bank on Vijzelstraat. I have a deposit to make."

"It's almost nine p.m. Good time to avoid the crowd," he said, laughing, as we headed out. "So how's your old man?"

"I spoke to him the other day," I said. "He said something about wanting grandkids."

"Did you explain that's not something you can do on your own?"

He made small talk as we drove, never asking me what went down on the cruise boat or what was in my duffel bag. It's something you learn in the corps. Respect the other guy's personal boundaries.

The bank was next door to an Indonesian restaurant on a wide, busy street. Kino parked directly in front. "I'll wait here till you're inside," he said.

"You don't need to do that," I said. I thanked him for his help, unzipped the duffel, and pulled out a stack of bills.

He waved me off. "What do I look like, a mercenary?"

"I came into some serious money," I said. "I want to spread it around."

"Put it in a college fund for those grandkids," he said.

"Thanks." I opened the car door and got out.

"Semper fi, bro," he said.

"Right back at ya," I said.

The lobby of the bank was well lit, and I walked up to the double glass doors and rang the after-hours bell.

A young man in khakis and an open-collar shirt unlocked the door.

"I'm Matthew Bannon," I said.

"We've been expecting you, Mr. Bannon," he said. "I'm Jan Schoningh. Come on in."

The bank was twenty-first-century techno architecture—mostly steel and glass—and completely devoid of old-world charm. But they still adhered to that old-world banking tradition that states, "We're always open late for a guy who shows up with a shitload of cash."

I expected Schoningh to escort me to a private office where I'd meet some venerable old guy in an expensive suit, but I guess these days it's the young bankers who get to stay late and service the late-night clientele.

There was a cashier waiting to count the money.

"This is Katje," Schoningh said.

Katje was blond with a knockout smile and a no-nonsense approach to handling seven million bucks.

She dumped the money on a table, unbanded the packets, and ran the bills through a machine.

Then she ran them through a second time.

The total came to $7,024,362.18. The exchange rate had shifted a few tenths of a point in my favor.

I guess you'd say I was rich. Mr. Schoningh did not seem overly impressed, though. "Do you want to deposit the entire amount?" he asked.

"Everything but eighty thousand euros."

Katje counted out the money and put it in a pale yellow bank envelope for me. We spent another twenty minutes filling out papers, and then Schoningh escorted me to the front door.

Kino was still parked outside.

He rolled down the window and called out to me. "Hey, Matthew, you need a ride to the airport?"

"You didn't have to wait. I could've caught a cab."

"Cabs are expensive," he said. "Get in, kiddo. I'm damn happy to do it."

And he was. I think the only thing that would have made Kino happier was if Marta Krall had still been around, taking shots at us.

Chapter 72

THE NEXT AVAILABLE flight to New York wasn't until two o'clock the next afternoon. That left me with seventeen hours to cool my jets at the airport.

But life changes when you have money. Maybe it can't buy happiness, but it sure as hell can get you where you want to go in a hurry.

Kino dropped me at the General Aviation Center. Two minutes later I was walking across the tarmac with Captain Dan Fennessy, pilot of the Falcon 900EX jet I had chartered.

By the time we got to the plane, I knew everything I needed to know about him. He'd been a pilot for thirty years, got laid off by Delta two years ago, and was happy to give me a bargain rate of only seven thousand dollars an hour so he wouldn't have to deadhead back to the States.

I paid cash.

The copilot was in the cockpit. "Where would you like to land?" he asked. "JFK, Newark, or Teterboro?"

"For forty-nine thousand bucks, I'd like to land on the corner of Bleecker and Perry in the West Village," I said.

The two flyboys laughed, and I opted for Teterboro, a small general aviation airport in New Jersey used mostly by corporate jets and small private planes.

"Good choice," Fennessy said. "Much less hassle with customs."

He gave me a short tour of the aircraft, pointing out the amenities and explaining emergency procedures.

"You have fourteen seats to choose from, Mr. Bannon," he said. "Too bad there's only one of you."

I'm sure it was his standard icebreaker. I didn't correct him, but as far as I was concerned, he had two passengers—Matthew Bannon and the

Ghost. And Vadim Chukov was determined to kill us both.

I sat down in a window seat and buckled myself in. Five minutes later we were wheels up.

If the Ghost had been calling the shots, we'd have been heading anywhere but New York. The Ghost was hardwired to be as emotionally detached as humanly possible. With the Russian mob after him, and seven million dollars in the bank, he would gladly disappear and start a new life elsewhere.

On the other hand, there was Matthew Bannon, the passionate, caring, wannabe artist, whose mission would be to fly home, win back Katherine's heart, and live happily ever after.

But there was a third choice. And after a lot of soul-searching, that's the one I finally made.

I was going back because I had screwed up the best relationship I'd ever had and I needed to apologize.

I was going back because, even though Chukov would be gunning for Matthew Bannon, I had put Katherine's life in danger, and I had to make sure that she was okay and that she stayed that way.

The old me never would have been on that plane. I was always so careful, so self-involved. But something had changed me. Actually, someone had changed me. Katherine. I loved her desperately. I didn't want to lose her. I wanted to set things right, and then maybe, just maybe, start my life over again.

Was that too much to ask? Probably, yeah.

Chapter 73

THE FALCON TOUCHED down at Teterboro at a few minutes after 10 p.m.

The customs and immigration agent who met our plane checked my passport and asked me why I went to Paris, Venice, and Amsterdam.

"I'm an artist on tour," I said.

He stifled a yawn. My name wasn't on his watch list, so he stamped my passport and sent me on my way.

A customs agent asked me if I had anything to declare.

"Only that I'm happy to be back in the good old U.S. of A.," I said.

He nodded like he'd heard it before. "Welcome home," he mumbled.

And that was it. Maybe in these times of young rock stars and baby-faced Hollywood celebrities, nobody wonders why a thirty-year-old in jeans and sneakers flies in from Europe on his own charter jet. Or maybe it was the end of a long day and nobody gave a shit.

Captain Fennessy had ordered a town car for me, and the driver took the Jersey Turnpike to the Lincoln Tunnel, then went down Ninth Avenue to Bleecker.

I got out three blocks from my apartment and walked south toward Perry. I checked the cars and the windows along Bleecker. Nobody was staked out waiting for me to come home.

I unlocked the front door and climbed the stairs to my apartment.

It was exactly as I'd left it.

I dropped my bag and stashed what was left of the eighty thousand euros I had taken from the bank in Amsterdam. Then I dug Marta Krall's Glock out of my bag. I had been ready to ditch it, but there had been no security at Amsterdam and even less at Teterboro. It was a nifty gun. A definite keeper.

And then I heard the scratching at the door. It

was followed by a long-drawn-out meow. My cat was home. I opened the door a crack and Hopper strolled in, looking well fed.

"What's new, pussycat?" I said.

I pushed the door shut, but it wouldn't close. I swung it open wide to see what was holding it back.

And there they were. Three men, armed to the teeth. "Welcome back," one of them said.

Then they shoved their way into my apartment and shut the door.

Chapter 74

"BOY, AM I glad to see you guys," I said.

Zach Stevens, Ty Warren, and Adam Benjamin are Marines Corps—to the core. We met in boot camp, trained together, and fought side by side against ruthless fanatics in the mountains of Afghanistan and the streets of Iraq. Once I decided to become the Ghost, I knew I couldn't do it on my own. And there was nobody I trusted more than these three. They were my best friends in the world.

So I had hired them to be my backup and my bodyguards, and they've been living in apartment 1 ever since. They are loyal, lethal, and, while you'd never know it to look at them, kind of lovable.

We exchanged bro hugs all around.

"You're lucky you didn't get shot sneaking in here," Adam said. "Why didn't you tell us you were coming back?"

"I was going to knock on your door at a more civilized hour. How did you guys know I was home?"

"You tripped the silent alarm," Zach said.

"No I didn't," I said. "I totally bypassed—"

"Sorry, boss," Zach said. "I'm talking about the *new* silent alarm. I installed it on the third step below the fifth-floor landing."

"You had a nasty-ass visitor the other day," Ty said. "We figured she'd be coming back."

"What did she look like?" I said.

Zach took a picture out of his pocket and handed it to me. It was a black-and-white screen grab from the closed-circuit camera at the front door.

"Her name is Marta Krall," I said.

"She tried to pass herself off as one of your art teachers," Zach said.

"Well, I guess I taught her a few things," I said. "And we don't have to worry about her ever coming back. She flunked the final."

None of them even blinked; kill-or-be-killed was in our DNA.

"We've been at threat-level red since she showed up," Ty said. "You think we should ease it back to orange?"

"If Marta Krall was the only one who wanted me dead, I wouldn't even bother locking the front door," I said. "But I've made a lot of new enemies recently."

"Don't worry about it, Captain," Adam said. "Nobody is getting in here."

"What are we looking for?" Zach asked.

I told them the whole story. Zelvas, Chukov, the diamonds, Paris, Venice, Amsterdam, Marta, and of course, Katherine.

"Where's Katherine now?" Adam asked.

"New York," I said. "At least I think she flew back to New York after she left me in Venice. I phoned her, texted her, but no response. She probably thinks I just want her back, so she's avoiding me."

"Knowing the Russian mob," Ty said, "if they can't find you, they'll go after her."

"You're right," I said. "That's why I came back here. I want them to find me. Fast."

I pulled my cell phone out of my pocket. Four rings later a voice that was laced with sleep and booze picked up.

"Chukov."

"This is the Ghost," I said.

Chukov woke up in a hurry. "Where the hell are you? Where are my diamonds?"

"I'm still in Amsterdam," I said. "Your diamonds are back in New York."

"Where? Who has them?"

"Matthew Bannon," I said. "He couldn't unload them. The kid is an amateur. He couldn't sell a fire extinguisher in hell. By the time I tracked him down, he chickened out and skipped town."

"Where's Bannon now?" Chukov said.

"He flew back home. He's holed up in his apartment, trying to figure out how to get rid of those stones," I said.

"He's in New York?" Chukov said. "That son of a bitch."

"Relax, Vadim. I'm catching a flight out of Schiphol in a few hours. I should be in New York by tonight to wrap things up. I'll call you then."

"I'll be waiting for you," Chukov said.

I hung up and turned to my three bodyguards.

"Let's ramp up, boys. The Russians are coming."

Chapter 75

CHUKOV'S PHONE RANG.

He clenched his teeth and picked it up. "Hello, Nathaniel. I was just going to call . . ."

"They sent for me," Prince screamed.

"Who sent for you?" Chukov said.

"Who do you think? The heads of the Syndicate. You've made so much goddamn noise trying to find my diamonds that they found out Zelvas was stealing and now they want answers."

"But Zelvas was only stealing from us," Chukov said.

"That's not the way they will see it. Now, where the hell are my diamonds?" Prince screamed.

"We're working on it," Chukov said. "We had a little setback."

"What? What kind of setback?"

"Marta Krall is dead," Chukov said. "From what I can put together, she tracked Bannon to Amsterdam and he killed her."

Chukov had to hold the phone away from his ear as Prince let out a torrent of insults aimed at Krall, Bannon, Chukov, and the mothers who spawned all three from their respective wombs.

"Nathaniel, I know it sounds bad, but it's under control," Chukov said. "I just heard from the Ghost. Bannon couldn't sell the diamonds, so he brought them back to New York. I swear I'll have them in another few hours."

"Natalia and I are at the airport now," Nathaniel shouted. "In another few hours, I'll be in Nassau and the Syndicate will have my balls in a vise. I want those diamonds back, and if Bannon already sold them, I want the money."

"I'll take care of it," Chukov said.

"That's what you told me when you hired Krall, may she rot in hell," Prince said. "And unless you get the diamonds now, you'll be joining her."

"Nathaniel, I promise you I'll—" Chukov stopped. Prince had hung up.

He grabbed a bottle of vodka from the bar, unscrewed the cap, and took a long swig. He had seen Prince go off the deep end before, but this was the worst.

He needed to put together a team. He called the top five professionals on his list. Three were out of the country on assignment, but both the Sicilian and the Jamaican were in New York and available. Then he called Nick Benzetti.

"Bannon is back in New York," Chukov said. "He still has the diamonds and my boss is going batshit."

"What happened to your sweet little German girlfriend who shoved the Glock in my face?" Benzetti said. "I thought she was handling the whole mess."

"She's dead," Chukov said.

"Aw, poor thing," Benzetti said. "Is she really dead, or are you just saying that to make me feel good?"

"I'm putting together a team," Chukov said. "I want the diamonds back and Bannon at the bottom of the East River. I have two men already. Do you and your partner want in?"

"Yeah, but we're not working for chump

change," Benzetti said. "Whatever you're paying the other two guys, we get the same."

"I can't afford to—"

"No problem," Benzetti said. "There are plenty of cops who work cheap. Just dial nine-one-one. Nice talking to you."

"Wait. Don't hang up." Chukov could feel his chest tightening. He grabbed his inhaler. "Okay, okay," he wheezed. "But it has to be now. We're running out of time."

"Relax," Benzetti said. "The guy is a dipshit art student. How long can it take?"

Chapter 76

NATHANIEL AND NATALIA caught the early-morning JetBlue flight to Nassau in the Bahamas. The Syndicate had rented a block of suites at the Atlantis, a sprawling ocean-themed resort with waterslides, river rides, a hundred-million-gallon aquarium, and almost as many slot machines. It was Disneyland, SeaWorld, and Las Vegas all rolled into one. The Princes despised it.

A limo picked them up at the airport and took them to the One&Only Ocean Club on the eastern end of Paradise Island. Once a private estate, it was now a gated community of ocean-front guest rooms, garden cottages, and luxurious villas.

"You've hardly spoken a word since we left

New York," Nathaniel said as soon as they were alone in their room.

"What is there to say?" Natalia said. "We're here for an inquisition, not a vacation."

"The inquisition doesn't start for five hours. Till then, let us enjoy life."

By noon Natalia was swimming laps in the pool, ignoring the stares of strangers who were trying to figure out the relationship between the voluptuous woman in the white bikini and the silver-haired man who looked old enough to be her father.

She toweled off and slipped on a pair of sandals. "I'm tired of giving those *mudaks* something to gawk at," she said. "Let's walk in the garden."

Directly behind the pool were the lush multi-terraced Versailles Gardens, the thirty-five-acre centerpiece of the Ocean Club.

They walked hand in hand past tropical trees, bronze and marble statuary, and a pond whose surface was graced with water lilies and lotus blossoms, until they reached the final terrace—the Cloisters—a twelfth-century monastery that had been shipped stone by stone from France and now stood overlooking Nassau Harbor.

The air was fragrant with the scent of roses, hibiscus, and oleander. Natalia sat down on a stone bench.

"Why are they persecuting you?" she asked. "Zelvas short-changed the customers and skimmed off the diamonds. You're the one who caught him. You're the one who had him killed."

But they both knew that was only a half-truth.

When Nathaniel found out that Zelvas was stealing, he knew he should report the violation to the Syndicate immediately and return the stolen diamonds to them.

"I have a better idea," he had told Natalia. "Let Zelvas take the fall, but we'll take the money."

He had recruited Natalia to get close to Zelvas.

"How close?" she asked.

Nathaniel didn't hesitate. "Whatever it takes."

And so Natalia worked her magic, the big, ugly Russian fell in love, and the cache of diamonds grew fatter.

It was all falling into place until the night Chukov got drunk and let Zelvas in on the family's most-guarded secret. Natalia's lover Nathaniel was also her father.

After that, it all unraveled like a Russian soap opera. Zelvas's love for Natalia turned into sheer disgust, and he made plans to leave the country.

Now it had come to this: Zelvas dead, the diamonds missing, the Syndicate ready to cut off Nathaniel's hands for stealing and put a bullet through his heart for betraying them.

"I'll be all right," Nathaniel said. It was a hollow promise.

And then he heard it—a soulful moan, like an animal in pain. It took several seconds before he realized the sound was coming from Natalia. She buried her face in her hands and began weeping.

He sat by her side and wrapped his arm around her. "What? What is wrong?"

"You swore—" Natalia said through her sobs. "Night after night you held my hand in the hospital and swore you would never leave me."

"And I haven't. All these years, I have always been here for you."

"But I know them, Papa. They'll kill you."

"All they want is money. The man who stole our diamonds has it, and Chukov will find him."

"And if he doesn't?"

"It may take everything I have," Nathaniel said, "but I'll pay it back, and the Syndicate will be happy."

She shook her head. "No. They're evil. They will still want their pound of flesh. They'll kill you. Please . . . please . . . don't go to the meeting. Let's pack our bags and run."

"We can't run. Zelvas tried to run. It doesn't work."

"But I need you," she wailed. "Now more than ever."

"No, *lyubimaya moya*. You are no longer a little girl in a hospital bed. You're a grown woman. Smart, strong, brave. I'm proud of you. You need me less than ever."

Natalia's body heaved with sobs. She wrapped her arms around his neck, and with tears streaming down her face, she kissed him again and again—his cheeks, his eyes, his lips.

"Papa," she moaned. "You can't leave me alone. Not now. I'm pregnant."

Chapter 77

THERE ARE TWELVE hundred and one rooms in the Royal Towers at the Atlantis Resort. Twelve hundred of them are just what you'd expect from a luxury hotel. But the twelve hundredth and first is beyond imagination.

The Bridge Suite is an expanse of ten rooms on top of the bridge that connects the two Royal Towers buildings. It overlooks the entire resort and marina, and at twenty-five thousand dollars a night, it's the most expensive hotel suite in the world.

It's where the Diamond Syndicate held their meeting.

Two men in dark suits picked up Nathaniel and Natalia at their hotel, drove them to the

Atlantis, and escorted them to the Bridge Suite by private elevator.

Nathaniel was patted down, then both of them were body-scanned—first with a metal detector, then with an EMF meter looking for bugs.

So much for trusting me, Nathaniel thought.

"You'll wait in the other room," one of the guards told Natalia.

He escorted her down a hallway while the other guard unlocked the front door of the suite and led Nathaniel into a lavish living room decorated in red, black, and lots of gold.

Six men sat on sofas upholstered in muted shades of silk damask. Nathaniel recognized the five Syndicate heads. The sixth man was a mystery.

Arnoff, the senior-ranking member of the Syndicate, spoke. There were no pleasantries, no foreplay, no invitation to sit.

"Did you know Zelvas was stealing from us?" Arnoff asked.

"No," Nathaniel said. "When he delivered merchandise to our customers, he would always come back with the exact amount of money I expected. My ledgers were balanced to the penny. You saw them every week. It was months before I finally found out he was short-changing the diamond merchants a few stones on every shipment."

"Those merchants are our loyal customers," Arnoff said. "Without them, we would be out of business. Every time he extorted a little bit from each client, he was doing damage to our reputation and goodwill."

Nathaniel was still standing. "Absolutely," he said. "That's why I had him killed."

"And what happened to the diamonds?" Arnoff asked.

"Unfortunately, they were stolen from Zelvas before I could retrieve them," Nathaniel said. "But I have my people looking for them. I'm confident we'll have them back soon."

"That's good to hear," Arnoff said. "Very reassuring. Have a seat, Nathaniel. Make yourself comfortable."

Prince lowered himself into a soft gold-and-white Queen Anne chair.

There was a brass samovar on the table in front of Arnoff, and he leaned across, turned the spigot, and filled a china cup with steaming aromatic coffee.

"Smells like home, yes?" He smiled. "It's imported from Leningrad. Can I offer you some?"

"Thank you," Nathaniel said.

"Liar!" Arnoff roared and lifted the samovar by the base, dumping the entire pot of scalding coffee on Nathaniel's lap.

Prince screamed. He leaped up from the chair, grappled frantically with his belt, and dropped his pants to the floor. His thighs were already burned red, and he shoved both hands into his underwear and cupped himself, but nothing could relieve the scorching pain.

"Zelvas was stupid," Arnoff bellowed. "We are not. He stole. You helped him."

"No. I swear on my mother's grave," Nathaniel said, blinded by the searing pain. "I run the North American operation. Why would I steal from myself?"

"Because you'd be stealing from all of us." Arnoff gestured to the other men in the room, all of whom nodded, corroborating the fact that they had been grievously wronged.

"Zelvas was the one who was disloyal,"

Nathaniel said, sobbing. "As soon as I found out, I had him killed. You must believe me."

Arnoff turned to the sixth man, the stranger in the room. "Do you believe this *svoloch*, Gutov?"

Gutov looked at Prince in disgust and spat out a single word. *"Nyet."*

Arnoff stood up. He was tall and muscular, with a perpetual tan and thick white hair that was combed perfectly in place.

"Anton Antonovich Gutov is your replacement. He doesn't believe you. I don't believe you. No one believes you."

Nathaniel stood there, his pants around his ankles, his legs and genitals burning hot, his dignity and his dreams gone.

"You were the golden boy, Nathaniel," Arnoff said, a hint of regret in his voice. "Another five years, and you would have been seated among us. But now, the gold is tarnished. The price of your mistake is ten million dollars. If you pay it, you can return to Russia and live out your days without threat from us. Your prior service has earned you that."

Nathaniel dropped to his knees, more

overcome by the blessed reprieve than the intense pain. "Thank you," he said, weeping. "Thank you."

Chapter 78

I WAS DESPERATE to find Katherine before Chukov did.

I phoned, e-mailed, and texted. No whining, no pining, no *please come back, I need you* messages—even though that's how I felt. I made it clear that the people who were after me could come after her and that I had to get her out of harm's way immediately.

By midmorning I still had no idea where she was.

But the Fortress was battle-ready. Ty had set up a surveillance post on the roof that gave him clear visuals of all points of access to the building. Zach was on the first floor, waiting in his apartment to flank our enemies and trap them inside when they charged up the stairs. Adam and I were in my apartment, tactical harnesses strapped on, magazines checked, going over our points of cover one more time.

"Déjà vu," he said. "Takes me back to Phantom Fury."

"Not a place I want to go back to," I said.

And yet I go back there in my head all the time.

Operation Phantom Fury had been part of the second battle of Fallujah. A year after Saddam fell, the insurgents had turned the city into a rat's nest of booby traps, IEDs, and snipers. Adam, Zach, Ty, and I were attached to Third Battalion, 1st Marines—the Thundering Third.

Our mission was to take Fallujah back one block at a time.

I was leading a squad of nine men when we took on enemy fire from the top floor of the Qukayh Hotel. We ducked into an abandoned apartment building and raced up the stairs to get a better shot at the hotel *hajjis*. As soon as we made it to the roof, two of our guys were hit. The rest of us scrambled for cover, but it was only a matter of time before they'd either pick us off or hit the roof with mortar fire.

I was about to give the order to head back down the stairs, when the insurgents stormed through the front door and started heading up.

Pinned down by fire from above and with the enemy blocking our retreat below, we radioed for an evac team. Tank support was still six blocks away, trying to navigate through a maze of IEDs.

We were carrying two wounded, running low on ammo, and didn't have enough cover to wait for air support.

There was only one way out. Down the stairs through a shitstorm of enemy bullets. I figured half of us would make it out alive. I was ready to go first.

I'd be dead if it hadn't been for Middleson. Jody Middleson was nineteen, a kid from rural Kentucky who spent most of his free time thumbing through a dog-eared Bible, playing the harmonica, and writing home to his mother, father, and his four sisters. I'd never seen him drunk, never heard him curse, and rumor had it he was still a virgin.

"No, sir," Jody said. "The squad needs you. I'll go first."

"Thanks, but it's not your call, Private Middleson," I said.

The kid had never disobeyed an order until that day.

He didn't argue. He just pulled the pins on two grenades and ran for the rooftop entrance to the hotel.

I screamed at him to stop but he kept running, miraculously making it to the doorway without being hit.

But as soon as he opened the door, five insurgents riddled him with bullets. He dived forward, letting the armed grenades fall from his lifeless hands.

In all my years in combat, it was the finest act of courage I had ever seen.

The explosions rocked the building, and the insurgents were either killed or stunned enough for the rest of the squad to finish the job. An hour later, the tanks got through and cleaned up the snipers' nest.

Jody Middleson was awarded the Medal of Valor.

I learned a hard lesson that day, one that neither the Ghost nor I ever forget. Consider every possible angle. *Think the unthinkable.*

Adam was right. It *was* déjà vu. But this time, I was on my home turf, and I had no excuse for being trapped in a desperate situation.

I made a promise that afternoon in Fallujah never to lose another man to poor planning.

The Russians were coming. And we'd be ready for them. We knew we had one big advantage. No matter what Chukov threw at us, we still had the element of surprise.

"I'm not going to second-guess you," Adam said, "but do you think this is the best idea?"

"What do you mean?"

"You let Chukov know where you are. We'll win this battle, but these guys are like cockroaches. You squash one, and the next day ten more crawl out of the woodwork. These maniacs will keep after you until they get their money or kill you—or, most likely, both."

"I have no choice," I said. "I need to get their focus off Katherine."

Adam shook his head. "All these years you've managed to keep the Ghost off everybody's radar. But the way this is shaping up, the Russian Mafia will be chasing Matthew Bannon. You'll be running for the rest of your life."

"I'm not running anywhere. Not until I can convince the woman I love to run with me."

"And if she says yes?"

I smiled at the thought. "They'll never catch me. I've got plenty of money and the three best bodyguards on the planet."

Adam put both hands to his heart and fluttered his eyes at me. "And the woman you love."

I punched him in the shoulder. It was like hitting granite. I'm sure I felt it more than he did. "Are you making fun of the guy who signs your paycheck?" I said.

"No, sir. Just let me and the guys know if you decide to change your handle from the Ghost to the Hopeless Romantic."

My cell phone rang. I checked the caller ID. It was Katherine.

I grabbed it. "Hello."

I heard her say my name, but it was a terrible cell connection and she was sobbing uncontrollably.

"Katherine, what happened?"

"Leonard . . . Leonard Karns. They shot him. He's dead."

This was no coincidence. Karns was about one degree of separation from me—the same as Katherine. I had to get to her. "Where are you now?" I said.

"Subway station. I just got off the—"

And then the phone went dead.

"Damn it!" I turned to Adam. "They killed one of the guys in my art class. An asshole, but still. We've got to find Katherine. We've got to find her right now."

I started to dial again, when my walkie-talkie crackled.

"Bartender to DJ, over." It was Ty on the roof.

Adam answered. "This is DJ. Go ahead, Bartender."

"I've got five dancers headed our way, looking to tango. They've come to the right place."

"Roger that. We'll start the music. Have Doorman let them in. Let's do what we do best. Over and out."

Chapter 79

THEY ARRIVED IN three cars—an Escalade, a Crown Vic, and a Mercedes S550—all black. They parked a block away, out of sight, but not out of camera range. Ty had a top-of-the-line Pelco surveillance camera pointed down onto Perry Street.

Adam and I went to the video monitor.

"Let's see couple number one," Adam said.

The two men in the Escalade were standing next to the car. Ty pushed the 22x optical zoom in on the first one, a black guy with a scar running from his left ear down past his collar and beyond.

"Umar Clarke," Adam said. "Jamaican hit man. Operates out of Brooklyn."

The camera panned to his partner. "Rosario Virzi," Adam said. "Complete scumbag. And from what I hear, racist. Chukov must be desperate if he threw those two together."

"I'm pretty sure he's desperate," I said. "He owes somebody a lot of diamonds."

"Couple number two," Adam said.

"Chukov likes to hire dirty cops," I said as Ty panned to the two men in the Crown Vic. "The one in the FedEx getup is Nick Benzetti. Partner is John Rice."

"*That's* their play?" Adam said. "*Knock, knock. Who's there? FedEx.* That's a goddamn *insult*. Do they think you're a complete idiot?"

"They probably figure all art students are as easy to pop as Leonard Karns. I guess I owe Leonard a debt of gratitude."

The driver of the Mercedes stayed behind the wheel. The camera zoomed through the windshield, and I saw a familiar face.

"Chukov," I said. "He must have the entire Russian mob up his ass to show up, but he's not going to storm the castle. He'll just sit there and watch."

"You realize Ty could take him out right

where he's sitting?" Adam said. "Do you have any wiggle room in your *don't clutter the neighborhood with dead bodies* policy?"

"None whatsoever," I said.

"Okay, I'm headed back to the first floor. Once you've drawn them up here, Zach and I will box them in from behind."

"Bartender to DJ," Ty said over the walkie-talkie. "Cue the music."

He pulled back to a wide shot. The four dancers were on the way.

Tango time.

Chapter 80

BENZETTI, THE COP in the FedEx outfit, entered the vestibule alone and rang my bell.

I responded on the intercom. "Who is it?"

"FedEx," he said. "I got a priority envelope for Matthew Bannon. That you?"

"Yeah," I said. "But I'm about to jump in the shower. Just leave it at the front door. I'll get it later."

"No can do, fella," he said. "Needs a signature."

"Who's it from?" I said.

"Katherine Sanborne."

"Damn," I said. "I can't come down. Do you mind walking up five flights of stairs?"

"No problem."

I buzzed him in. He opened the door. He was oblivious to the CCTV camera, and I watched him slap a piece of duct tape on the latch. The door closed but it didn't lock. A few seconds later, the other three followed him into the building.

Zach called in from apartment 1. "FedEx man and two others on the way up. They left a sentry at the front door."

Thirty seconds later, Benzetti rapped on my apartment door. "FedEx."

"Door's open," I said.

Three of them stormed in—Benzetti, Clarke, and Virzi—pistols drawn and suppressed and ready to shoot. But there was nobody to shoot at. They slowly fanned out around my living room.

"Where are you?" Benzetti called out. "I got deliveries to make."

"Be right out," I yelled. "I'm in the john."

Hearing my voice, Virzi pushed Benzetti aside and rushed to the bathroom door. Planting his boot inches above the doorknob, he splintered the jamb and sent the door crashing inward. I put a bullet through his head before the door even struck the wall. He never crossed the threshold.

As soon as Virzi hit the floor, I could see the Jamaican charging toward me from behind him. I fired, but the bastard was quick. He lunged straight at me, his body going horizontal, narrowly ducking my shot. He plowed into my midsection and we both went down in a heap on my bathroom floor.

Benzetti, more accustomed to shakedowns than shootouts, began firing in our direction. I'm sure he didn't care if he killed the Jamaican, too, as long as he kept himself alive. But Umar Clarke cared. When a bullet shattered the tile an inch above both our heads, his eyes grew wide and the scar on his face seemed to flush. He turned his attention away from me and fired a pinpoint shot at Benzetti. The bullet passed through Benzetti's thigh and the cop fell back against the wall.

Benzetti staggered toward the door, and the Jamaican turned to me. We had both held on to our guns, but his knee was pressing mine to the floor. I desperately grabbed his wrist, twisting the barrel of his gun away from my face. He pressed so hard, I felt the trigger guard of his Beretta jammed under my nose. He strained to turn the barrel a few more inches so he could fire a 9-millimeter slug through my left eye.

If he had been smart, he would have hauled back and pistol-whipped me. It might have stunned me and given him the edge he needed to get off a shot.

But he wasn't smart. He was strong. Stronger than I was, and he knew it. And as he forced the barrel of the gun closer and closer to my face, he grabbed me by the jaw and twisted my head, trying to angle it for a better shot. I could see he was determined to win this one on brute strength alone.

Macho bullshit. Not my style. Certainly not my father's style. Rule number one according to Dad was "There are no rules. Do whatever you have to do to win. Kick him, pull his hair, gouge his eyes out, fight like a girl, bite him."

I bit him.

With his giant palm pressed under my jaw, his fingers digging into my face, I got my teeth around the first joint of his thumb and clamped down hard. Real hard. They passed through the skin, through the flesh, and right between the joint of his first knuckle. I spat the end of his thumb straight into his eye.

The Jamaican yanked his bloody hand to his chest, and as his body lurched backward, his knee lifted off my gun hand.

I shoved my gun under his nose and fired. At point-blank range, one bullet was more than enough. Covered with blood and bits of gray matter, I reeled out of the bathroom and toward the door in pursuit of Benzetti.

His leg was bleeding and he was limping toward the top of the steps.

Adam was standing directly below him on the fourth-floor landing, a 9-millimeter Glock in his hand. Benzetti fired his gun. Adam fired his. The only difference was that Adam took the time to aim. Benzetti toppled forward and bounced noisily down the stairs.

Rice yelled up from the first floor. "Nick. Nick. You okay?"

Then I heard him running toward us. I counted ten frantic steps before I heard the whispered pop of Zach's gun.

It was over. And since everybody used suppressors, there was almost no noise. Just death.

The walkie-talkie sprang to life. "Bartender to DJ. Chukov knows there's trouble. One of his guys must have entered the building with a wire or an open cell connection. He jumped in the Benz and drove up. He's right in front of the building. I can drop him."

"Stand down, Bartender," Adam said. "Hold your fire."

I expected Ty to say, "Roger that," but instead he came back with "Oh, shit. Matt, it's Katherine."

I grabbed the walkie. "What do you mean, 'it's Katherine'?"

"Big as life," Ty said. "She's walking down Perry, headed straight for us."

Zach's voice came on. "Matt, I'm going out there to get her."

"Stand down, stand down," Ty yelled. "Chukov has a gun trained on the door. He'll drop you before you get to the top step."

"Where's Katherine now?" I said.

"Thirty feet from the building," he said. "Oh, shit—*he sees her.* No question—he recognizes her."

So much for my good-neighbor policy. I keyed the walkie. "Take him down," I said. "Now."

"I don't have a shot," Ty yelled. "He grabbed her!"

Zach jumped in. "I'm going after him. Cover me. Oh, shit—he has her, Matthew. He took Katherine in his car. She's gone."

Chapter 81

"MATT, I'M REALLY SORRY," Zach said, and my friend looked incredibly sad. "I should've—"

I held up my hand. "No apologies. You couldn't have seen this coming. I should have, though. Oh, man. Katherine is Chukov's negotiating tool. He'll trade her for the diamonds."

Almost on cue, my cell rang. It was Katherine.

"Where are you?" I said.

"I don't know," she said. "I'm in a car. A man grabbed me."

"Bitch!" It was Chukov's voice. "Give me the phone."

I could hear Katherine crying as Chukov grabbed the phone and screamed at me. "Bannon, can you hear what's happening to your girlfriend?"

"Let her go," I said. "This is between you and me."

"*You* and me?" he bellowed. "I don't even know who the fuck *you* are. But I'll bet you know who I am. I'm Chukov, the man whose diamonds you stole, and I want them back!"

"Okay, okay, just don't hurt her."

"I haven't hurt her. Not yet. Right now she's in the front seat of my car, stretched out nice and comfortable with her head in my lap."

"You touch her, and I swear to God, I will hunt you down and there'll be nothing left of your lap but a bloody stump."

"Tough guy," Chukov said. "You're not just some art student, are you, Mr. Bannon?"

"I would be if you assholes would leave me alone. I want my girlfriend back."

"And I want my diamonds," Chukov said.

"I have them right here," I lied. "I'll trade you. You can have your goddamn diamonds—just give Katherine back to me. Untouched. Unharmed."

"Now you're getting smart," Chukov said. "There's a self-storage warehouse under the Williamsburg Bridge—"

"No. I'll bring the diamonds to the exact same

place where I found them," I said. "The main concourse of Grand Central."

"Too crowded," Chukov said.

"I like a crowd," I said. "It's safer. We'll do it after rush hour. Ten p.m. It'll be quiet, but there'll still be people around. If we both behave, this can be a civilized exchange. Nobody gets hurt; everybody's happy."

"I'm happy right now, Mr. Bannon," Chukov said. "You know, your girlfriend has a beautiful ass." I heard a smack and Katherine screamed.

Chukov belched out a sickening laugh. "Ten o'clock, Bannon."

Chapter 82

I HAD SET the grand finale exchange with Chukov for the main concourse—center stage at Grand Central Terminal.

Chukov wasn't too happy about it, but he agreed. He probably believed that Matthew Bannon the art student would feel safer surrounded by people walking through the terminal.

But the reality was that Matthew Bannon the Ghost had picked the spot because it offered the best field of fire.

Adam and Zach were already scoping out the building when Ty and I arrived. Then we worked together to map out the best possible combat plan.

Ever since the night I threw those smoke grenades and turned Grand Central into total pandemonium, security had been beefed up. This meant that four strapping ex-Marines standing in the middle of the main concourse on a recon mission would definitely attract cops.

So we opted for aerial surveillance. A table for four at Michael Jordan's Steak House on the north balcony of the terminal, overlooking the rendezvous spot. It was an excellent vantage point. Plus, we were all starving.

We ordered, then sat there and quietly studied the traffic patterns below. When you're standing in the middle of the terminal, it seems like people are crisscrossing the concourse without rhyme or reason. But from twenty feet up, the perspective changes, and they begin to look more like a colony of ants, each one racing about with purpose.

Very few people come to Grand Central to stroll through it aimlessly. Everyone is on a mission—headed for a stairwell, a train, a Starbucks, an exit. If the concourse floor were a giant lawn instead of a vast expanse of polished marble, you'd be able to see where the steady stream of travelers had trampled the grass and created distinct pathways.

"Right down there," I said, pointing at an area where almost no one had walked for fifteen minutes. "That looks like the smartest place to make the exchange."

Adam nodded slowly. "The *exchange*," he said, a sardonic little smile crossing his lips. "Which exchange are we talking about? The one where Chukov trades us Katherine for the diamonds, or the exchange of bullets that will start flying as soon as he realizes that he just gave up his ace in the hole for a bagful of worthless glass?"

I couldn't show up completely empty-handed, could I? So in the afternoon, we had found a theatrical prop shop on Twelfth Avenue that sells loose rhinestones for twenty-five dollars a gross. Zelvas's medical bag was now filled to the brim with them.

"How long do you think it will take Chukov to realize he's been played?" Ty asked, digging into a bowl of Louisiana Crawfish Chowder. The rest of us were chowing down on the only thing you go to a steak house for: meat.

"They look like the real thing from a distance," I said. "That'll help me get close to

Katherine, but I guarantee that Chukov will know they're bogus as soon as he gets his hands on them."

"And I guarantee you that as soon as he does that," Adam said, "he and his squad of Russian goons will start shooting up Grand Central Terminal."

That was our biggest challenge—collateral damage. You do your best to minimize it, but sometimes it's unavoidable. Innocent people getting killed is part of the reality of war. As dangerous as this operation was, it was complicated by the potential for civilian casualties once the bullets started flying. And knowing how desperate Chukov was, that seemed inevitable.

I would be wearing a vest. But some weary advertising executive trudging out of the Graybar Building toward Track 17 hoping to catch the 10:14 to Larchmont wouldn't have the benefit of Kevlar.

And neither would Katherine.

Chapter 83

WE LEFT ZACH behind to patrol the area in and around Grand Central and call us if he saw any sign of Chukov's men arriving early and taking up positions. The rest of us took the subway back to the Fortress.

There was only one thing more intimidating than facing Chukov and his Russian triggermen. That was facing my father.

He knew what I did to earn a living. Hell, he had gotten me into the business. I think he naturally expected that I would be as good—and as lucky—as he had been.

But this time was different. Going into Grand Central to trade diamonds for my kidnapped girlfriend was a suicide mission. And the fact that I didn't even have the diamonds made it all the more impossible.

If somebody had tried to hire me to do it, I'd have said no thanks and walked away—I don't care how much they would have paid me. But this wasn't about money. This was about Katherine's life. I didn't care if I took a bullet. I just had to save her.

I called my father. It was midday in Colorado. My mother picked up.

I spent five minutes answering all her excited questions about my trip to Paris.

"It sounds so romantic," she said. "I wish your father would take me."

"I'll tell him," I said. "Is he around?"

"He's in his workshop with his harem," she said, using her favorite expression for Dad's gun collection. "I'll buzz him on the intercom and tell him to pick up."

I could picture my father in his shop with a gun-cleaning kit and a bottle of Hoppe's solvent, carefully going through the same ritual he taught me, and his father taught him. "A clean gun is a mean gun," he always said.

It's a philosophy I had lived by. At least so far.

"Hey, boy," Dad said, answering the phone. "How you doing?"

I told him the whole story, from the night I found the diamonds to the last phone call from Chukov—everything I hadn't told him when I called from Milan. As usual, he listened without saying a word.

When I was done, he simply said, "Anything I can do?"

I gave him all the information he'd need to get the money out of the Dutch bank. Then I told him how to divide it. "Half gets split up evenly among Adam, Zach, Ty, and Katherine. The other half goes to you and Mom."

He laughed.

"What's so funny?" I said.

"I'll never see a penny of that money," he said.

"Why do you say that?"

"Because if anything happens to you, your mom will kill me faster'n look at me," he said. "So listen up, and listen good, boy. You're gonna get through this. You're gonna get through this because you know that not only is your life and Katherine's life on the line, but so's your old man's. *Ooooorah*."

"Thanks," I said. "I love you, Dad."

"Love you, too, boy."

Chapter 84

AT 5:30 ZACH called in. *This was it.*

"Two guys showed up fifteen minutes ago. Early twenties, dark suits, dark turtlenecks, gold jewelry, Russian accents. They scoped out the drop zone."

"They're probably trying to figure out choke points," I said.

"Choke points would require some military intelligence," Zach said. "These guys are thugs, not tacticians. They're counting cops and checking out security cameras. It's like they're planning to stick up a Seven-Eleven."

"I'm insulted," I said. "They still don't seem to think I'm even a threat."

"Try not to take it personally," Zach said. "As

far as they know, you're some fey art student. They're worried about the cops."

"So am I," I said. "What else did you get?"

"I can give you the three spots where Chukov is going to position his men."

"How'd you get close enough to hear that?" I asked.

"Matt, I didn't have to get close. These idiots were broadcasting. They were pointing *there, there, and there*."

Adam leaned into the speakerphone. "Tell us where, where, and where."

I had sketched a map of the main concourse while I was wolfing down my rib eye at Michael Jordan's. Zach rattled off three locations, and Adam marked them on the map.

"Where are they now?" I asked.

"The Oyster Bar, getting primed for the showdown with a few vodkas. Do you want me to follow them when they leave?"

Zach is tough and confident. Sometimes too confident, sometimes too tough. Even if he could follow Chukov's men without getting caught, I didn't want him to even think about rescuing Katherine on his own.

"No," I said. "Let's just stick to the plan. Did you find a good spot for the rabbit?"

"Best place is across the street from the Vanderbilt Avenue entrance," Zach said. "I counted half a dozen uniforms who circulate between the main concourse and the lower level. When they're not on patrol, they cluster upstairs near the Vanderbilt door on the north balcony. One rabbit ought to take care of most of the cops."

"What about K-nine?" I asked.

"Oh, they got dogs. I haven't seen any so far, but I chatted up the counter guy at Starbucks, and he told me there are cops with bomb-sniffing dogs who patrol the main concourse randomly. Seems like another reason why the rabbit is better outside the terminal."

"Good job," I said. "Call us if anything pops. Otherwise we'll meet you at nineteen hundred hours."

I hung up.

The feeling I had in the pit of my stomach was all too familiar. Pre-combat butterflies. Anyone who tells you it doesn't happen to him is lying to you. Or to himself.

"It sounds like we took out Chukov's best men, and he called in a bunch of amateurs," Adam said.

"I think that works against us," I said. "Amateurs tend to panic and go trigger happy. I don't want civilian casualties."

"Matt's right," Ty said. "We signed up for this. The people who'll be walking through Grand Central tonight didn't. Katherine didn't. Our job is to make sure none of them gets hurt."

"Oh, they won't get hurt," Adam said, "but when those T-four-seventy-ones go off, they'll wish they'd never gotten out of bed this morning."

"You only have a narrow window before the Russians shake off the T-four-seventy-ones and start shooting," I said. "As soon as Katherine is out of the field of fire, take them out. Every one of them. Fast."

"Don't worry, Matt," Ty said. "We're gonna kill the bastards who took Katherine, and we're gonna bring her home safe."

We had gone into battle before. But this time, I swore to myself, would be different. No matter what the outcome, this battle would be my last.

Chapter 85

BY 7 P.M., the four of us were in Position Alpha.

We had three hours to wait for Chukov to arrive, which in our line of work we could do standing on one leg with a full bladder. Waiting in complete silence, barely breathing for hours, even days, at a stretch is what we're trained to do.

Ty was on East 43rd outside the entrance to the Lexington Avenue subway. Adam was on 42nd, covering the south side of the terminal. Zach was at 45th and Vanderbilt with the rabbit.

I was inside, my hand clutching the medical bag, my eyes scanning the commuters who poured out of the MetLife Building to take the escalator down to the main concourse.

The four of us were fitted with the same

wireless communication system the Secret Service uses. Micro earbuds, transmitter necklaces under our collars, and invisible microphones in our lapels. The protocol was for each of us to check in with an update every quarter hour.

Ten o'clock came and went. Ten fifteen. Ten thirty. Ten forty-five. No sign of Chukov.

At eleven o'clock, Adam was the first to check in.

"Cab Forty-two to Dispatch. Our passenger is still MIA. What do you make of it?"

I radioed back. "Dispatch to Forty-two. He'll be here. He just wants to see me sweat. It isn't working."

One of the most critical skills a combat Marine has to hone is patience. I had once sat in a sniper's nest for seventy-two hours without moving. This assignment was much harder. Knowing that Katherine was in the hands of a sadistic maniac like Chukov made every minute drag and every quarter hour endless.

I paced from one end of the waiting area to the other. The escalator from the MetLife Building whirred quietly. No one had set foot on it for twenty minutes. The traffic in Grand Central had thinned out dramatically. That, at least, was a plus. Fewer people. Less chance of hitting an innocent bystander.

I was ready. My team was ready. But where the hell was Chukov?

Eleven fifteen. Eleven thirty. Eleven forty-five.

At three minutes before midnight, my cell rang. The caller ID said it was coming from Katherine's phone. I answered. The voice on the other end was ice cold and menacing. It was Vadim Chukov.

"It's over," he said.

"Over? Where are you?" I said. "I've been standing here in Grand Central with your diamonds since ten o'clock."

"Shove them up your ass," he said.

"What are you talking about? We have a deal."

"The deal is off," he said. "You lied. You sold the diamonds in Amsterdam."

"That's crazy," I said. "I tried, but I couldn't. I have them right here in my hand."

"You want to know what's in *my* hand, Bannon?" Chukov said. "A seven-inch carbon steel knife, and as soon as my men have finished gangbanging your pretty little girlfriend, I'm going to use it to slit her throat."

He hung up.

I stood there shaking. Unable to breathe. Sweat pouring off me.

Chapter 86

"FORTY-THREE TO DISPATCH."

It was midnight, and Ty was doing his quarter-hour call-in from Lexington Avenue.

"Slow night," he said. "No passengers."

"This is Dispatch to all cabs," I said. "I just got a call. The Russian isn't coming. He's backing out of the deal."

None of us said a word as each man on the team let the bad news penetrate. And then Adam broke the silence.

"Forty-two to Dispatch. We may have some signals crossed. You said the Russian isn't coming, but his Benz just pulled into the loading zone at the Grand Hyatt."

The Hyatt was next door to Grand Central.

"There are a lot of Benzes in this city," I said. "Are you sure it's his?"

"Hold on," Adam said. "Let me put on my reading glasses."

Adam's reading glasses were a three-thousand-dollar pair of 13x Steiner sniper-grade binoculars.

"Affirmative," he said. "He's in the front seat, passenger side. There are people in the backseat, but I can't get an angle on them."

"Forty-five to Dispatch." It was Zach calling in from Vanderbilt. "I have three men looking for a taxi. I recognize two of them from this afternoon. You should see them in a few seconds."

Even as he spoke, three men in dark suits walked through the Vanderbilt entrance and down the stairs. One of them pointed to the three spots we had targeted on the map, and each headed for his assigned place.

I tried to process the new information. Chukov was outside the terminal. His men were taking their positions inside. I was trying to make sense of it all when my cell rang.

It was Chukov.

"So, Mr. Bannon," he said. "Do I have your attention?"

"Undivided," I said.

"It's painful when you think that something you love is gone forever, isn't it?" He didn't wait for an answer. "That's how I felt when you ran off with my diamonds. You have experienced only a moment of pain, but I have the power to make your pain last a lifetime. Do you understand?"

"Perfectly," I said. "I want to see Katherine."

"And I want to run my blade from her perky little nipples to her creamy white thighs. Let's see which one of us gets what he wants. Where are my diamonds?"

"Right here in my hand," I said. "I didn't sell them."

"I didn't think you did," Chukov said. "I don't think you could. You know why? Because you don't have the brains and you don't have the balls. Where are you now, Bannon?"

I gave him my exact location.

He hung up.

A few seconds later, Adam reported in.

"The Russian just got out of the Benz. The back doors are both opening. People are getting out. One man . . . a second man . . ."

I held my breath.

Finally Adam came back on. "And a woman. Matt, it's Katherine. She's headed your way."

I exhaled and gave the command I had been waiting to give all night. "Dispatch to all cabs— go to Position Bravo right now. Let's do this."

Chapter 87

THE NEXT THING I saw made me want to throw up.

Vadim Chukov—the short, fat, tattooed, asthmatic turd who had sat naked, sweating, and in total fear for his life that morning in the Russian and Turkish Baths—was walking down the wide marble passageway from 42nd Street. He was brimming with confidence, and he was arm in arm with Katherine.

I'd always told her that it was impossible for her to look anything but beautiful. Even when she wakes up with bed-head and no makeup, she exudes a beauty that comes from her soul.

But now that soul was badly damaged. I wanted to blame it all on the fat bastard at her side, but I knew the truth. It had started with me. First I brought Katherine into my life; then I dragged her into my world.

Chukov and Katherine stopped at the foot of the passageway. Two more Russian punks stood behind them. High above them was Old Glory—the giant American flag that had been suspended from the ceiling in those dark hours following the terrorist attacks on September 11, 2001.

Chukov spotted me instantly. Then he looked up at the vast expanse of stars and stripes—the flag I had fought for, the colors so many of my fellow Americans had laid down their lives for—and the Russian son of a bitch slowly extended his middle finger.

He looked back across the vast cavern of Grand Central and threw me a mock salute.

He took his phone from his pocket and dialed. Seconds later, my cell rang.

"I'm ready to do business," he said. "Bring the diamonds here."

"Send Katherine over here," I said. "I'll put the diamonds down and we'll leave quietly."

"*Nyet*. She's not going anywhere until I see

them," Chukov said. "Start walking toward me. Nice and easy. I've got three guns pointed at you and three on her."

I muted my cell.

"Ready to tango, boys?" I said softly.

Ty's voice came back first. "In Position Bravo, dancing shoes on."

Then Adam. "I was ready to stomp all over him as soon as he gave the flag the finger."

Then Zach. "The rabbit and I are hopping mad. Let's kick some Russian ass."

There were about two hundred feet between Chukov and me. I started walking toward him. Operation Nighthawks was under way.

The city that never sleeps was living up to its name. Even though the crowds had thinned, there were still hundreds of people all around us—some chattering away upstairs in the restaurant, some waiting for a late-night Metro North commuter train, and a steady stream of straphangers on their way to catch a Lexington Avenue subway or the shuttle to Times Square.

"Lots of foot traffic," Adam said.

"We've got a pair of eyes on the Vanderbilt balcony checking out the main floor," Zach said.

"A cop. I can't tell if he's focused on you or just staring into space."

I was halfway there, a hundred feet to go. I didn't look up at the cop. I just kept walking.

I could see Katherine clearly now. Her tan pants were stained with dirt and grease, her hair was matted from sweat, and her eyes were red, puffy, and filled with dread.

When I got thirty feet away, I stopped and unmuted my cell phone. "This is as far as I go, Chukov," I said.

I put the phone down, unlatched the medical bag, tipped it forward, scooped up a fistful of rhinestones, and let them trickle through my fingers and run back into the bag.

A smile spread across his jowly mug, and I knew that the worthless glass had passed for the real thing. I closed the bag and picked up the phone.

"You wanted to see them?" I said. "You've seen them. Now send one of your men over here with Katherine and he can have the diamonds."

Chukov hesitated.

"Don't take too long," I said. "There's a cop on

the west balcony who is starting to get interested in this little tableau, and I think we all should get out of here before he decides to ask embarrassing questions."

Chukov looked up at the cop who was standing on the balcony. He turned to one of his men: a big, burly, stoop-shouldered Eastern European.

"Grigor," he said. That was all I understood. The rest was in Russian.

Chukov let go of Katherine's arm. Grigor stepped in, gently tapped her shoulder, and said, "We go. Please."

They walked toward me and stopped less than two feet away. I could feel the fear coming off Katherine's body.

"Take the bag," I said to Grigor. "Take it back to Chukov and get the hell out of our lives."

I waited for him to bend down and pick it up. He didn't. Instead, he nudged it into position with his foot, then kicked it hard. It skittered across the floor and stopped directly at Chukov's feet.

It would take Chukov less than ten seconds to open the bag and realize the diamonds were fake. Grigor stood silently, one hand on his gun, the other on Katherine.

I tilted my head down toward my lapel.

"Release the rabbit," I said.

Chapter 88

THE BEST WAY to get a greyhound to race around a track is to give him a mechanical rabbit to chase.

Our rabbit was an olive-drab rucksack packed with smoke grenades like the ones I had thrown the night I found the diamonds. As soon as Zach pushed the remote detonator, it exploded outside the prestigious Yale Club at 50 Vanderbilt Avenue, across the street from the terminal.

Our mission was to create chaos outside Grand Central before all hell broke loose inside.

It worked like gangbusters.

The explosion was not much more than noise and smoke, but the earsplitting boom was enough to cause a coronary a block away, and the billowing acrid cloud of smoke could have blanketed a football field.

The blast was far enough away that down on the main concourse it sounded like a muffled car backfiring. Those who heard it waved it off—a classic case of *This is New York. I have my own problems. That noise ain't one of them.*

Not so with the cops at the door. For them, standing around hour after hour, day after day, night after night, this was a *holy shit* moment. The shoe they had been waiting to hear drop.

And despite the fact that the streets of New York are the sole jurisdiction of the NYPD, the MTA state cops bolted out the door like a pack of greyhounds from the starting gate, racing to nail the exploding rabbit.

Katherine heard it, too. If she could be any more petrified than she already was, the noise pushed her to the edge. After her body twitched from being startled, fresh tears made tracks over the ones already dried on her dirty cheeks. I desperately wanted to wrap my arms around her and apologize for the pain and suffering I had caused, and vow to spend the rest of my life making amends for it. But all I could do now was make that promise to myself. I turned my attention back to Chukov.

The noise didn't faze him. He was too busy opening the bag. He reached in and grabbed a handful of the glittering stones. A second later his head snapped around and he screamed at me. The words were in Russian, but I needed no translation. It was the cry of a man who had just come up with a fistful of worthless glass.

"Light it up," I yelled into the wireless.

Chukov flung the rhinestones to the floor and went for his gun. I reached for Katherine and screamed, "Close your eyes! Cover your ears!" as I shielded her with my body.

She was too dumbfounded to follow through with my instructions. I pressed her face to my chest, covered her ears with my arm, and braced myself.

Unlike the benign smoke grenades that had drawn the cops onto the street, the ALST471 magnum ultra-flash grenade produces a brilliant flash, a deafening concussive blast, and a shower of white-hot sparks. It's the military's nonlethal version of shock and awe—developed as a stun device for a variety of tactical operations, including hostage rescue. Launch one into a crowd and it leaves everyone temporarily blind, deaf, and totally disoriented. Adam and Ty launched two.

The flash grenades hit their marks and rocked the place. Even with my eyes closed and my ears covered, the white light and the thunderous noise were like a lightning strike.

The shrieks and cries of the throng who were caught by surprise bounced off the marble walls and echoed from the domed ceiling.

I screamed into my wireless for Zach, opened my eyes, and saw him running toward me.

"You're safe, you're safe," I yelled at Katherine as I passed her over to Zach. "Zach, don't let her out of your sight. Go, go, go!"

Chapter 89

ZACH PUT HIS arm around Katherine and half dragged, half carried her toward the stairway to the north balcony, our designated safe zone.

The rest of us had six incensed Russians to deal with. Like everyone around them, they were still stunned, unable to fight back.

First, Grigor. He was flailing, still blinded, trying to get his bearings. I gave him a vicious chop to the larynx with the blade of my hand. The blow drove quantities of blood into his lungs. He dropped to his knees, gasping for air and coughing up thick red puddles. I grabbed his jaw with one hand, put my other hand behind his neck, and twisted. Hard. Harder than I would if I were trying to get a stuck lug nut off a wheel.

Even over the screams echoing through the cavernous train station, with its high ceilings, I was close enough to hear the wet *pop*, and I let him fall to the floor.

"Tango down," I told my team.

A volley of gunfire reverberated through Grand Central. It was coming from above. Adam and Ty had raced up the stairs into Michael Jordan's Steak House. They'd taken positions on the north balcony.

One of Chukov's young punks had parked himself under the New Haven line departures board. He was still dazed from the flash grenade when Adam fired. The man's chest tore open like a pumpkin that's been hurled off a rooftop. His shirt turned red and he dropped in a heap.

"Tango three is on the west balcony," I said.

Ty came back. "I don't see him."

"He hit the ground when the grenades went off. He's hiding behind the marble balustrades."

Ty kept talking. "Chickenshit bastard is socked in good. I can see a sliver of his punk ass between the sixth and seventh column."

The balustrades were only inches apart, and

Ty was at least two hundred feet away. Hitting the target would be like driving a golf ball through a chain-link fence.

"Do you have a shot?" I asked.

"No . . ."

Then there was a loud crack.

"But I took one, anyway," he added. "Tango three is down."

I watched as a trail of blood flowed through the marble balustrades on the west balcony and dripped to the floor below.

"Nice work," Adam said.

The place was sheer bedlam. I had used flash grenades in combat and seen the effect it had on the enemy. But this was a hundred times worse. The people around us had no training. Many of them were suddenly blind, deaf, or both. It was temporary, but they didn't know that. And now bullets were flying, too.

Random screams filled the air. People calling out to God. People cursing out the unseen enemy. People proclaiming their love for parents, spouses, and children they thought they would never see again. I could smell the fear.

In the midst of all the insanity, the Russians

were reeling and unable to find a target. Ty and Adam had excellent vantage points, but they had to be careful not to shoot innocent bystanders helplessly stumbling through the mob.

One of Chukov's men who still didn't have his vision completely back began firing wildly up toward Adam and Ty, riddling the marble railing, shattering glassware, and popping the overhead lights.

"We've got a loose cannon down there," Adam yelled.

Ty stood away from his cover. Just for a second. One of the Russians spotted him and fired. The round caught Ty square in the chest. He went down hard, and I moaned.

"Son of a bitch, that smarts," he said, pulling his six foot six frame off the floor. He tapped the body armor that had stopped the bullet. "God bless you, Mr. Kevlar."

He got back in position and opened fire on the shooter. Not just one shot, *three*—a double tap to the chest, one through the forehead. A perfect Mozambique Drill.

"Tango four is down and out," I said. "Talk about overkill—"

"Yeah, well, that's what happens to people who piss me off."

"You okay?" I asked.

"Fine. Vest is a little torn up."

"For the record," I said, "there's no Mr. Kevlar. You should be thanking Mr. DuPont."

"Noted," Ty said.

There were two shooters left. Chukov and his number two. They were coming out of their daze, and Chukov, his gun now in his hand, screamed, "Shoot the bitch! Kill her!"

Then Chukov turned his gun on me. I dived as bullets chewed up chunks of marble behind me. I rolled and pulled my own gun. The Russian going after Katherine was already thirty feet away from her, moving fast. I had one shot. Maybe. I drew a quick bead, exhaled, squeezed the trigger lightly. The bullet drilled straight through the back of his neck. He pitched forward, driving his face into the marble staircase.

"Matt, behind you!"

I spun around and Chukov's first bullet caught me in the chest. The second one ripped a hole in my left shoulder. The pain was immediate and excruciating. I hit the floor hard. Truth was, I'd never been shot before.

Chapter 90

EVEN OVER THE mayhem, I could hear Katherine scream when I got shot. Then I heard Adam's voice in my earpiece. "Junkyard Six is down."

That was me. I hadn't been Junkyard Six since we left Iraq, but in the heat of battle, Adam reverted to familiar territory.

"Cover him, cover him!" Adam yelled.

There was a hailstorm of bullets. My guys were laying down suppressive fire at Chukov, forcing him to take cover and stop shooting at me.

I was in pain, but I was grateful. The bullet that Chukov fired at my chest was lodged in my body armor and not in my body. But the force of the concussion had knocked the wind out of me, and I felt like I had a couple of cracked ribs.

The bullet in my shoulder was what the medics casually refer to as a *flesh wound*. But it's impossible to be casual when it's your flesh that's wounded. I struggled to get up.

"Matt, Matt, are you okay?" Ty said.

"Where's Katherine?" I yelled.

Zach jumped in. "Shaken but safe. Are you okay?"

"No. And I won't be okay until we get Chukov." I stood and looked around. "Where is he?"

"Running up the south ramp," Adam said. "I don't have a clean shot from the balcony. Matt, how bad were you hit?"

"Enough to really piss me off. I'm going after him."

I could see Chukov barreling his way up the ramp through the frenzied crowd toward the 42nd Street exit.

My shoulder was burning as I headed toward the ramp. Chukov looked back and saw me. Then he looked at the bottleneck in front of him. Hundreds of people were screaming in terror as they fought to squeeze through doorways that were designed to handle one person at a time.

Ten more seconds and I'd have him.

There was a second ramp—one that went down into the subway. It was wide open because nobody wanted to go down there. The lessons of 9/11 were still fresh in people's minds. Grand Central was under attack. Get out of the building. Don't risk being trapped underground. Only a crazy person would head down there.

The mob kept clawing at the front doors. One crazy person broke off from the pack and raced down the ramp toward the spiderweb of subways below.

Chukov. He had realized he'd never make it out the narrow door.

A second person, bleeding, in pain, and probably just as crazy, followed.

Me.

Chapter 91

THE GRAND CENTRAL subway station is a labyrinth of uptown, downtown, and crosstown options. Along with its sister station under the Port Authority Bus Terminal in Times Square, it is one of the busiest stations in the entire system, so it's easy to get lost in the subterranean maze, even if you don't want to.

Chukov definitely wanted to.

By the time I made it down the ramp, he was out of sight.

There were dozens of subway riders who had just gotten off a train and were walking through the passageways oblivious to the chaos going on above them.

I stopped the first man I saw. "Did you see a

short, fat guy? He was probably running—"

"Whoa, man," he said. "You're bleeding real bad."

I hadn't realized what I looked like. "I'm okay," I said. "Did you see—"

He held his hands up and backed away. "Didn't see anyone. You better get to a hospital, dude."

There were half a dozen staircases and at least that many passageways that Chukov could have taken.

I tried to weigh the pluses and minuses using the same logic he would have used. The passageways would eventually lead him to a street exit. But the streets would be clogged with cops responding to the bomb blasts and the gunfire. The stairs would take him to a subway. He could be miles away in minutes. That was the best option.

But which subway? Uptown? Downtown? Local? Express? Flushing line? Times Square shuttle?

I was headed for the downtown staircase when I heard the scream.

A woman came running up the opposite

stairwell, shouting, "Run! There's a man down there with a gun!"

I charged back to the Lexington Avenue uptown and took the steps three at a time.

The platform was deserted. No passengers. No cops. No Chukov. He had just been here, but the screaming woman had sent him running again.

The tracks. Chukov was a madman. Would he be crazy enough to try to escape through the tunnel?

I stepped to the edge of the platform and looked into the semidarkness. There was enough light to navigate the tunnel, and I realized that if he was smart and careful, he could make his way uptown to 51st Street this way.

"Turn around."

I froze. The madman was behind me. My gun was tucked in my belt. Even without looking, I knew where his gun was—aimed right at my back.

I turned slowly, and there he was, pointing a semiautomatic Marakov PM at my chest.

His eyes were on fire, and I could hear the asthmatic rattle in his lungs as he breathed. I knew what was coming next—the diatribe, the rant, the blistering harangue cataloging every injustice I had inflicted on him, followed by threats of retribution he would bring down on me and everyone connected to me. And then, one last negotiation. He still wanted the diamonds, and even though I had duped him on the exchange, he still believed I had them.

Scream at me all you want, I thought. *I need as much time as I can get to figure a way out of this.*

But I was wrong. He didn't utter a word. He just aimed the gun at my heart and squeezed the trigger.

The bullet slammed into the shock plate of my body armor and blew me backward off the platform onto the tracks. The pain was unbearable, but once again the vest under my sweater had saved my life.

But only for a few seconds. Chukov stepped up to the edge of the platform and pointed the Marakov at my head.

"*Do svidaniya*, modderfocker," he said.

Chapter 92

BULLETPROOF VESTS SAVE lives, but they don't do much for bones. I have twenty-four ribs, and it felt like every one of them was broken.

Chukov aimed at my head. Every ounce of my training told me to roll before he pulled the trigger, but I could barely breathe, much less dodge a bullet.

I was a dead man.

I heard the gunshot and saw the muzzle flash, but I wasn't dead. The tile wall behind me shattered and a mighty bellow from Chukov echoed through the tunnel as his body flew off the platform.

Someone had hurtled down the stairs and slammed into Chukov from behind, sending the bullet wide and pitching his fat Russian ass onto the tracks.

It wasn't a miracle. *God bless Adam, Zach, and Ty*, I thought. I sat up to see which one had saved my skin. But it wasn't any of them.

"Matthew, get his gun, get his gun!" It was Katherine.

Chukov's gun had skittered along one of the rails when he landed. My adrenaline surged. I managed to get to my knees and dig for my own gun. Chukov was already up. He swung his foot into my jaw. That hurt. Plus, it raised hell with the hole in my shoulder.

I went sprawling, and Chukov grabbed for the gun in my hand. He dug his fingers into my face with one hand and yanked at the weapon with the other.

The pain was blinding. I almost lost consciousness. I did lose the gun.

"You stupid piece of shit," he screamed, pointing the muzzle at my face.

I was out of strength. And I knew that as soon as Chukov finished me off, he would shoot Katherine. I had to get her to run. I looked up at the platform.

And there she was, hoisting a New York City Transit Authority trash can high over her head with a strength that must have been born of fear and red-hot anger. She hurled it at Chukov.

It hit him square in the face and knocked him off balance. The wire mesh left a bloody grid on his cheek.

Totally enraged, he pressed his palm into my shoulder, pushing himself up and once again sending waves of agony through my body.

And then I heard it. The number 6 train.

Chukov heard it, too. After a darting glance between me and the platform, he decided to save his own ass and let the train take care of me.

With my gun still in his hand, he leaped toward the platform like an overweight mountain lion.

Katherine screamed.

Chukov threw his right leg onto the platform and screamed back at her. "I'll kill you, you goddamn bitch."

I lunged and clawed at his left foot. I jerked hard, and we both toppled backward onto the tracks. I rolled as we fell, so that by the time we got our bearings, I was straddling his chest.

I grabbed his head and whacked it against the rail. I leaned forward to pry the gun from his grasp, but Chukov slammed his oversize forehead into my face. I felt my nose break.

Down the track, the headlights of the Bronx-bound subway were bearing down on us fast. The whistle screamed.

I bet the motorman screamed, too. He of all people would know that no matter how hard he applied his brakes, he wouldn't be able to stop in time.

I heard the squeal of metal on metal as the train's wheels skidded along the track.

Chukov and I had been engaged in a battle to the death. In a matter of seconds, the battle would be over.

Chapter 93

CHUKOV AND I had our hands wrapped around the gun. The way we were going, there could only be one winner: *the number 6 train.*

I knew I was out of time. So I let go of the gun. I threw my good shoulder back and drove my right elbow into his left eye. I think I heard bone crack as I drilled down into the socket.

Then I jumped up. Kicked the gun out of his hand. Planted the other foot on his throat.

Katherine leaned over the platform. She peered down the tunnel at the oncoming train. "Matthew," she yelled, "get off the tracks *now!*"

I looked into the darkness. The train's headlights, which had been pin dots only seconds ago, were brighter and looming larger.

Chukov struggled to get up, but I had weight and leverage on my side.

"Matthew, please—he's not worth it," she begged. "Please, please run."

I couldn't. If I took my foot off Chukov's throat, he'd still have enough time to vault the platform. I had to finish this.

And then I remembered. I pictured Chukov sitting in the steam room with the bronchodilator on his lap. Chukov the asthmatic.

I lifted my foot off his throat and slammed it down on his chest. The compression was more than his lungs could take. He began gasping for air.

I reached down and scooped up a fistful of the black dirt and subway soot that lay between the ties. And just as Chukov inhaled deeply, struggling to breathe, I flung it in his face.

He sucked it all in.

I grabbed another handful of the powdery filth and threw it at his nose and mouth. He was now in a full-blown asthma attack—choking, spitting, screaming half-gurgled Russian. His eyes bulged with fear.

I leaned in close to his face. "What's the

matter, Vadim? You look like you've seen a Ghost."

Chukov's eyes grew even wider as the truth sank in and he realized whom he had been up against all along.

I took one final look into the face of evil and drove both fists into his failing lungs.

"*Do svidaniya*, modderfocker," I said.

I started to run. Chukov didn't follow.

"Matthew, hurry!" Katherine yelled. "The train is coming."

As if I needed a reminder.

The whistle screamed and screamed and screamed. I turned as best as I could. I could see sparks flying off the wheels as they scraped the metal rails. I could even make out the outline of the motorman in the front cab. I could only imagine the sheer horror in his eyes.

The front of the station was maybe five hundred feet away. I'd never make it. I couldn't get out of this. I was going to die.

Chapter 94

I RAN FOR my life anyway.

Katherine ran right alongside me on the platform.

"Take my hand," she screamed down. "I'll pull you up, Matthew."

"No," I shouted. "I'd pull you down."

"I don't care," she said.

Her words rushed over me, and if they were the last ones I'd ever hear, I'd die happy.

Well, maybe not happy, but a little more at peace with the world.

"I'm sorry for everything," I yelled, hoping she could still hear me over the roar of the number 6 train. "I love you." And then I broke into a sprint—or as much of a sprint as I could muster with multiple fractures and heavy blood loss.

Grand Central is a four-track subway station. Two single tracks on each side and a double set of tracks in the middle. If I had been on the center set of tracks, I could have stood between them and let the train pass me. But the outer track is a death trap—a platform on one side and a wall on the other. The only possible escape was a service door set in the wall.

I could see one twenty feet ahead.

I looked back. The train had just entered the station—sparks flying, whistle blowing—and now I could see the motorman's face: absolute panic when he saw one man lying on the tracks and another running toward the tunnel.

And then I heard the thump.

If Chukov had any air left in his lungs, he might have screamed when the train hit him. But he didn't. All I heard was a flat, dull *whoomp,* like a tennis racket slapping a mattress. It was unmistakable. Chukov was dead.

I reached the service door that was tucked into the wall below the platform. I pulled the handle. *Locked!*

Another hundred feet still lay between me and safety.

The train was slowing down. Maybe I could outrun it after all. And then my foot caught a railroad tie, and I fell face-first into the bed of debris and muck between the tracks.

It was over. I took comfort in knowing that the most evil son of a bitch in the world was dead and the most wonderful woman in the world was alive and safe, which was what I had set out to do.

Mission accomplished.

The squeal of the brakes was deafening now. Even an art student knows a little physics.

The train couldn't stop in time. Inertia wins.

I lose and die on the train tracks.

Chapter 95

ZACH HEARD THE crying before he reached the platform. He raced down the stairs. It was Katherine. She had her face buried in Ty's shoulder and was sobbing uncontrollably.

"Ty, am I glad you found Katherine," Zach said. "Matt would kick my ass if I let anything happen to her. Let's round everybody up and get the hell out of here."

"Zach . . ." Ty hesitated.

"What?" Zach snapped back. "What's going on?"

"Matt's dead," Katherine said.

"Matt and Chukov went head-to-head down on the tracks," Ty said. "The train took them both out."

The last three cars of the number 6 train were still inside the tunnel. The doors to the train remained closed. A handful of passengers were pressed against the front window wondering why the motorman was on the ground, his back against a steel column, his legs stretched out in front of him. A transit cop was kneeling beside him.

"Oh, God," the motorman said, breathing hard. "Oh, God, I can't believe it."

"Try to stay calm, Mr. Perez," the cop said, putting her hand on his arm. "The paramedics are on the way."

"Paramedics?" he said. "For what? They're both dead."

"For you," she said. "They'll be here for you. Try to calm down."

"I had green lights all the way from Thirty-fourth," Perez said, "so we were moving. But legal. A hundred percent legal."

Katherine let out a mournful wail.

The cop turned sharply and looked at her. "I'm trying to get a statement here. Can somebody please—"

"Hey!" Ty snapped at the cop.

"Hey, I'm sorry," she said, "but we got a situation here."

She turned back to the motorman. "Did they fall, did they jump, what happened?"

"I don't know. They were already there when I saw them. One guy was on the track and couldn't get up. It looked like maybe the other guy was helping him. I hit the brakes as soon as I saw them, but the man on the tracks was too close to the rear of the station. He never had a chance."

He closed his eyes and buried his head in his hands.

"And the second guy?" the cop said.

"He started running. The train had slowed down to four miles an hour. He could have made it, but he fell. It wasn't my fault."

Five cops came bounding down the stairs. One was a sergeant.

"Sarge," the cop said. "We have two civilians under the train. The motorman is in shock. I told the conductor to keep the doors closed until I can get someone here for crowd control."

"Any witnesses?" the sergeant said.

"That woman," she said, pointing at Katherine.

By now a dozen passengers had moved forward to the front car. One started pounding on the window and yelling, "Let us off. Let us off." The others immediately picked it up.

"Keep her on ice," the sergeant said. "Let me deal with the passengers first."

"I'll wait with her," Adam said and put his arm around Katherine.

"We have to get you out of here," he said in a whisper. "*Now*. While the cops are still busy."

"I can't," she whimpered. "Matthew's still down there. His body's there."

"Katherine, you don't want to see him," Zach said.

"He's gone," Adam said. "We can't do anything for the captain. He wanted us to keep you safe. That's what we're going to do."

He tried to move Katherine toward the stairs.

But she dropped to her knees. "Matthew. I love you so much. I love you," she said, sobbing. "And I forgive you."

A faint voice came from under the train. "If you can find someone who can get this train off me, you can tell me in person. I love you, too."

Chapter 96

I WAS LYING right under the second car, maybe twenty feet from Katherine. I had managed to fall flat into the track bed. Forty-odd tons of the 6 train had passed over me before it finally came to a stop.

I don't know how long I was unconscious. Between losing blood and whacking my head when I fell, I was out of it for a while probably. But when I came to and heard Katherine saying she loved me and forgave me, I had another reason to get out of there.

Up on the platform, I could hear Katherine crying and my guys laughing and screaming and then orders from someone in charge.

"Don't move," the voice said.

"Don't worry," I responded. "I'm not going anywhere."

"Matt!" It was Adam. "You okay?"

"No," I said. "You know how disgusting it is on these tracks? I'll probably die from being facedown in subway grunge."

I heard Ty next. "At least we know his sense of humor is still awful."

It took half an hour before the power to the third rail was turned off so the fire department guys could pull me out. EMTs laid me on a stretcher on the platform. I looked up, and the next person I saw was Katherine. "Nice shot with that trash can," I said.

She knelt down and pressed against my filthy, foul-smelling, bloody body. She kissed my face a dozen times before the EMT guys pried her off.

"Ma'am, we've got to get him to the hospital. You can ride with us."

Four firefighters and two EMTs lifted the stretcher, and we headed for the stairs.

"Wait. I have to talk to him. *That guy there*."

It was the motorman. He came forward and stood over me. His face was ashen; he was crying.

"I'm sorry. I couldn't see you till it was too late. I'm so sorry."

I was the one who should have apologized. It was I who had left Chukov gasping for air on the tracks and made this poor man feel like an executioner.

"Don't apologize," I said. "That guy on the tracks—he was evil. He tried to kill this beautiful woman, Katherine. He was on the tracks trying to kill me. You saved both of us. Thank you."

He nodded, but his expression didn't change, and I knew his life would never be the same.

He was a killer now, too.

Chapter 97

THEY TOOK ME to Bellevue Hospital, where the ER docs removed the bullet from my shoulder, gave me a blood transfusion, and told me that my broken nose and three cracked ribs would heal on their own in about six weeks.

Then they pumped me full of painkillers and let me sleep. Katherine slept in the chair in my room, and my three buddies spent the night in the hospital, taking turns standing guard at the door.

At four in the afternoon, I had my first visitors. Detectives Steve Garber and Nathan Watt, NYPD.

"We're trying to piece together what happened last night," Watt said. "Do you mind if I ask you both a few questions?"

"It's all a blur," I said. "This crazy man attacked me and my girlfriend. I tried to fend him off, but the New York subway finished the fight."

Katherine nodded in total agreement.

"Did either of you know this guy?" Watt said.

"No."

Watt smiled. "Vadim Chukov. He had a record on two continents. Smuggling, arson, robbery, murder—the list goes on—but this is the first time he ever tried to pick a fight with an innocent young couple waiting for the subway. Are you sure you didn't know him?"

"I don't know anyone like that," I said. "I'm just a struggling art student."

"A struggling art student and a war-hero Marine who served in Iraq and Afghanistan," Garber said.

"My Marine days are over," I said.

"Were you aware that Chukov and five of his men launched some kind of terrorist attack in Grand Central Terminal earlier last night?" Garber asked.

"It was in the paper this morning," Katherine said.

"Was anybody hurt?" I asked.

426

"Counting Chukov, there are six dead. All bad guys. It seems like somebody knew they were coming and cleaned up the mess without any help from the cops."

"Good Samaritans, I guess," I said.

"But you weren't there," Watt said.

"No," I said.

"It's easy enough to check," Watt said. "They have the whole incident on video."

Katherine's eyes opened wide, and she squeezed my hand.

"Oh, crap, I just remembered," Garber said. "The terminal is not our jurisdiction. That's MTA—the state cops."

"Then I guess there's no sense in looking at the tapes," Watt said. "We're just here to ask questions about the incident down in the subway. Does either of you have anything else to add?"

"No, sir," I said.

"Then I think we've got it all," Watt said. "Detective Garber, why don't we let this young war hero and his girlfriend get some rest."

They headed to the door. Watt stopped and turned around.

"Mr. Bannon, I have to take issue with just one thing you told us."

"What's that?"

"You said your Marine days were over," Watt said.

"Yes, sir."

"They're never over. My partner and I both served in Desert Storm." He grinned. "Semper fi, bro."

He threw me a wink and a salute, and the two of them walked out the door and never came back.

Chapter 98

WE FLEW TO Paris and rented a funky studio on the fourth floor of an art deco building in the Quartier Saint-Germain-des-Prés. The mattress was too soft and the toilet was temperamental, but the northern light that streamed through the floor-to-ceiling windows made it an artist's dream. My broken nose healed. My cracked ribs healed. And three months after that night in the subway tunnel, my relationship with Katherine was also mending rather nicely. She had told me she loved me in the heat of the moment, but I wanted to make sure that she could forgive me for the life I had led and for dragging her into it.

It was a Sunday morning in September. I

woke to the aroma of fresh-brewed french roast, the sounds of Coldplay on the stereo, and the sight of Katherine in jeans and a paint-spattered tank top, sitting on the sofa. There was sunlight on her bare shoulders, and my cat, Hopper, was curled on her lap, purring gratefully.

"Hold that pose," I said. "I'll get some coffee and a paintbrush."

"You don't do portraits," she said.

"I do nudes," I said with a smile. "You know where I can find one?"

"I just happen to have one under here," she said. Then she peeled off the tank top. She scrambled out of her jeans. Lord, she was good at undressing.

"The coffee can wait," I said.

Morning sex for us was usually fast, urgent—kind of like *an asteroid is heading for the planet and we only have a few minutes left* fast.

That morning we took the better part of an hour.

"I hate to be practical, especially at a time like this, but we should shower and get dressed," Katherine finally said.

We were lying in a heap of tangled sheets,

skin to skin, soaked in sweat. I was still inside her. More or less.

She put her lips on mine, kissed me gently, and found my tongue with hers. That's all it took to reboot my libido.

"We need to go, Matthew," Katherine said. "We have to get up."

"As you may have noticed, I'm pretty much up," I said. "Give me two good reasons why we should leave this bed. Ever."

"Your mother and your father," she said. "We're meeting them for brunch at ten o'clock."

"We'll be late," I said. "They'll understand."

Chapter 99

AN HOUR LATER we were sitting at a sidewalk café, eating duck eggs Benedict and buttery *petites brioches,* while my mother, giddy on half a mimosa, extolled the joys of Paris. She was like a Colorado schoolgirl on her first holiday. Even my father was smiling some.

It was our *au revoir* brunch. My folks had spent a week in Paris, and now they were moving on to Rome, Florence, and Venice. They were capping it all off with a two-week Mediterranean cruise. It was outrageously expensive, but it only put a small dent in the seven-figure account I'd opened for them at my Dutch bank.

We drove them to the airport and went back

to the apartment, where I painted for six hours straight, breaking only for coffee and a few words of inspiration.

At seven, Katherine and I sat on our tiny terrace, sipping a light white burgundy while watching the steel-gray western sky slowly turn spectacular shades of red, orange, and indigo.

The doorbell rang.

"Poor man," Katherine said. "I hate to put him through this."

"It's good for him," I said.

We were expecting company, but old habits die hard, so before buzzing our visitor in, I checked the tiny security camera I had installed at the front door.

He tromped noisily up the steps, stopping often to catch his breath or complain.

"My darlings," Newton gushed as he finally made it to our front door. "You're coming down in the world."

"Meaning what?" Katherine said.

"The first time we met, Matthew was a starving artist living on the top floor of a five-story walkup. Today you're on the fourth floor. I look forward to the day when you are rich and famous, and I can ride the elevator to your penthouse in the sky."

"You're full of shit, Newton," Katherine said. "The day Matthew is rich and famous is the day you'll go off and find another poor struggling artist with no money and lots of stairs to climb."

Newton laughed. "She's right. Now let me see what I came for."

He stepped in. "Oh, my," he said as he took in my latest work. "Oh, my, my, my. Genius."

"Really?" Katherine said. "You think Matthew is a genius?"

"Oh, heavens, no. I'm the genius. I said he'd get better, and he has. The lad has discovered color. And hope. And passion."

"Keep talking, Newton," Katherine said. "Every word of praise is going to cost you more money."

Newton shrugged. It wasn't his money.

He picked out five paintings.

"Someday these will be worth millions," he said. "Until then, I'd peg them at ten grand apiece."

He wrote me a check for fifty thousand dollars. I couldn't believe it.

"There's one catch," he said, waving the check in my face. "You must let me buy you dinner."

"Shouldn't I be buying?" I said. "I mean, that check will cover a year's worth of dinners."

He laughed. "Not where we'll be dining, my boy. Have you ever heard of La Tour d'Argent?"

"I have," Katherine said, gently plucking the check from his hand. "We accept your generous offer."

"Excellent. I'll pick you up at eight forty-five."

As soon as Newton left, Katherine started rummaging through her closet. "I have nothing to wear," she said. "*Rien.* Nothing."

"You look fabulous in nothing. It's my favorite look for you."

"You're not helping," she said. "Hurry up and get dressed."

"One question," I said. "Why is he taking us to dinner?"

"Because he loves to eat, he has a big fat expense account, and he wants to be seen in public with a handsome *artiste Américain* and his ugly professor who doesn't have a thing to wear. Why else would he take us to dinner?"

I didn't know. And that made me nervous.

Chapter 100

LA TOUR D'ARGENT has been a Paris institution since the sixteenth century. Perched on the river Seine in the heart of Old Paris, it's a mecca for people who live to eat. Not exactly the kind of place where you pop in and ask for a table for three.

And not just any table. Ours had a sweeping view of the river and Notre Dame Cathedral.

"How'd you manage to get such a good table at the last minute?" I asked.

"All it takes is charm and money," Newton said. "I supply the former and my employer has oodles of the latter. *Voilà*. We're in."

The sommelier handed him a wine list.

"This is the manageable version," Newton

said, handing it to me. "They have half a million bottles of wine in their cellar, and the complete wine list is four hundred pages."

He ordered a bottle of 1990 Louis Roederer Champagne Cristal Brut that cost more than my first car.

"A toast," Newton said once our glasses were filled. "To our blossoming young artist, Matthew Bannon."

"And to the beautiful woman who made it all possible," I said, "Katherine Sanborne."

"And to Matthew's generous new patron," Katherine said. She looked innocently at Newton. "What's his name, anyway?"

"I'm afraid I can't say," Newton said. "He's a lovely man but rather secretive." He smiled at me. "I'm sure you understand, don't you, Matthew? We all have our little secrets."

"But we're toasting him," Katherine said. "He has to have a name."

Newton grinned. "In that case, feel free to give him one."

"Copernicus," Katherine said. "Newton and Copernicus—both drawn to the stars."

We all drank to Copernicus.

"So, Newton," I said, "are you as secretive as your boss, or can you tell us a little bit about yourself?"

"Secretive? *Moi?* Heavens, no. My life is an open book. In fact, I plan to write one someday. I already have the title—*Confessions of an Art Whore.*"

"I can't wait for the book," Katherine said. "Tell us some of the good parts."

"Actually, my dear, they were all good parts. When I was twenty years old, I fell in love with Andy Warhol. Some people dismiss him, but he was the bellwether of the art market," Newton said. "Notice I said art *market*. Andy was the rare artist who mastered the delicate balance between art and commerce. Are you familiar with one of his early works—*Eight Elvises?* It recently sold for a hundred million dollars."

"And you knew him personally?" Katherine asked.

"Intimately," Newton said. "Andy introduced me to Timothy Leary, who of course introduced me to LSD."

"You took LSD?" Katherine said.

Newton shrugged. "It was just a phase, but

who among us didn't experiment in the eighties?"

"I know what you mean," I said. "I was hooked on breast milk back in nineteen eighty. But it was just a phase."

Newton let out a guffaw, and we spent the next few hours swapping stories of our lives. Mine were carefully edited. His were delightfully entertaining, but I'd be willing to bet they were more bullshit than substance.

By one o'clock I felt like I had learned very little about this man whom I knew only by a single name. Hopefully he knew even less about me.

On the ride home, he had the driver open the moonroof. The three of us rode in silence and gazed at the sky.

"For my part, I know nothing with any certainty, but the sight of the stars makes me dream," Newton said when we arrived at our apartment.

"That's beautiful," Katherine said.

"Vincent van Gogh said it first. Off to bed with you now," he said with a wink.

Which is exactly where we went.

That night, we undressed each other slowly,

gently touching, exploring, caressing. There were no threatening asteroids hurtling toward us. I knew in my heart there would be lots and lots of bright, beautiful tomorrows. At least, that's what I wanted to believe on that perfect night in Paris.

Chapter 101

IT WAS A warm September evening when Nathaniel Prince set out on his five-mile jog through the streets of Moscow. A half hour into his run, the fine mist that had been in the air turned into a pelting rain. Two minutes later, it stopped as suddenly as it started, but Nathaniel was already soaked to the skin.

He laughed. He didn't care. Soon he'd be home, and Natalia would draw him a hot bath, and then they would sit down to their traditional Sunday-night meal: borscht, golubtsy smothered in sour cream, and his favorite—sweetbrier berry kissel.

A jog, a bath, a home-cooked dinner, and then a few hours of mindless Russian television before bed. Life was simpler now. Nathaniel found it impossible to comprehend, but for the first time since he was a boy, he was happy. More than happy. He was at peace.

It had come at great expense. His power, his home, and his wealth were all gone. In exchange, he and Natalia had been allowed to live.

That night at the Atlantis Hotel in Nassau, he still held out hope that Chukov would recover the diamonds and he could humble himself to Arnoff and the other members of the Syndicate. But within hours of the meeting, Chukov and five of his men were dead and the diamonds were lost forever.

Nathaniel sold the house in Park Slope, raped his bank accounts, and with Arnoff's guarantee of amnesty without forgiveness, he and Natalia moved back to Moscow.

Even after forking over the ten million, they were far from poor, and Natalia had found a beautiful apartment in a vintage Stalin-era building on the Frunzenskaya embankment. Six spacious rooms, high ceilings, and a wide terrace with sweeping views of the Moskva River.

It was a family neighborhood, and in another

three months, he and Natalia would be pushing a baby pram through the tree-lined streets, over the pedestrian bridge to Gorky Park and the Neskuchny Gardens on the opposite riverbank.

A father again at the age of sixty. Three months ago, he thought the Syndicate would have him killed. Now he had everything to live for. *Who knows?* he thought as he reached the front door of his apartment building. *Maybe that bastard Zelvas did us all a favor.*

He stretched his calves and his hamstrings and took the elevator to the tenth floor.

Even before he opened the door, the heady aroma of meat and onions wrapped in cabbage and simmering in a pot of creamy tomato sauce welcomed him home.

He entered the apartment and saw the intruders. Instinctively he reached for his gun. But of course he didn't have one in his wet jogging suit.

The men in the apartment had guns. All four of them.

Natalia was sitting in the middle of the living room, tied to a dining room chair. Her eyes were red and puffy, her mouth taped shut.

"How dare you!" Nathaniel screamed. "What is the meaning of this? Do you *muzhiks* know who I am?" He charged forward to untie his daughter.

One of the men slammed him in the face with a gun barrel, and Nathaniel reeled backward, spitting blood and teeth.

Nathaniel studied his attacker. One side of the man's face was covered with scars and skin grafts. It was a face that was difficult to look at, but Nathaniel knew that if he had ever seen it before, he would surely remember it now. But this man was a stranger.

"Sit," the man said.

A second dining room chair was pushed under him, and Nathaniel was shoved into it.

"Who authorized this? Who sent you?" Nathaniel demanded as one of the other men tied him to the chair.

The man with the scarred face seemed to be in charge. "Nobody sent us," he said, winking at the others. "We heard there was a party tonight, so we came on our own—no invitation."

The other three laughed.

But Prince didn't see the humor. He was

incensed. "I gave those Syndicate assholes ten million dollars, and they agreed to let me live in peace as long as I never returned to the United States again," he said. "We had a deal. Ironclad. Bound by the *Vorovskoy Zakon*."

"I see," the leader said. "A deal. An agreement between the Diamond Syndicate and the illustrious *Mr. Nathaniel Prince*. Or should I call you Mr. Nikita Primakov?"

It had been decades since Nathaniel had heard his real name.

"I don't care what you call me. Just untie me and get out. You've made a big mistake. None of the senior members of the Syndicate would ever choose to violate the *Vorovskoy Zakon*."

"That may be true," the gunman said, punching Nathaniel in the mouth and shattering more teeth. "But we are not from the Diamond Syndicate."

Chapter 102

AS SOON AS Natalia's father took the blow, muffled screams erupted from under the duct tape that covered her mouth.

One of the men slapped her face. "Shut up, bitch."

Prince strained against the ropes the men had tied around him. "I'll kill you," he screamed.

"Your killing days are over," the leader said, driving a fist into Prince's left ear.

Nathaniel could feel the vital tiny bones in his ear splinter. But he couldn't hear them break. His left ear could no longer hear anything.

The punch perforated his eardrum. Fluid leaked from his inner ear and he became dizzy and nauseated. He tried to focus.

Not from the Diamond Syndicate?

For a moment he felt a flash of justified anger. His gut feeling had been right—the Syndicate would never do this to him. *But who would?*

"Who are you?" he asked, the bloody shards of his two front teeth flying out as he spoke.

The leader pointed to his men and each one answered in turn.

"Fyodor Dmitriov."

"Kostya Dmitriov."

"Leonid Dmitriov."

"And I am Maxim Dmitriov," the leader said. "We are what remains of the Dmitriov Cab Company. You murdered my father and my uncles, you killed our brothers, our cousins—"

"And my son," Kostya growled. "My only son, Alexei. He was eighteen, and he died in the fire that morning in the garage."

"I was late for work that day," Maxim said. "By the time I arrived, the garage was an inferno. Twenty-seven of my friends and family were locked in a storeroom. I tried to get to them, and this is all I got for my efforts."

He rolled up his shirtsleeves. Covered in skin

grafts, his arms looked even more gruesome than his face.

"My bride-to-be was locked in that storeroom," Maxim said. "She didn't even work there. She came to show me photos of our wedding cake. We were going to be married in two more days. You killed her."

"Not me," Nathaniel said. "It was Chukov. Vadim Chukov—"

A swift cuff to the right eye silenced him.

"Chukov was your puppet," Maxim said. "You pulled the strings. You lit the match."

"What happened was not my fault," Nathaniel said. "I swear. I was in the hospital. My own family had just been run down by one of your drivers."

"One!" Maxim screamed. "Not twenty-seven. Not three generations of an entire family."

"I know your pain," Nathaniel said. "We were both injured parties. Let me try to make it up to you. I have money—not a lot, but some. I could make restitution for Chukov's evil deeds."

"Money? You think we're here for money?"

"Everybody needs money," Nathaniel reasoned. "Tell me what you want."

"You took what we want. You murdered what we need. Now, like they say in America, you have to face some music."

He took a cassette player from his pocket and pressed a button.

"Wedding music," Maxim cried out.

Even with only one good ear Nathaniel could make out the fiddle, the mandolin, and the garmoshka playing the joyful sounds of his homeland's traditional folk music.

"Everyone," Maxim said, "a toast to the bride."

The four men lifted their imaginary glasses.

"*Nazdaróvy!*" they shouted. Then they began to dance around the bride.

Natalia.

"This is the wedding dance you stole from me," Maxim shouted.

Fluid was seeping out of Nathaniel's inner ear. The room was spinning, and watching the four men dance in a circle around Natalia made him even dizzier.

Maxim ripped the tape from Natalia's mouth, and she gasped for air.

"Raise the bride up high," he bellowed.

The four men each grabbed a leg of the chair

and hoisted it almost to the top of the ten-foot ceiling.

Natalia screamed in terror. "Papa!"

And in that moment Nathaniel knew.

"Please," he begged. "I'll give you everything I have. Three million dollars. You can have every penny."

"This will be payment enough," Maxim said, as the four men danced toward the terrace door.

Leonid kicked it open, and now Natalia, too, realized her fate. "Please," she screamed. "You can see I'm pregnant."

"I hope," Kostya Dmitriov said, "with a son."

"Death to the whore," Maxim yelled, and they heaved the chair, the woman, and her unborn child over the balcony rail.

Natalia's screams were loud and piercing, but Nathaniel couldn't hear them. He was vomiting. He was still gagging on his own puke when he realized the chair underneath him was being lifted up. He closed his eyes and felt the cool September air as it penetrated his wet jogging suit.

The last thing he heard was the voice of the scar-faced man.

"Feed this incestuous pig to the pigeons."

Epilogue

PAYBACK

Chapter 103

A FEW WEEKS after our dinner with Newton, Katherine flew back to New York to attend the annual College Art Association conference. I went with her. I had some unfinished business that I couldn't do by fax, phone, or e-mail.

I met Ty, Zach, and Adam at one of our favorite hangouts—the White Horse Tavern. It's on Hudson Street at 11th Street, a few blocks from the Fortress, but its reputation has spread across continents.

Urban lore has it that the White Horse is where Dylan Thomas drank himself to death. He pounded down eighteen whiskeys, went home to his room at the Chelsea Hotel, and croaked. The restaurant has perpetuated the legend by turning one of their rooms into a shrine for the Welsh writer.

The yuppies and the tourists go there to soak up history and possibly even plop their asses on the very same bar stools that Thomas and other artsy boozers fell off. The guys and I go there because they have excellent burgers at reasonable prices and seven different kinds of beer on tap.

We found a quiet four-top under a red-and-white umbrella on the Hudson Street side. Guys, especially Marines, don't get all gushy about reunions, but after ten minutes and one beer, we were into that *Bro, it's so good to see you* shit you see in lame beer commercials.

But damn, it was so good to see them.

The burgers came, and after a few more minutes of "How's Paris?" and "What's up with you?" Adam got down to the nitty-gritty.

"What's next?" he said.

"Yeah," Zach said. "We're just sitting around getting old and fat. We're itching for a job."

"That's why I'm here," I said. "I've got one for you guys. A big one."

"Lay it on us," Ty said.

"We have to eliminate someone," I said.

"Who?" Adam asked.

"First let's do this," I said. I had three envelopes and handed one to each of them. "I'm paying you up front."

They each took an envelope and started to stuff it into a pocket.

"No, you gotta open it," I said.

"Hey, Matt," Zach said. "Whatever it is, we're in."

"Open it."

I got a couple of eye rolls, then one by one they opened the envelopes, and one by one they reacted. Ty just sat there with his mouth open. Zach responded with "Holy shit." Adam looked at me dumbfounded and finally said, "Who do we have to kill? The President?"

"No," I said. "The Ghost."

"Matt, you're not making any sense," Adam said. "I think somebody slipped something funny in your soufflé while you were in France."

He passed his check over to Ty and Zach. "Is this what you guys got?"

They nodded.

"A million bucks apiece for *what*?" he said. "To kill the Ghost?"

"Since I'm the Ghost, I don't want you to actually kill him. But I've decided to eliminate him," I said. "It's over, guys. This is the Ghost's retirement party and all my loyal employees are getting bonus checks."

"Matt, this is a million bucks," Ty said. "This is like Wall Street money."

"Hey, I made a killing in the diamond market. I believe in sharing the wealth."

"Why?" Zach said. "Why quit?"

"Because I'm happy with the life I'm living now, and I don't miss the life I had."

"You're going to miss us," Zach said.

"You're not going anywhere. You're my buds. We can fish, we can hunt, we can play poker. Shit, now that you got money, I'm gonna take you for every dime."

"Matt, I understand you want to give up the life. But a hundred percent? Why not just do a few jobs a year?"

"You know me, Zach. Everything I do is whole hog. From now on, my hundred percent is going to go toward building a life with Katherine."

A busboy came over and cleared our dishes.

The four of us just sat there in stony silence. Finally, we were alone again.

Adam raised his beer. "To Matthew and Katherine. A long, happy, and healthy life."

"And to the Ghost," I said. "May he rest in peace."

Chapter 104

AFTER LUNCH, I walked to Sixth Avenue, caught the uptown F train toward Jamaica, and settled in for the forty-five-minute ride to the Union Turnpike station.

I emerged on Queens Boulevard, one of the busiest roads in the borough. And with twelve lanes of bus, car, and truck traffic, one of the deadliest.

I weaved my way through streets I'd never seen before, but I'd mapped them out and committed them to memory that morning.

I love my Fortress in lower Manhattan, but it was nice to walk the streets of New York and not be surrounded by SoHo-chic models, aging hippies, or Trump wannabes. I walked along

Metropolitan Avenue past a United Nations of food options that in one block alone offered up Mexican, Chinese, Korean, Italian, Caribbean, and glatt kosher.

The only thing missing was a sign that said REAL PEOPLE LIVE HERE.

I turned right at the Yeshiva Tifereth Moshe onto 118th Street and saw him. The person I was looking for. He was wearing cutoffs and a Mets T-shirt and raking up the few leaves that had fallen onto his tiny plot of grass.

He saw me and dropped the rake.

"Matthew Bannon," I said. "Remember me?"

"Until the day I die," he said, wrapping his brown arms around me. "It's good to see you vertical. I'm sorry I didn't visit you in the hospital. I was just too . . . I don't know . . . I was kind of messed up for a while."

"Hey, Mr. Perez—"

"Manny."

"Manny, no apologies necessary," I said. "How are you doing now?"

"I'm on disability. The union said they can't fire me, but I'm not sure when I'll be ready to go back to driving a subway. Maybe never."

"You getting any help?"

"The Transit Gods sent me to a lady shrink. She's young and cute, and she gave me some anti-depression pills for the PTSD, but I never took them. How about you?"

"I decided to take my broken bones and my girlfriend to Paris for a while."

"Sweet."

"Manny, do you know anything about the other guy who was on the track that day?"

"'On the track.' I like that. You mean the guy I killed? They said he was some kind of a Russian businessman. No family—that was the good part."

"There are no good parts to that man. He was a murderer, a thief, a smuggler, an arsonist—you name it. Vadim Chukov lived a life of crime, and the only thing you did was help put it to an end."

"I'll remember that when I wake in a cold sweat at two in the morning."

"I was in the Marines," I said. "Three combat tours, so I know what you're going through. Middle of the night is when a guy can really get self-destructive."

He looked away and I knew I'd hit a hot

button. The good Catholic had been wrestling with thoughts of suicide.

"But you *can* get better. It won't happen overnight. You need a good therapist—one who's experienced and smart, not young and cute. You need to stop standing on your front lawn in the middle of September waiting for leaves that won't fall off the tree till October."

"You sound like my wife. She thinks I'll feel better if we take a vacation."

"She's right," I said.

"Not so easy when you're living off disability checks."

"Then live off this for a while." I handed him an envelope exactly like the ones I had given Adam, Zach, and Ty.

He opened it, put one hand to his mouth, and lowered himself to the ground. I sat down next to him.

"Is this a joke?" he said.

"No, it's real."

"Where does a kid like you get a million dollars?"

"Chukov owed me some money. I settled with his estate. I figured you deserve a piece."

"A 'piece'?" He took another look at the check. "Why are you doing this?"

"You got kids?" I asked.

"Two daughters, a son, and four grandkids."

"I'm doing it because your wife and your family need you. I'm partly responsible for taking you away from them. I want to be responsible for helping you get back."

He waved the check at me. "If this can't do it, I don't know what will." His brown eyes glistened. "Matthew, you're changing my life."

"It's a two-way street, Manny," I said, finally standing up.

He stood up next to me. "You tired of French food? Stay for dinner. My wife Nilda makes a mean arroz con pollo."

"That would be great," I said.

My cell phone rang.

"Excuse me," I said. "Probably Katherine. My girlfriend."

"She's invited, too," he said.

I answered the phone.

"Matthew?"

It wasn't Katherine. It was somebody I didn't expect.

"This is Newton. Matthew, I'm calling to tell you my employer is very impressed with your work."

"Your employer? You mean the guy we call Copernicus?"

He laughed. "Yes. Copernicus is a big fan. Actually, he wants to hire you."

"You're kidding," I said. "He wants to commission a painting?"

"No," Newton said. "He has a job for you, though. You and your three Marine buddies, Zach Stevens, Ty Warren, and Adam Benjamin. Are you interested?"

I was standing right there on the lawn, but my legs were feeling unreal. So was the rest of me. Manny Perez had moved away to give me some privacy. He was up on the front steps, waiting for me to come in. His face was radiant. I knew he couldn't wait to go inside and tell his wife the unbelievable news.

Newton repeated the question. "Are you interested? At least just to talk about it?"

I hesitated a few more seconds. "No," I said. "Not today."

A NEW THRILLER

NYPD Red

James Patterson
& Marshall Karp

NYPD Red is a special task force charged with the city's highest-profile cases affecting the powerful, rich, and famous – and a criminal mastermind has plotted a script of total destruction.

When an all-star cast of Hollywood's stars and executives arrive in New York for a film festival, NYPD Red is put on high alert.

On the festival's first day, a world-famous producer is poisoned at his power breakfast and NYPD Red moves into action. Detective Zach Jordan and his new partner Detective Kylie MacDonald – who is also his ex-girlfriend – catch the case. Before the day is over, they have two more wildly theatrical killings, and two more dead stars, and a city erupting in complete chaos. The killer has every murder and every escape planned down to the last detail – and he's scripted the most explosive finale ever.

With larger-than-life action, relentless speed, and white-knuckle twists, *NYPD Red* is a mega-blockbuster of a thriller.

Century · London

Read on for a sneak preview of

NYPD RED

HENRY MUHLENBERG CLAMPED his hand down hard over Edie Coburn's mouth. She sank her teeth into the soft flesh of his palm and threw her head back, but he didn't let go. The last thing he needed was for some idiot to walk past her trailer and hear her screaming.

Her body convulsed. Once. Twice. Again. Again. She shuddered and went limp in his arms.

He eased his hand off her mouth.

"Get me a cigarette," she said. "They're on the counter."

Muhlenberg slid off the sofa and padded naked to the other side of the trailer. He was twenty-eight, a German wunderkind who made edgy films that critics loved and nobody went to see. Fed up with driving a ten-year-old Opel and living in a one-bedroom apartment in Frankfurt, he sold his soul for a Porsche 911, a house in the Hills, and a three picture film deal.

The first picture had tanked, the second made six mil—a home run for an indie, but in big-studio speak a colossal failure. If this one didn't blow the roof off the multiplexes, he'd be back in Deutschland, shooting music videos for garage bands.

It was his final at-bat, and now that bitch Edie Coburn was screwing it up. He had come to her trailer to negotiate a truce between her and her asshole husband, Ian Stewart, who unfortunately was also her costar. Negotiate? More like grovel.

"Edie, please," he had said. "We've got a full crew and a hundred extras standing around with the meter running. It's costing the studio a thousand dollars for every minute you refuse to come out and shoot this scene."

"Ian should have thought of that before he started banging that brainless bundle of silicone and peroxide."

"You don't know that for a fact," he said. "The rumor about Ian and Devon is just that—a rumor. Probably started by some flack at the studio to get advance buzz about the movie."

"I don't know about Germany, Herr Muhlenberg, but here in New York, all rumors are true."

"Look, I'm not a marriage counselor," he said. "I know you and Ian have problems, but I also know you're a professional. What'll it take to get you into wardrobe and onto the set?"

She was wearing a short royal blue kimono that was busy with floral designs and peacocks. She tugged on the sash, and the kimono fell to the floor.

Revenge fuck. Muhlenberg complied.

At a thousand bucks a minute, the sex cost the studio fifty-four thousand dollars. Edie wasn't nearly as good as the underage star of his last film, but if you had to bang a forty-six-year-old diva to save your career, you could do a lot worse than Edie Coburn.

He lit the cigarette for her. She sucked in hard and blew it in his face. "I hope you're not waiting for a standing ovation," she said. "This was strictly business."

"Right," he said. "Then I can tell Ian you'll be on the set in thirty minutes."

"Yeah. You might want to put some pants on first."

"SETTLE DOWN, PEOPLE," the assistant director bellowed. "Picture is up. Roll sound."

Henry Muhlenberg took a deep breath. He was finally back in control. Thirty feet away, looking elegant in a vintage *Casablanca* black shawl-collar tuxedo, the Chameleon had the same thought.

"Speed."

The clapper board snapped shut, and the assistant director called out, "Background action."

The Chameleon and ninety-nine other wedding guests slid into character, chatting, laughing, drinking, all without making a sound.

"And action," Muhlenberg called.

The bride and groom, Devon Whitaker and Ian Stewart, stepped onto the dance floor, and the assembled guests stopped pretending to talk and pretended to be enthralled as the happy couple began to dance.

The band pretended to play. The music would be added to the sound track in postproduction. Ian and Devon twirled around the room.

"Dancing, dancing, dancing," Muhlenberg called out, waiting for the couple to hit their marks. "And now!"

Edie Coburn stepped into the scene, wearing a pair of wide-legged, high-waisted Katharine Hepburn trousers and a loose-fitting chocolate-gray silk blouse.

"Well, well, well," she screamed, pointing a 9-millimeter SIG Pro at the couple. "The former Mrs. Minetti finally gets to meet the current Mrs. Minetti."

The crowd reacted with appropriate horror. Muhlenberg looked at the video monitor of the close-up camera. Edie Coburn was calm and cold on the outside, but seething with rage on the inside. Hardly a stretch for her to play the jealous ex-wife, Muhlenberg thought, but still, she was brilliant.

Ian turned to her, his eyes filled more with anger than fear. "Put the gun down, Carla. If this is another one of your stupid melodramatic—"

Edie fired at the bride. Once. Twice. Blood stained the lace front of the wedding gown, and Devon collapsed to the floor. Ian let out a wail and charged toward Edie. She fired again. Blood spread across his white shirt. He staggered, and she fired again. Arterial spray spurted across the dance floor, and Ian fell down hard.

It was a spectacular film death, and Henry had it covered with four cameras. "And cut," he yelled. "Brilliant."

The assistant director helped the bloodied bride to her feet. "Ian, you need help?" he asked.

Ian Stewart didn't answer. He gasped for air and let out a groan that turned into a full-throated wet gurgle as blood gushed from his windpipe and onto the parquet floor.

The special-effects guy was the first to figure it out. The blood squibs on the wedding gown had exploded right on cue, but the blood pouring out of Ian Stewart was very real.

"Live fire," he shouted as he barreled his way onto the set, grabbed Edie Coburn's arm, and wrested the gun from her hand.

Henry Muhlenberg was right behind him. He

dropped to the floor and lifted the actor's head. The blood had slowed to a trickle. Ian's face was contorted, mouth agape, eyes wide open, seeing nothing.

"Get a doctor," Muhlenberg screamed, knowing it was futile.

The extras were on their feet, some stunned, some crying, some shoving their way to the front to get a better look.

The Chameleon stood in their midst, motionless, just another horrified face blending in with the crowd.

Also by James Patterson

ALEX CROSS NOVELS

Along Came a Spider • Kiss the Girls • Jack and Jill •
Cat and Mouse • Pop Goes the Weasel • Roses are Red •
Violets are Blue • Four Blind Mice • The Big Bad Wolf •
London Bridges • Mary, Mary • Cross • Double Cross •
Cross Country • Alex Cross's Trial (with Richard DiLallo) •
I, Alex Cross • Cross Fire • Kill Alex Cross •
Merry Christmas, Alex Cross

THE WOMEN'S MURDER CLUB SERIES

1st to Die • 2nd Chance (with Andrew Gross) • 3rd Degree (with
Andrew Gross) • 4th of July (with Maxine Paetro) • The 5th
Horseman (with Maxine Paetro) • The 6th Target (with Maxine
Paetro) • 7th Heaven (with Maxine Paetro) • 8th Confession
(with Maxine Paetro) • 9th Judgement (with Maxine Paetro) •
10th Anniversary (with Maxine Paetro) •
11th Hour (with Maxine Paetro) • 12th of Never (with
Maxine Paetro, to be published February 2013)

DETECTIVE MICHAEL BENNETT SERIES

Step on a Crack (with Michael Ledwidge) • Run for Your Life
(with Michael Ledwidge) • Worst Case (with Michael Ledwidge) •
Tick Tock (with Michael Ledwidge) •
I, Michael Bennett (with Michael Ledwidge)

PRIVATE NOVELS

Private (with Maxine Paetro) • Private London (with Mark
Pearson) • Private Games (with Mark Sullivan) • Private: No. 1
Suspect (with Maxine Paetro) • Private Berlin (with
Mark Sullivan)

NON-FICTION

Torn Apart (with Hal and Cory Friedman) •
The Murder of King Tut (with Martin Dugard)

ROMANCE

Sundays at Tiffany's (with Gabrielle Charbonnet) •
The Christmas Wedding (with Richard DiLallo)

We support

I'm proud to support the National Literacy Trust, an independent charity that changes lives through literacy.

Did you know that millions of people in the UK struggle to read and write? This means children are less likely to succeed at school and less likely to develop into confident and happy teenagers. Literacy difficulties will limit their opportunities throughout adult life.

The National Literacy Trust passionately believes that everyone has a right to the reading, writing, speaking and listening skills they need to fulfil their own and, ultimately, the nation's potential.

My own son didn't use to enjoy reading, which was why I started writing children's books – reading for pleasure is an essential way to encourage children to pick up a book. The National Literacy Trust is dedicated to delivering exciting initiatives to encourage people to read and to help raise literacy levels. To find out more about the great work that they do, visit their website at www.literacytrust.org.uk.

James Patterson